VALHALLA GOLD

Rob Jones

ISBN-13 978-1533565853
ISBN-10 1533565856

This novel is an action-adventure thriller and includes archaeological, military and mystery themes. I welcome constructive comments and I'm always happy to get your feedback.

Website: www.robjonesnovels.com
Facebook: http://bit.ly/RobJonesNovels
Email: robjonesnovels@gmail.com
Blog: http://robjonesbooks.blogspot.com
Twitter: @AuthorRobJones

DEDICATION

Once again, for T – never give in and never give up

VALHALLA GOLD

PROLOGUE

Newfoundland, Canada

The Mi'kmaq Cultural Museum was a tiny clapboard building perched on the jagged granite cliffs of eastern Newfoundland. The Mi'kmaq were a proud First Nations band and had lived in the Maritime Provinces of eastern Canada for thousands of years. Along with other museums scattered across the Maritimes, this modest building housed what few archaeological treasures remained of the tribe.

Far below, the savage rising swell of the Atlantic powered against the rocks and sprayed sea foam dozens of feet into the cold air. The wind was cutting up from the Grand Banks, some of the most plentiful fishing grounds on Earth and it looked like another short summer was reaching its end.

Bill Smith turned his back on the view, unlocked the main entrance and shuffled inside. He had been the curator since the place opened fifteen years ago, and was rarely overworked, but he was proud of his partial

Mi'kmaq heritage and spent his days organizing cultural events and studying the language of his forefathers.

He watched the sun struggle to break through a split in the thickening cloud out on the horizon and returned to his work in the museum. He was in the middle of renumbering a collection of arrowheads recently discovered by archaeologists in the Gros Morne National Park.

Irritated that some were named incorrectly, he was shaking his head and sighing when he heard the sound of a helicopter's rotors somewhere above the museum. He frowned and set down the arrowheads before walking to the window. The only chopper that came around these parts was the Bell 412 Griffin, a twin-engined affair used by the Canadian Coast Guard, but that was painted red with a white stripe on the side. This one was a dull gray and much bigger. It looked almost military.

He opened the front door and stood on the top of the steps, putting his hands in his pockets to keep them out of the cold. Why anyone would be landing a helicopter that size right outside his little museum was anyone's guess. He already had a bad feeling about it and was starting to consider if he should call the local police when the chopper's chunky rubber tires touched down with a gentle crunch on the gravel outside the museum. He sucked on his asthma inhaler and grew more anxious.

The side door swung open and a man in a cheap suit emerged. Behind him another man and a woman both in paramilitary fatigues jumped out. Both the military personnel were carrying submachine guns over their shoulders. Bill took a step back toward the door, but didn't break eye contact with them. As they drew closer, he saw the paramilitary man had a tattoo of a flaming grenade on his neck. Like the woman, he was wearing a dirty green-colored beret.

The man in the suit told the others to wait and jogged up the wooden steps toward the entrance. "Mr Smith, I presume?" He held out his hand to shake.

Bill Smith nodded, but declined the handshake.

"I'm Dr Nate Derby – we spoke on the phone."

Bill looked at Derby and then peered suspiciously over his shoulder at the people behind him. He had spoken to Dr Derby on the phone a few days ago and they had arranged a meeting to discuss something that had bothered the old curator for all of his life. The academic seemed trustworthy and had promised to keep it to himself, but now he saw he'd been wrong to trust him and was struggling to understand why this man would need a military helicopter to make the visit. He raised his chin in the direction of the people standing further back with the weapons. "I thought we agreed this was just between us?"

Dr Derby gave an awkward shrug of the shoulders. "I'm sorry, sir. But after our conversation I talked to some colleagues."

"What do you need an army for?"

The paramilitary man stepped up. "We're here on behalf of the Canadian Government."

Maybe Derby seemed normal enough, but Bill thought there was something not quite right about this other man. While he could write off the French accent to him being Québécois, the unmarked chopper and grenade tattoo made him doubt these paramilitaries were representing the Canadian Government. What they were doing accompanying Dr Derby up here bothered him greatly.

"You got any ID?" he asked, trying to hide his nerves.

"We don't carry ID, sir. We're Special Ops."

Bill frowned. "What about you, Dr Derby?"

3

Derby smiled. "Sure." He pulled out an ID from the Memorial University of Newfoundland and flashed it in his face. "Department of Archaeology."

Smith eyed the laminated badge. It looked genuine enough. "You can come in as we arranged, but not these guys."

Derby looked out to sea for a second and then fixed his eyes back on Bill. "I'm afraid I can't agree to that, Mr Smith. We believe you have something vital to national security policy in this building."

"You guys are kidding right?" He offered a laugh but he saw things were getting out of control.

"Please, Mr Smith – open the door."

"And what if I don't? What if I call the police?"

The man with the grenade tattoo gave a wicked smirk and lifted the submachine gun from his shoulder. "You think you can get to the telephone before I can squeeze this trigger?"

Whoever the hell they were, Bill thought, it wasn't Government, and Derby had obviously lied to him on the phone about keeping things between the two of them. He thought about backing into the door and slamming it in their faces, but his five years in the Royal Newfoundland Regiment told him what those guns would do to the wood and vinyl clapboard siding of the museum. It would look like a sieve in less than twenty seconds, and so would he.

Grenade Tattoo stepped closer. "So, you show us where they are, then, oui?"

The casual reference to *they* told Bill all he had to know. They all knew why they were here, and there was no point in playing games. Derby had breached his trust.

Looking at the menacing muzzle of the submachine gun in the man's gloved hands, Bill offered a reluctant nod and opened the door. As they trampled up the steps and dragged mud and grit into the small museum, his mind filled with terror as he finally realized they weren't going to let him live through this. He had seen their faces. He knew what they wanted from him.

They wanted evidence of the Invisible One.

Or what was left of him – he who dwelt by the lake in ancient times and could not be seen – the great warrior who walked among enemy tribes like a ghost. Now they wanted his power, and it was all his fault. He had opened an ancient secret to the world to satisfy his own curiosity. Until his call to Derby, only he knew about the precious objects – the secret passed to him by his father on his deathbed. He had only ever told one other living soul, and he knew she would never betray him. No, what would unfold would be on his conscience alone.

"I don't suppose it's worth me denying they're here?" he asked, trying to sound calm.

A humorless shake of the head was the response. "No, and stop trying to play for time. Take us to them right now, or…" Grenade Tattoo cocked the gun and pointed it at his chest.

Derby looked almost as nervous as Bill felt, and he wondered if the academic was also being coerced. Either way, the old curator understood what he had to do. He shuffled slowly through the museum until he reached the back room – a nondescript state of affairs with three cases of ancient fishing tools. He stopped and pushed one of the cases away from the wall. Beneath it was a loose floorboard which the old man manipulated out with his leathery fingertips.

The intruders drew closer around him, forming a small circle as he leaned over the hole.

"Don't worry," he said. "It's not a gun down here."

No response.

Bill pulled out a tin box and blew a thick layer of dust off the lid. "What you want is in here, and may God forgive me for what I have done today." The look of disgust he gave Nate Derby was worth a thousand words.

He opened the box and in a second pulled an old Smith & Wesson on the men. He aimed it at the man with the tattoo and fired.

Nothing happened.

Bill looked down at the jammed gun with horror on his face.

They all laughed, and Grenade Tattoo knocked the weapon from his hand. It landed with a loud smack on the floorboards.

"Now, we do it my way," Grenade Tattoo said, and struck Bill in the face with the butt of his submachine gun.

The old man staggered backwards, knocking over one of the cases and sending old fishing hooks all over the floor.

"No, wait!" Derby shouted. "We agreed no one would get harmed."

"Shut up!" The woman shouted. She blew a large purple bubblegum bubble and it popped all over her lips.

Bill spat out a wad of blood as he staggered back to his feet. "All right... all right. What you are looking for is in there." He pointed a shaking hand to a grille on the wall which was used to pull warm return-air from the small room and send it back to the furnace downstairs. His long-planned feint had failed to save what he had protected for most of his life.

Grenade Tattoo ordered the woman forward. She scowled at Smith as she walked past him, raised her machine pistol and blasted the grille and a good chunk of the plasterboard surrounding it to oblivion.

"Get it, old man," Grenade Tattoo commanded. "Any more tricks and you're dead."

Bill Smith put his hand in the hole and pulled out a small leather bag which he handed to the woman. She snatched it from his trembling hand and passed it back to Grenade Tattoo.

He opened it at once and whistled in awe. Several long moments passed as the man with the grenade tattoo stared at the tiny beads now in his hand, barely able to believe what he was seeing – or more accurately what he *wasn't* seeing. Instead of seeing his palm, he was looking at the floorboards of the museum directly beneath it. It looked like he had a hole in his hand. He smiled and shook his head gently in wonder as he tried to make sense of what his eyes were telling him.

Smith wheezed as his asthma began to worsen. "If you're on the trail of the Invisible One, it will lead only to your painful deaths."

Grenade Tattoo ignored him and continued to stare at the strange beads, utterly fixated. Without looking at Bill Smith, he raised his machine pistol and fired a burst of bullets into him, tearing his chest apart and smashing him back into the shredded plasterboard behind him. He slumped slowly to the floor stone cold dead, leaving a trail of his blood smeared down the wall behind him as he went.

Derby staggered back in horror, unable to believe what his eyes had just seen. "What the hell did you do that for?"

"For the same reason I'm going to do this." He raised his pistol and aimed it at Derby's heart.

"What are you doing? Wait, please... don't shoot! We agreed..."

Grenade Tattoo fired twice and Derby crumpled to the floor beside Bill Smith.

"All right, we're out of here," he said.

The woman put her boot on Bill's blood-soaked chest to tighten one of the straps and then picked up her gun. She blew another cherry-flavored bubble and giggled. "Back to the chopper!" she screamed.

Both of them left the museum, their boots crunching on the broken glass and Mi'kmaq artefacts as they went. Outside, the rotors began to whir faster as the pilot powered up ready for takeoff.

A storm was blowing in off the Atlantic as they climbed inside the chopper, and a heavy rainfall began just as they lifted off the ground and spun the airborne machine around. Seconds later the mighty helicopter was blowing the old clapboard museum into matchwood with liberal use of the M230 Chain Gun mounted on its chin turret.

Moments later the building was ablaze, and the helicopter disappeared up into the thick gray clouds, gone forever.

CHAPTER ONE

Elysium

"Afraid you'll lose?" Joe Hawke said, revving the Yamaha WaveRunner jet ski and giving Lea Donovan the smuggest of all possible smiles. He shaded his eyes from the tropical Caribbean sun with his hand and watched as a look of amused indifference crossed the Irishwoman's slim, tanned face.

Lea ignored the comment and studied the curve of the bay. "So, first one around the island wins, yeah?"

Hawke slipped on his shades and nodded confidently. "That's what we agreed. If you want to back out then just say so."

Lea revved her Kawasaki Jet Ski in response. "You've got to be joking, *Josiah*. Playtime's over, baby."

The use of his full name was met with raucous laughter from Ryan Bale and Maria Kurikova. They were sitting on the pier a few yards behind the jet skis. Hawke smirked at them, pleased his name could bring so much amusement to the group. It didn't bother him in the least. Over the last few days he had settled easily into a playful sort of life on Elysium – hiking, swimming, diving and his favorite – playing around on jet skis.

"So are we going for it or not?" asked Lea.

Without saying another word Hawke raced away, taking care to cover Ryan and Maria in a heavy spray of sea water from the discharge nozzle at the back of the WaveRunner.

"Hey – no fair, you cheat!" Lea called out, and immediately raced after him. She was parallel within seconds.

"Frightened I'm going to win?" he shouted over his shoulder to her.

"Not a bit of it," she called back, her voice barely audible over the roar of the 1.8 litre engine. She turned the throttle and the fuel-injected 4-stroke responded straight away, pulling her through the warm ocean effortlessly.

"We'll see about that," Hawke said with a grin, and took off once again in another burst of sea spray.

He raced across the bay to the northeast of the island, cutting across the shallow water in a diagonal path and heading out to where a low cliff jutted into the sea. Thousands of years of hydraulic action had eroded a beautiful archway into this part of the cliff, which as he accelerated toward it, Hawke noted with excitement was about the same size as a jet ski. In another thousand years it would collapse leaving a stack separated from the headland and towering up out of the sea, but today it made a perfect tunnel to zoom through. He raced toward it.

It was just after midday now and the air was hot and humid. To his right he was aware of the looming presence of the island – the tropical canopies stretching over the twin mountains and the sparkling glass and steel structure that formed ECHO headquarters. Behind him he heard the roar of Lea's Kawasaki as she closed in on him, determined to beat him around the island and win the race.

He ducked his head as he powered the WaveRunner through the hole in the cliff and steered hard to the right.

The hot wind buffeted him as he turned south and accelerated the machine to its maximum of just under seventy miles per hour.

Glancing behind him, he was impressed to see Lea had taken the same shortcut through the erosion hole. He watched as she steered the Jet Ski to the right and leaned over to expedite its turn in the warm water. He knew how much she wanted to win and show him that he wasn't just going to waltz down here to the island and show everyone how everything was done. He knew that she considered winning to be a serious business – almost as serious as losing, he thought.

He was now reaching the end of the southwest tip of the island and turning north for the final part of the race. Ahead was the home-straight, where a slightly intoxicated Ryan Bale had promised to wave in the winner of race.

He approached the finish line and saw Ryan and Maria were no longer on the pier to witness his victory.

Racing across the line, he powered the WaveRunner down and even had time to moor it at the end of the jetty before Lea pulled up and shut her engine off.

"That doesn't count as a win," she said.

"Sure it does."

"You cheated."

"Let's talk about it over a nice, cold beer."

*

Hawke pushed open the double doors of the HQ's entrance and strolled casually into the chilled climate-controlled complex. Behind him, Lea was still arguing about how he forfeited the race when he started before Ryan gave the signal, and he knew she was right but he didn't care. All was fair in love and jet ski races.

After pulling two cold beers from the fridge and tossing one to Lea, they stepped in to the sunken living area and relaxed. Hawke was horrified to see that while they had been on their race Ryan had undergone some kind of transformation. He was now wearing Bermuda shorts and the loudest Hawaiian shirt he had ever seen.

"It's true what they," Hawke said, patting Ryan on the back and looking at his clothes. "Some things really cannot be unseen."

Alex Reeve laughed and agreed with a nod of her head, but Maria looked lovingly at the new, bright Ryan from where she was working in the kitchen.

"Hey!" she called over the counter. "He looks great!"

"Yeah," Ryan said, smiling. "Don't knock it till you've tried it."

They collapsed on the sofa in front of the enormous plasma TV and Hawke took a long, slow drink of the beer. Beside him, Scarlet Sloane was sitting with a cigarette in one hand and what looked like a banana daiquiri in the other, while Maria was still in the kitchen trying to make chicken noodles. It didn't smell like it was going too well.

"I still can't believe I'm actually here, in ECHO HQ," Hawke said. He paused to look over the large space again, glancing up at the swirling fans on the ceiling and then bringing his eyes down to the enormous window wall which gave a view of the sparkling turquoise ocean beyond. "What does ECHO stand for again?"

"It stands for the Eden Counter-Hostile Organization," Scarlet said confidently.

Lea looked puzzled. "I thought we agreed on Eden Covert History Organization – or maybe even the Eden Covert *Heritage* Organization?"

"No, that's what *you* agreed on," Scarlet said. "Everyone else thought it was naff and went with Counter-Hostile. Makes us sound much harder."

"But we spend our time in the world of covert history," Lea whined.

Scarlet scoffed. "Covert History or Covert Heritage makes us sound like those nimrods who dig up old coins with Tony Robinson."

"Hey!" Ryan said. "I like those programs – and it's *Sir* Tony Robinson to you." Maria entered the room with a couple of bags of chips.

"What happened to the noodles?" Scarlet asked.

"They went black," Maria said. "And very hard... like little shards of detonated wood."

"Yummy!" Scarlet said.

"Hey – hold up," said Ryan.

"What is it?" Lea asked.

Ryan craned his neck over the sofa and tried to look up the circular staircase to see into Eden's study. "Eden's on the Bat Phone."

Scarlet leaned back in her chair and slowly pulled the cigarette from her mouth. "So if you take a call on it, Ryan, would that make it the Twat Phone?"

A general rumble of laughter went around the room.

Ryan gave Scarlet a withering glance and slowly extended his middle finger in her direction as he made his reply. "But let me get this straight," he said, deadpan. "Didn't you shoot the President of the United States?"

Maria laughed and handed Ryan the bag of chips.

Scarlet sighed and rolled her eyes. "Not this again."

"But you did, yeah?"

"Well... *sort of*, but it was for his own good."

Hawke recalled the moment he'd watched as Agent Doyle dragged President Charles Grant from the Hudson River, the two of them looking like a couple of drowned rats... and then the moment the President had thanked him for saving the nation.

"But technically," Ryan continued mischievously, "it was an assassination attempt – am I right?"

"Oh, do shut up, *boy* – you're getting tiresome. It was no such thing and you know it. I made the call to get the President in the water because I knew Doyle was a strong swimmer from when we had initially attacked the Perseus, and Kiefel was about to shoot him. He still had three shots left in his weapon at that point. It was the only way I could think of to get Charlie to safety."

"Charlie?"

Scarlet gave a smug smile. "Sure, that's what he asked me to call him when we spoke on the phone."

"*Please* tell me you're not having one of your lurid affairs with the American President," Ryan said. "Unlike most of your victims this one's not disposable. You realize that, right?"

Hawke listened with amusement, but kept one eye on Eden who was now descending the staircase on his way to join them in the main area.

Scarlet sighed and got up from her chair, picking up a cushion as she went. "I am not having an affair with Charlie, so keep your pants dry." She smacked the cushion into Ryan's face and pretended to smother him. He fought her off somewhat unconvincingly and when he was free of the cushion he saw she too was now watching Eden as he drew closer.

"What's the matter, Rich?" Lea said.

"I think we might have a problem."

Scarlet looked serious. "What's going on?"

"I just took a call a second ago."

"We know," Scarlet said. "We saw you on the Tw... Bat Phone."

Her comment didn't register with Sir Richard Eden. "It was Lady Victoria Hamilton-Talbot."

Lea nodded. "I've heard you talk of her – who is she again?"

"Her father, the viscount, was an old friend of mine."

"And what did she want?"

Eden looked troubled. "She's just told me that a mutual friend of ours was murdered and that she thinks it might have something to do with Thor."

Silence followed as Eden furrowed his brow and sat down gently in his leather chair. Outside the window they all heard the gentle chirping of a mangrove cuckoo hidden somewhere in the canopies of a line of nearby coconut palms.

Hawke, who had noticed a look of discomfort on Lea's face at the mention of Thor, was the first to break the silence. "Thor – you're serious?"

Eden fixed his eyes on the former SBS man. "When have you ever known me not to be serious?"

Hawke accepted the rebuke. True enough, he thought. "Did she say anything else?"

Another long period of silence followed.

Eden lowered his voice. "She's not sure exactly what happened but the police found his body in a burned-out museum in eastern Canada. They say he'd been shot twice in the heart." Involuntarily, Eden rubbed his forehead as a deep sigh emanated from his lips.

"I'm sorry, Rich," Alex said quietly.

"This is terrible news, Rich," Lea said. "I don't know what to say – you must be in shock."

"I am, and it gets worse… She had a telephone message telling her to stop asking questions about his death or she'll be next."

"Does she know what it's all about?" Ryan asked,

Eden looked gloomy. "Nate – her friend and former supervisor – spent his life researching the local tribes of the Canadian Maritimes. I met him on more than one occasion and he was a damned decent sort. American, from Connecticut. She said that for some reason he'd started talking to her recently about Thor, the Norse god and she's sure it must have something to do with his death."

"But what's our interest in this?" Scarlet said. "Aside from gold, of course?"

"Our *interest* as you put it," Eden said, "is that Victoria's father was a very old friend of mine. If she needs my help then I'm going to give it to her."

"Sounds fair enough to me," Ryan said, looking at Scarlet. "Anyway, I thought everyone was interested in Thor?"

Scarlet snorted and swept her pack of cigarettes off the table as she made her way to the door. "I'm interested in anything that promises me a pay off, *boy...* and gold is the best promise of all."

"We're not just interested in bloody gold, Scarlet," Eden said sharply. "ECHO is about more than that. We're not just treasure hunters."

Scarlet took the point and looked apologetic as she put the cigarette in her mouth.

"Anyway," Eden said, a look of foreboding on his face. "We're going to get into this because if this has anything to do with Thor and the Norse legends then this is exactly what we're all about. Plus, if there's a chance this might lead to anything of archaeological significance then I want it here, with us, not disappearing into some government archive."

"Looks like I'm going to need to change into my Batman t-shirt," Ryan said seriously.

"So where are we going?" Hawke asked.

"The Buccaneer Palm Resort," Eden said quietly, obviously still bothered by the phone call. "She has a place there. It used to belong to her father."

"You mean in the Florida Keys?" Lea asked.

"Yes, Little Torch Key," Eden replied. "I want a jet fuelled and in the air within the hour and all of you on it."

And Hawke thought that sounded like the best idea he'd heard all week.

CHAPTER TWO

Florida Keys

The Gulfstream touched down at Florida Keys Marathon Airport less than two hours after Victoria Hamilton-Talbot's telephone call to Sir Richard Eden. Hawke, Lea, Scarlet and Ryan made the team, with Eden keeping Alex on the island to man the computers and Maria for security.

The flight passed without any problems, but from the air they had seen Hurricane Jasmine far on the eastern horizon just as they landed. Now, from their new vantage point on the ground it was just as impressive, but too far away to be of any danger to them. This was life in the tropics.

They hired a self-drive SUV from the airport and Hawke took the wheel while Lea called Eden and informed him of their arrival. They headed southwest on Rick Turner before hanging a right onto US-1 S. The drive was flat and mostly featureless as they drove along the Overseas Highway.

Passing Bahia Honda Key and the State Park, they hit Big Pine Key and then crossed Pine Channel. Watching the sun-soaked landscape drift past the car window, Lea's mind turned to her recent journey to Ireland, and how it all fitted together with why she was now in Florida. It couldn't be a coincidence that her father's research notes had been focussed on the Norse goddesses of healing and now a man connected with research into Thor had been killed.

Now, she was feeling guilty that she had kept the contents of her father's research file to herself when she'd returned from Ireland. When she'd landed she had taken the file to her quarters, scanned the contents onto a disc and copied them to a flash-drive, and then put the notes in her filing cabinet – but she had told no one. She had no idea why her father was researching the Norse legends, and she wanted to keep it to herself until she'd looked into it more, but now that looked like a bad plan. Clearly all this had to be connected.

"We're here," Hawke said, casting an eye on the Sat Nav. "Little Torch Key."

He indicated left and turned the SUV off the road. They drove across a small gravel car park and pulled up outside the exclusive resort. It was set over several acres of expensive beachfront real estate and while some here owned their properties most rented. Just inside the entrance was a long, low building which was clearly the main reception and a few people in broad sunhats were meandering along the winding paths inside the compound. The place offered the sort of peace and tranquillity that could only be bought for several thousand dollars per night.

Victoria's place was at the south end of the resort and the walk took them several minutes through the center of the compound until they finally weaved their way to the luxury residence. It was hidden among a burst of tropical plants and shaded from the sun by several towering palm trees which swayed gently in the warm breeze now coming off the Straits of Florida.

The young woman waved to them from the veranda and they walked slowly up the steps to join her.

"You must be Lea Donovan?" she said. "Dickie's told me a lot about you."

Hawke gave Scarlet a questioning look and mouthed the word *Dickie* at her, but Scarlet shrugged her shoulders and said nothing.

Victoria caught the shared glance and turned to Scarlet. "And you're the woman who tried to kill President Grant, right?"

Scarlet opened her mouth to reply but Hawke put his finger over her lips. "She's kidding, Cairo."

Victoria smiled wanly and addressed all of them together. "Please, all of you – come in. You're most welcome."

*

Inside turned out to be even more sumptuous than outside, and Ryan stared at the plush drinks cabinet and mosquito net-covered beds down the corridor with unconcealed jealousy. Through the open window, beyond a neat strip of sand, the strong, clear Florida sun pitched down on the turquoise water.

"Woah," he said finally.

Scarlet sniffed. "I've never heard such a well-articulated exclamation of appreciation."

They sat in the main room, which was part of an open-plan lower level with polished hardwood floorboards, wooden slat walls and Louvre windows. Victoria poured everyone iced tea, which elicited a look of disgust from Scarlet Sloane.

"Haven't you got anything stronger, Victoria? When I'm saving the world I tend to run on heavier fuel than this."

"Of course," Victoria said. Her long brown hair blew gently in the cross-ventilation from the Louvre windows. She opened the double doors of the walnut veneer drinks cabinet and made a dramatic sweeping gesture with her hands. "The bar is open... and please, call me Vikki."

"A vodka'll do me, Vikki," Scarlet said unceremoniously.

Even though she had heard Eden talk several times of Victoria Hamilton-Talbot, Lea had never met her before and she knew very little about her. She was an academic by training, specializing in maritime archaeology and her former supervisor, with whom there had been rumors of an affair, was Dr Nate Derby. She also knew from Richard that she happened to be the daughter of Lord Peter Hamilton-Talbot, the Viscount of Weston, and that entitled her to the title Lady Victoria Hamilton-Talbot, but she never used it.

Now Victoria brought the small-talk to an end as she deftly steered the conversation back around to business. "One of these days someone's going to have to tell me where old Dickie's little hideout is," she said in an attempt to make everyone relax.

No one replied.

"Why are we here, Vikki?" Hawke said flatly.

Lea watched the woman carefully as she surveyed the group, and then lowered herself slowly into a wicker chair beside the open window. "As I'm sure Dickie will have briefed you, a few days ago my old boss Nate was found dead in a burned-out building up in Canada. I think he was murdered."

"Yes, Rich briefed us on it," Lea said taking the lead. "We're very sorry for your loss – were you close?"

"Our academic partnership was extremely close, yes, but that was the extent of our relationship."

"Why do you think he was murdered?" Hawke asked.

Victoria hesitated, and Lea thought she looked like she was calculating something before answering. "I can't be sure, but I think it's got something to do with what he was researching... on the side."

"What was his specialist field of research?" Ryan asked.

"Pre-historic archaeology in the Maritimes, but he'd started researching Thor."

"And you think something to do with this got him killed?" Hawke asked.

Victoria sighed. "Maybe, yes, but it all seems to strange."

"What makes you say that?" Lea said.

"Nate had started acting rather peculiar lately – missing important lectures and other professional appointments, ignoring his cell whenever I tried to call him, and also he'd started drinking... that wasn't like him."

"He wasn't all bad then," Scarlet said under her breath.

"But this Thor business," Victoria said, the hesitancy almost palpable in her voice.

"What about it?" Lea said.

"He started talking to me more and more about it. He became obsessed with Thor."

That name again. Lea felt the anxiety rising as she considered if all this could be a coincidence. Could her attack in Ireland for a file containing research into Norse legends, and now the murder of a man obsessed with Thor, really be connected somehow?

Her thoughts were broken by the sound of Hawke's voice. "We're going to need more than this if we're going to help, Vikki."

Victoria offered a shallow nod and looked away for a moment. Lea thought she looked scared. "More specifically then, Nate kept talking to me about Thor's

Hammer – you've all heard of Thor's Hammer, I presume?"

"Of course," Ryan said. "Every man and his dog's heard of Thor's Hammer – but that might not extend to Joe, of course."

"I know what Thor's Hammer is, Rupert."

"Hey! I thought I was safely out of Rupert territory? What happened to *mate?*"

"If you behave like a Rupert, you get called Rupert. Easy."

"What's this all about, Victoria?" Lea said, interrupting the banter. "What would a professor of Atlantic Canadian archaeology have to do with Thor's Hammer?"

Ryan leaned back and folded his arms behind his head. "I would have thought that was obvious."

Hawke sighed and shook his head. "What did I just say about acting like a Rupert, Rupert?"

Lea rolled her eyes. "Guys, *please.*"

"Obvious to some, maybe," Victoria said curtly with a glance to Ryan. "As some of you may know, the Vikings had a long history with Atlantic Canada, specifically the L'Anse aux Meadows site on the northern coast of Newfoundland. Archaeologists discovered the site in 1960 and our research dates it to at least the year 1000 AD, making Viking settlement in North America well over a thousand years old."

"It's what they call Pre-Columbian trans-oceanic contact," Ryan said chirpily.

"I'm impressed," Victoria said.

"Thanks, *babe,*" Ryan said with a wink.

Victoria looked with horror at the man in the Batman t-shirt.

Hawke rolled his eyes. "Ignore it, Vikki... and please continue."

"As I say, Nate started talking to me about Thor recently, so I began to research it as well, on the side. I got particularly interested in Valhalla, but then I realized that there were other agencies involved."

Hawke frowned. "What do you mean, *other agencies*?"

"I don't know, but Nate wasn't working alone. I think he got mixed up with others."

Victoria continued but Lea walked slowly to the French doors and stepped out on the deck. There was a ceiling fan out here on one of the roof beams, but it wasn't switched on and without the gentle whir of the blades she instantly felt the heat of the day move up her neck and over her face.

As Victoria meandered meekly through her story, Lea took a second to scan the area for any trouble. All that bothered her was a single yacht a few hundred meters out to sea – it looked like a big one worth at least a couple of mill, but that wasn't such a surprise around here, she guessed.

Further along the coast to the south she saw what looked like a Seabreacher X partially obscured by a scraggy line of mangroves. It was moored to a private jetty at the bottom of a property to the south of the resort – which also made sense. She and Hawke had seen a program on the TV about them recently and they were somewhere around the fifty K mark. If the TV program was right, they went through the sea like a torpedo and could even submerge for short durations, allowing you to see underwater through the acrylic canopy. Boys and their toys, she thought, and returned to the air-conditioned room behind her.

"All quiet on the Eastern Front?" Hawke asked.

"I think so... there's a nice Seabreacher out there I know you'll want to check out."

"A Seabreacher?" Hawke asked with interest.

"One of the neighbors owns it," Victoria said dismissively. "Makes a bloody noise half the time going up and down outside my house. Anyway, very recently," she continued, "we've been able to study the latest satellite images of the Province and they've revealed a real treasure further south on Point Rosee."

Scarlet downed her vodka and leaned forward in her seat. "Treasure, you say?"

Victoria nodded vehemently. "Oh yes, absolutely. Point Rosee is a peninsula on the southern coast of the Province and these new satellite images are strongly hinting at human social activity in the region. It's incredibly exciting."

Scarlet sighed and poured another vodka. "But no gold?"

Victoria looked confused. "Gold?"

"And ignore that, too," Lea said, taking a seat. "What has all of this got to do with Nate's death and Thor?"

Victoria sighed and tied her hair back with a small band. She looked lost. "I really don't know... I guess I'm just wondering if Nate found something up in Newfoundland that relates in some way to Thor's Hammer – he mentioned something to do with a Tesla coil – does that mean anything to anyone?"

Ryan stared at her, the blood running from his face. He had lost Sophie Durand fighting against people who wanted to destroy Tokyo with a Tesla device.

Lea saw the change in his expression. "Ry – are you okay?"

"I'm fine... Many people have surmised that Thor's Hammer might have been an ancient doomsday weapon that operated somehow like a modern Tesla coil, but nothing's ever been proved. I for one am sceptical about it."

Victoria looked glum. "I can't know or be sure what Nate was researching – but it's certainly what he was starting to talk about more and more. I'm no scientist but as I say, he did mention to me something about a Tesla Coil."

Ryan leaned forward. "Did he elaborate at all?"

"Just that Thor's Hammer wasn't actually a reference to a hammer at all, not as we see it anyway. He claimed it was more like what today we'd call a Tesla Coil. I'm not even sure what one of those is to be honest."

"It's a type of induction coil which generates alternating high-frequency currents." Ryan frowned, aware that everyone in the room was now staring in his direction in hope of a better explanation. "It's very dangerous."

"Sounds like it," Victoria said.

"But so was Thor's Hammer," Ryan said. "Mjölnir, using the Old Norse word to describe it, was one of the most terrifying weapons in Norse mythology. In fact I'd say it was probably up there with Poseidon's trident."

"This is all sounding very dangerous," Scarlet said, sipping the vodka. "Which is just great."

Victoria sighed again. She looked desolate. "But what has any of this got to do with why Nate was killed in Newfoundland?"

Ryan's eyes widened. "Maybe it's got something to do with Thor crossing the ocean thousands of years ago and winding up in Canada, like the Vikings did?"

"It can't be…" Victoria said in almost a whisper. "Thor was a mythological figure! Obviously he couldn't have existed…"

"Obviously," Scarlet said quietly. The vodka glass raised to her lips obscured her eye-roll from Victoria.

"But then again," Victoria continued, beginning to sob, "Nate was an extremely accomplished and highly respected archaeologist. If he was talking about Thor and this hammer all the time then maybe – just maybe there's something to it after all."

"That's a good theory," Lea said, steering Victoria away from the subject. "I'm no expert when it comes to archaeology, but if you say Nate was onto something then that's good enough for me."

Victoria looked up at Lea and the others and dried her eyes, smearing mascara on her cheeks. "Do you mean it?"

Lea nodded and rubbed her shoulder. "Of course."

"So you don't think I'm insane?"

"We've heard a lot worse," Hawke said. "Believe me."

Lea shot him a quick, covert *shut up* look and handed Victoria a handkerchief.

"Thank goodness for that," she said, pulling herself together again. She swivelled in her chair and hit the play button on her answer-phone. "Because I got a call yesterday and I know I'm not imagining *this*."

The room was suddenly filled with a man's low, gravelly voice as the message on the machine played: *"Lady Victoria... you talk to anyone about Dr Derby and you get the same treatment he got. Keep your mouth shut."*

Victoria jumped in her seat as the line disconnected violently. "Damn thing gets me every time!" she said, almost in a whimper. "I must have listened to it a hundred times since it came in yesterday just to make sure I'm not going mad and imagining it."

Hawke frowned. "You're definitely not imagining it, Vikki." He turned to the others. "Any ideas?"

"French, obviously," Scarlet said.

Ryan snorted. "Hardly – that's a Belgian accent."

Lea felt herself grow cold. Now she knew this could be no coincidence and that she had to tell the others the details of what she'd found in Ireland.

"Lea?" Hawke asked. "What's the matter?"

"That voice... it sounds exactly like the voices of the men who tried to kidnap me in Ireland."

Victoria sighed. "Well, whoever they are, I know they must have killed Nate and I know it had something to do with this Thor business."

"Whatever's going on," Hawke said, "we need to get to Newfoundland and see if we can make sense of what happened to Nate. Hopefully we can find a lead up there and then we might be able to work out what happened to him and get to the bottom of this Thor stuff. If we're talking about some kind of ancient doomsday weapon we can't waste time."

Victoria nodded her head "All right, in that case I think we need..."

She stopped talking and her face froze into a rictus of fear. She pointed at the open doors and screamed.

Within the space of a second the tranquillity of the beach hut was turned upside down as the boat Lea had spied earlier passed along the seashore at the end of the garden. Then a number of heavily armed gunmen on the deck fired submachine guns at the property.

"Get down!" Hawke yelled.

"Bastards are doing a drive-by shooting in a frigging motor yacht!" Ryan shouted.

All around them bullets drilled into the luxury room and tore the place to pieces.

CHAPTER THREE

Hawke hit the floor in a heartbeat, and then immediately scanned the room to check on everyone else. Lea was already behind the cover of the sofa and she was returning fire in no uncertain terms, but Victoria looked like the proverbial rabbit in the headlights, so Hawke dived for her and grappled her to the floor with his arms tight around her waist. Lea caught the move in the corner of her eye but said nothing. Everyone else followed suit as the first wave of bullets tore over their heads and wrecked the rear wall.

On the other side of the room, Scarlet had dived for cover and grappled Ryan to the floor with her arms around his waist. They landed with a crash on the mahogany floorboards, and Ryan yelled out as Scarlet fell down on top of him. "If you want me all you have to do is ask," he said, putting his arms around her waist.

"Gross," she said "I just saved your life and that's what you're thinking about? I hate to break it to you, *boy*, but I see you in approximately the same way a praying mantis sees a fly."

"Roger that," Ryan said glumly.

"Or *not*, in your case," she replied.

Hawke peered over a shredded sofa and saw the speed boat had turned around in a sharp arc and was pulling up to the jetty at the bottom of the garden.

"We've got to get out here!" he shouted. "We're out-manned and out-gunned, and not even *I* am that good."

Lea shook her head and sighed. "If you were a Mr Man you'd be Mr Modest, I reckon."

Hawke gave her a sarcastic grin and told everyone to stay calm, but Victoria began to panic and scrambled closer to Lea by the door.

"They're trying to kill me again!" she screamed, and ducked down behind Lea with her head in her hands. "I need to get out of here!"

"Just take it easy," Hawke said as he unloaded a second magazine through the Louvre windows. He tried to calm her but between the answer-phone message and this attack she could hardly be called paranoid. Someone out there obviously wanted her dead and it had to be connected to Nate Derby's murder in Canada, but now his focus was on the vicious assault approaching from the waterline.

Outside the boat had now moored on the pier and the gunmen were making their way through the garden, using the lush tropical undergrowth for cover. Hawke counted four of them including a woman with a crew cut, and the way they moved made him think they were ex-Special Forces of some kind. As they got closer, he recognized a tattoo of a burning grenade on one of the men's necks – the same as the one he had seen on Reaper, which could mean only one thing.

Now, he and the rest of the team returned fire as Victoria grew more hysterical.

"They've come to kill me! You have to stop them!"

The assault team in the garden split into two groups, with three of them remaining in the original assault position while the woman disappeared from view.

"Where has she gone?" Scarlet said. "The woman's disappeared."

"They're opening a second front somewhere!" Hawke said, ducking again to avoid taking a bullet. It traced over him and smashed into the wall sending plaster puffing up into the air.

In the chaos of the fire-fight, Lea yelled: "I'll find her!"

"Where are you going?" Victoria said, panicking. "You can't leave me alone!"

"Just stay here with the others while I make sure the kitchen's clear!"

Before Lea could make another move, Victoria panicked and bolted for the kitchen door. Hawke cursed, guessing her intention was to try and escape out the front but that was exactly where the woman with the crew cut had gone to create the second front in their assault.

Lea stayed low and made a move toward the kitchen to try and stop Victoria but she was through the door in a second. If the assault team really were thinking of a pincer movement and coming in through the kitchen, Victoria would be in a lot of trouble.

Hawke picked off another of the men in the garden, sending him spinning around into the shrubbery where he got tangled and ended up hanging there like a macabre scarecrow. The SBS man nodded in appreciation of his work when he heard Ryan shouting from across the room.

"Er... *guys!*"

"What is it, Ryan?" Scarlet shouted. "If you want someone to change your nappy I'm afraid the grown-ups are rather busy at the moment and if you..." She stopped talking when she saw the look on his face. "Ryan?"

Ryan said nothing, but raised a hand and pointed over Scarlet's shoulder.

Hawke turned to see someone holding Victoria hostage. It was the woman he had seen in the garden with the crew cut. She was tall with a powerful athletic body and a thin, jagged scar ran from the corner of her mouth and snaked away behind her left ear. She blew a large purple bubblegum bubble which popped and she pulled it back into her mouth. Whoever she was, she was holding a knife to Victoria Hamilton-Talbot's slender throat. The serrated blade pushed into the soft flesh and started to draw blood.

Then she spoke. "All of you – drop your weapons or she dies, right in front of you."

Hawke watched an expression of total fear color Victoria's face as he processed the woman's accent. It sounded Russian, he considered – maybe a southern dialect. He hated to give the order, but he knew had no choice. "Do as she says!"

Scarlet spoke next. "All right, just take it easy, darling," she said, never taking her eyes off the woman. "I'm going to climb away from the geek and stand up, with my hands above my head – I'm not armed."

The woman peered at Ryan for a second before giving Scarlet a slow nod of approval to stand up.

Scarlet moved away from Ryan, hands up to show she was unarmed, and made her way slowly into the center of the room.

Hawke studied the woman carefully as she spoke and measured up the threat: left-handed, Russian accent, and a coldness in her eyes that reminded him of someone he had met before.

Then she screamed another order. "All of you, guns down! I won't tell you again."

Hawke cursed inwardly, but gently set his gun down on the floorboards. "Just let her go and tell us what you want."

Before he finished speaking, the sole surviving gunman from the garden stepped casually through the rear doors and stood in the center of the room. This was the man with the tattoo of a burning grenade on his neck. He too was tall but sported slicked-back hair and had a solid, prominent nose. He spoke in rapid French to the woman holding Victoria and then looked down at Hawke on the floor.

"Could this be the mighty Joe Hawke?" he said.

"Right first time," Hawke said sourly. "And who are you?"

With no warning, the man kicked Hawke in the face and sent him flying back into the upturned drinks cabinet. "My name is Leon Smets and never forget it."

Hawke wiped the blood from his mouth with the back of his hand and crawled back up to his knees. He noticed the yacht at the bottom of the garden was slipping out of view to the south of the resort.

Smets surveyed the small group for a few seconds and nodded with appreciation. His dark eyes settled menacingly on Victoria. "Are you Donovan?"

She shook her head.

"Where is Donovan?" he said, looking around at the others, all kneeling on the floor. "Give me her or this woman dies right in front of you." He nodded dismissively at Victoria who was still trembling in the woman's grip.

Hawke knew what Lea had to do. He knew she couldn't watch an innocent woman die to protect herself, but why Smets could possibly want her and not Victoria was a mystery to him.

Lea turned her face up to Smets and spoke. "I'm Lea Donovan... what do you want with me?"

He grabbed her by the hair and yanked her to her feet. "You know what we want. Come with me, and no more fucking questions." His voice was cold and emotionless.

Hawke reached out to her as she passed but they all knew she had no choice but to surrender. That hunting knife was pushing deeper into Victoria's throat and the woman holding it looked like she wanted to kill her more than she wanted to take her next breath.

When Lea was beside Smets, the former Foreign Legion man gave a nod to the woman and she pushed Victoria away. Smets put his gun in the small of Lea's back as Victoria gasped with a strange mix of relief and horror. She tumbled to the floor beside Hawke.

"I'm so sorry..." she said quietly.

"Forget it," Hawke said. "People like this don't play fair."

Smets grinned, but there was nothing in the eyes except hate. "Now we go, and you stay here like good little puppies or the Irish woman gets her throat slit."

They moved Lea away into the kitchen and silence fell in the room as the ECHO team looked at each, stunned.

Hawke knew there was no time to waste, so he grabbed his gun and ran to the kitchen. He went through the narrow door and turned the corner with the weapon raised but found an empty room. The flyscreen door was closing slowly behind them. They had gone, and he had to act fast if he was going to rescue Lea. Why they had gone to all this trouble to take her was a question he could answer later, but how had they known they were in Florida?

He smashed his way through the wedged-shut outside door and scanned the back yard for Lea and her kidnappers. He felt the adrenalin pounding through his body as his mind raced with visions of her being subjected to another kidnapping, and maybe worse. He wasn't going to let that happen again.

"I see them!" he shouted to the others. "The bastards are dragging her toward the boat!"

The yacht he had seen going south was slowly moving further along the coast from Victoria's beach hut to where it was covered by the curve of a tree-lined beach. The Englishman now saw it was a Maritimo M58, a luxurious sixty-foot motor yacht with several opulently appointed decks not to mention some pretty chunky hardware under the hood. Whoever was behind this operation had funds.

"We can't let them get away!" Ryan shouted, pulling out his phone.

"Thanks for that contribution, Captain Obvious," Scarlet said as she smoothly reloaded her SIG. "And now is hardly the time to play Final Fantasy, is it dear?"

"I'm not playing Final Bloody Fantasy," he replied. "I'm taking their picture. If they're Foreign Legion our friend from Marseille might be able to help identify them." He zoomed in on them and started snapping pictures.

"Ah, yes," Scarlet said. "I was waiting to see how long it would be till you thought of that."

Hawke ignored the comments as he tracked the attackers' progress through the resort. They were keeping off the central path and using the gardens of the beach huts for added cover as they made their way to the boat.

"The yacht has to come into the coast to pick them up." Scarlet said.

From their position in the garden they were able to look down the side of the property at the coast and watch as the luxury boat sailed calmly away from them.

"They're going to rendezvous further down the coast behind those palms!" Hawke said.

"There's a short-cut through here!" Victoria said. "It's a narrow track which is used by the garbage trucks once a week. If they're trying to get back to the coast then this is the fastest way to try and catch them."

"Right," Hawke said firmly. "Scarlet, you stay here with Vikki and Ryan – I'm going after Lea."

Scarlet rolled her eyes. "Babysitting again?"

"We're not sure if they're planning on attacking again or if they have other men here we don't know about. The last thing we want is for us both to go after Lea and get back to find Vikki and Ryan with their heads blown off."

"Er *yeah*…" Ryan said with a look of horror on his face. "That's definitely the last thing we want."

"Heads blown off?" Victoria said, going white. "You don't mean that literally, do you, Mr Hawke?"

Scarlet sighed. "I will do literally anything if you let me go for Lea while you stay here with these two."

"Sorry, Scarlet, but not this time."

"Bastard, but go… just go!"

Hawke didn't reply, but just started running.

He sprinted down the track Victoria had suggested and kept his eye on the progress of the yacht. His boots crunched on the gravel and he made his way along the backs of the luxury huts at speed, calling out an apology as he ran through the middle of someone's garden picnic and getting snagged in their birthday bunting.

He saw the yacht was slowly drawing away from him, and the humidity of the Florida day was dragging on him like a weight as he sprinted. He leaped over a low wooden fence and sent a shower of startled Bahama mockingbirds flying from an orange tree up into the air. It was then he realized he was starting to lose the race.

He increased speed, but they were still too far away. He vaulted over another low fence and made his way toward the shore, noticing an Innespace Seabreacher X moored to a pier. It must have been the one Lea had seen earlier.

Now Smets was dragging Lea along the jetty and waving his gun in the air as he screamed at his underlings. He turned, saw Hawke and fired a series of casual shots in his vague direction to keep the

Englishman from getting any closer, but Hawke slipped into parkour mode to dodge the bullets and executed a couple of high-speed shoulder rolls as he drew closer.

Now he felt like his lungs were about to burst as he finally got to the beach, only to see Smets hauling Lea roughly into the back of the large boat and shouting commands at the man in the wheelhouse.

Without thinking of his own safety, Hawke took a deep breath and started to sprint to the jetty. He'd let Lea slip through his fingers before and he was damned sure he wasn't going to let a man like Smets get his hands on her.

But even running as fast as he could, he knew he wasn't going to get there in time, and as he hit the foreshore and vaulted up onto the jetty he watched in agony as the Maritimo's powerful engines roared loudly and pushed the boat out into the ocean.

CHAPTER FOUR

The Maritimo raced away from the shore, its twin Volvo engines powering the sixty-foot motoryacht toward the eastern horizon with an impressive roar. Hawke raised his gun and shot one of the men at the rear of the boat. He tumbled toward the bright blue water clutching at his neck before hitting the surface with a loud splash and disappearing into the white foam in the boat's wake.

Leon Smets was still holding a gun to Lea's throat. A faint smirk was visible on his face as the boat moved further out to sea. As they accelerated away, he turned and dragged her below decks. The woman with the shaved head stopped to flip the bird at Hawke and then followed Smets and Lea into the cabin.

Hawke knew he had seconds to give chase, and scanned the area for a solution. He saw plenty of boats bobbing up and down in the marina, but that was a five minute sprint and by the time he got there a boat as powerful as the Maritimo would have built up too much of a lead.

Then he remembered the Innespace Seabreacher X he had seen earlier – the one Lea had told him about back at the beach house. That was less than half the distance and those things were fast enough to eat up any lead generated by the motoryacht.

He sprinted to the private jetty and climbed aboard the Seabreacher. It was a semi-submersible watercraft painted to look like a shark, and as watercraft went it was in a different league to just about anything else on the water. Thanks to the TV show he'd watched with

Lea he knew they worked on a three dimensional axis with pitch, roll and yaw, the way aircraft moved. He also knew it had a top speed of almost fifty knots, which was nearly twice as fast as the Maritimo could manage.

He wasted no time in dexterously unscrewing the ignition and hotwiring the boat, and seconds later he felt the revs of the lightweight supercharged Rotax engine all around him. This was the fighter jet of the ocean.

Behind him he heard the sound of a man shouting and screaming. He turned in the seat and saw a man with a white hat running toward him. "Get out of my boat you god-damned thief!"

Time to go, he thought.

He closed the cockpit hatch and secured it before strapping himself in and squeezing on the joystick. Instantly he increased in speed and shot away from the jetty, leaving nothing behind him but a lengthy wake and a massive spray of seawater.

Looking ahead he saw the Maritimo, and squeezed down on the trigger once again to increase his speed. As the rapid acceleration pushed him back into his seat he felt like he was riding a bullet, but now he was getting close enough to the motoryacht to start making the gunmen suspicious. They assembled on deck with their weapons and watched with interest as he piloted the Seabreacher closer and closer to their boat.

After much pointing and arguing they decided he was a threat and started firing on him. Hawke reacted in a heartbeat, steering into the yacht's wake and pushing down on the joystick. The Seabreacher pushed through the wake and descended beneath the waves for a few seconds – just long enough for Hawke to steer the high-velocity watercraft away from its original vector and bring himself across to the yacht's portside.

He pulled back on the stick and the Seabreacher broke the sea's surface at high speed, shooting up into the air like a dolphin racing alongside the prow of a cruise liner. Now he was on the portside of the Maritimo and the men raced from the rear of the yacht, lined up along the left side of the boat and began to pour fire on the compact watercraft with their submachine guns.

Hawke heard the familiar metallic *pings* as their bullets sprayed up the side of the Seabreacher's reinforced glass-fibre hull. He cursed and steered sharply to the left and then pushed down on the stick sending the craft under the waves once more. Correcting his course to the right, he crossed in front of the Maritimo just as he emerged from the surface again and shot into the air barely avoiding a collision with the bow of the yacht. The Rotax engine revved wildly as he shot into the air and landed with a smack at ninety degrees to the boat.

Now on its starboard side, he decided playtime was over and hit the hatch release. The glass dome slid back like the cockpit on a fighter jet and allowed him to return fire. He slowed the craft until the boat pulled parallel with him and smiled warmly at the men who had now reassembled on the starboard side, giving them a cheery wave.

For a second his disarming smile seemed to confuse them, but then he raised his gun in his left hand and fired a series of shots at them while still controlling the boat with his right hand. The Seabreacher slipped around on the surface back and forth and the salty water sprayed up into the now open cockpit as Hawke struggled to control the craft while simultaneously aiming at the gunmen.

It paid off as he successfully picked off another of the men and sent him flying off the back of the yacht, but the men returned fire and this time they had more success. The Seabreacher's incredible speed and versatility in the water was dependent on its amazing design, part of which was the inclusion of shark-like fins. The men's second volley of fire had blasted one of these fins to pieces and raked a series of holes in the hull and now Hawke felt the craft slipping out of his control.

With the Seabreacher now veering all over the place, he knew there was only one move left to play, and that was the move he was here to make anyway, so he did his best to navigate the craft over to the yacht and then pulled back on the stick. The speeding watercraft launched into the air and flew towards the yacht's rear deck.

The men scrambled for fear of getting hit by its lethal whirring propellers, but it flew past them just as Hawke had planned. On its way past the yacht he leaped from the small cockpit and grabbed hold of the yacht's rear deck. Somewhere behind him the Seabreacher spun upside down and hit the water at full speed, sending a massive explosion of fire and sea-spray into the hot afternoon.

Half immersed in the water as the yacht raced forward, Hawke scrambled up onto the stern and clambered over the railing to the relative safety of the rear deck.

But it was only a relative safety, because a second later a man emerged from the yacht's galley and fired an uncompromising quantity of hot lead at him from the flashing muzzle of a Heckler & Koch MP5. Hawke ducked behind the lazarette, the small storage area at the rear of the yacht. Ryan had once told him this was named after Lazarus, because he was placed on board an old sailing ship in such a place after his death. *Thanks for that, Rupert*, he thought as he reloaded his gun and prepared to fight back.

Hawke's death nearly ensued seconds later when the man returned fire and his bullets punctured their way through the lazarette and drilled into the teak deck, splintering all around him. He waited until the assault was over and the man tried to reload before he spun around and fired at him, but the man had wedged himself behind the cockpit's folding doors for cover. Hawke's bullet smashed the panel of strengthened glass but it did no more damage than cause a spider web fracture and further obscure the man from view.

He ducked again as the man returned fire, but then the gun jammed, and Hawke took advantage of the situation by firing two more bullets at him, planting them in his chest and neck. He collapsed like a sack of potatoes and Hawke leaped to his feet and crossed the small deck to the cabin.

As he went, he saw Leon Smets and the woman with the crew cut zooming away from the Maritimo in a Nautilus 12 DLX – a luxury console tender attached to the larger yacht. They were moving away at some speed from the Maritimo, the Suzuki outboard roaring away as the vessel cut through the surface of the water. He cursed himself for letting them get away, but it was then he heard Lea screaming from somewhere below decks.

He had only seconds to make the call and went with his heart – save Lea. He knew that the Maritimo was faster than the Nautilus, so maybe Smets had made a mistake and would pay for it later. With the decision made he moved toward the cabin. It was empty, but he knew there was another man somewhere on the top deck – someone was controlling the boat after all – and this was confirmed a few seconds later when a man began firing at him from above. He dodged the burst of bullets from the goon and turned to go in the main cabin for cover.

He was now in a sumptuous open-plan room surrounded by a horse-shoe shaped white leather couch and a sparkling glass coffee table. He ran right over the top of the table, booting the centrepiece out the way as he went, and headed for the lower decks. Somewhere down there was Lea Donovan, and he prayed she was unharmed.

He kicked open a polished wooden door, gun raised, but saw nothing except a gleaming galley replete with bowls of fresh fruit and orchids. It reminded him of the catamaran Reaper had acquired back in the Ionian Sea, but if anything it was even more stunning.

He heard a noise above him and looked to his left to see a man trying to make his way down a series of steps leading to the galley from the upper portside deck. It was the goon from the wheelhouse who had been piloting the yacht. By Hawke's reckoning this man must be the last remaining man on board, but it only took one to knock you out of the game.

Hawke fired a shot at his legs and hit the man's knee. He screamed in agony and tumbled down the steps until landing with a smack on the hard teak decking. Hawke smiled at him before piling a fist into his face and knocking him out. "Nighty night."

He then helped himself to the man's machine pistol and moved through the saloon and into the lower corridor. With no one at the controls the yacht turned sharply to starboard and everything tipped to the left. Hawke had to grab a handrail to stop himself from being thrown into one of the guest cabins.

"Fuck it!" he screamed.

"Joe?"

It was Lea's voice coming from behind a heavy wooden door opposite the guest cabin.

"Sorry about the language."

43

"Is that you, Joe?"

"No, it's King Edward the First... who do you think it is?"

"Just get on with it Your Majesty!"

He blasted the lock before moving inside and was faced with a large double bed in what was obviously the VIP suite, but there was no sign of Lea.

"Where the hell are you?" he asked.

"In the toilet."

"If it's at sea it's called the head," he said.

"Oh sorry – is that like if you're at sea you're called a dickhead?"

Hawke rolled his eyes and aimed the machine pistol at the door, setting it on single shot. "Stand away from the door – I wouldn't want to accidentally hit you and deprive the world of your cutting wit."

"Sorry," Lea replied, her voice muffled by the heavy door. "Did you say you were a cunning shit?"

Hawke ignored the comment. "Stand back, Lea!"

He fired and blasted the lock off the door. The force of the explosion smashed the door back against the compact shower cubicle and revealed a smiling Lea Donovan. She winked at Hawke and kissed him on the cheek. "My hero!"

"All right, that's enough of that," Hawke said, handing her his pistol. "Here, take this."

"Why do you get the MP5? I want the MP5!"

Hawke sighed and switched guns. "Fine, you have the MP5 if it means that much. At least with a rapid fire weapon you stand a chance of actually hitting your target."

"Seriously now, Josiah – why did you give up your comedy career?"

Hawke held her shoulders and looked her in the eye. "You said these were the same men who attacked you in

Ireland... the same men behind your father's death. I'll only ask you once, Lea – why did they take you?"

He watched as she agonized over her answer. "I'm sorry, I should have told you all earlier... especially you."

"Told me what?"

"We've no time now, Joe – but when I went to Ireland I found something, a file containing research about the Norse legends. It was written by my Dad... I put the information on a flash-drive and..."

"And these goons just took it?"

She nodded glumly. "I think the plan was to torture it out of me or something, but when they found the flash-drive they thought all their birthdays had come at once. Please tell me you took them all down on the deck?"

"Sorry, but no... I think I know where your flash-drive is though."

"Where?"

"Follow me!"

They ran up to the deck and Hawke cursed when he saw the Nautilus was nowhere in sight. "Damn it – they've gone!"

"Don't tell me – half-man, half-ape with a Reaper tattoo?"

Hawke nodded. "That's the one – he took off on a tender with Miss Congeniality."

"And you let them go?"

"I made the call to save you instead."

"And this is why I *love* you, Josiah Hawke."

"I thought we agreed you weren't going to call me that?"

"We did – sorry... but talking of names – we need to run Smets through our computers."

"Agreed. We can do it when we get back to shore – and we need to get Alex to resend your father's research files to your phone, but in the meantime let's get after the bastards. We can easily track them down in this."

Lea shook her head.

"What is it?" Hawke asked.

"No fuel left – I heard Crew Cut Lady and Smets talking about it. That's why they took off in the Nautilus."

"Bloody fantastic, and they've got the research files as well."

Hawke determined they had enough fuel to go the short distance back to shore and slowly turned the yacht around, taking control and sailing her home with what little remained in the tanks. Arriving at the jetty and securing the yacht with a mooring rope, a small man in Bermuda shorts and a white bucket hat came running up to them, waving his fist in the air.

"Hey! You – I recognize you!"

"Who's *that?*" Lea said, narrowing her eyes with confusion.

"Leave it to me."

"You stay right where you are, buster!"

"Afternoon!" Hawke said chirpily as he tied off the mooring rope.

"You took my Seabreacher – where the hell is it?"

"Gone but not forgotten, mate," Hawke said flatly.

"What the hell! That thing cost me fifty grand!" The man put his hands on his hips but took a step back when the Englishman straightened up to his full height and covered him with his broad shadow.

"Here," Hawke said, casually tossing him the keys to the Maritimo. "Have this instead – it's worth two million dollars."

CHAPTER FIVE

Newfoundland, Canada

Lea woke up after a short sleep just in time to see the tops of thousands of pine trees flashing beneath the plane as they descended onto the runway in St. John's. The island was a largely untouched wilderness on the eastern coast of Canada, still bearing the ancient glacier scars of the last ice age on the sparse face of its boreal landscape. It was hard to believe this was part of the same continent they had taken off from just a few short hours ago.

This was the island that the Icelandic Viking explorer Leif Erikson had sailed to over a thousand years ago. He had called it Vinland because of the grapevines he had discovered growing all over the island. This was the island where Portuguese explorers had come to find the legendary Northwest Passage. This was the island where Sir Humphrey Gilbert, Sir Francis Drake's half-brother, had started the entire British Empire when he claimed it under Royal Charter for Elizabeth I in 1583. This was an island with history.

After the plane had taxied into the small airport they were soon on their way west, skirting the shores of Windsor Lake in a hired Land Rover Evoque. Less than fifteen minutes later they reached the small community of Portugal Cove on the Avalon Peninsula and drove the Evoque into the back of the Bell Island ferry.

"Did you know," Ryan said, "that Portugal Cove was one of the first settlements in the entire New World?"

Scarlet sighed. "Do try and control your nerd, Lea."

"He's not my nerd," Lea said with a shrug. "He's Maria's nerd."

"Hey!" Ryan said, indignant. "I'm right here!"

Scarlet dragged on her cigarette and winced. "Like I could ever forget."

Lea smiled at the banter. She had felt better since telling everyone about the research files and having Alex get them from her room and re-send them. At least now they were working as one again. She looked out across the waters of Conception Bay. Even now in summer they looked cold and gray, which wasn't surprising considering they often still got winter snow and ice well into April or sometimes later.

She felt a sense of serene calm about the place and took the opportunity to relax as the ferry trundled slowly across the bay on its way to the island. After she'd explained about Ireland and the files on the plane journey, Ryan had enlightened the team about their destination, and while much of what he'd said could only ever be of interest to a person like Ryan, some of it had stuck in her mind.

The largest town was the community of Wabana, where they were headed now. The town's name meant 'the place where the sun shines first' in Beothuk, the language of the first people to live here. More recently, the town had suffered U-Boat attacks in World War II in the Nazi drive to destroy Allied cargo ships transporting much-needed iron ore to the steel mills of Nova Scotia.

Today, just a few thousand people lived on the small island, and they were all dependent on the ferries for their connection to the rest of Newfoundland. When the ferry service stopped for whatever reason, helicopters had to be used to take people to the mainland for any emergencies.

It didn't take long for them to make the short drive to the center of the island and then down a gentle slope to the northwest side where Martha Parsons had lived alone in her small white clapboard house for over thirty years. When they had started researching the blaze at the museum in which Nate Derby had died they had quickly discovered the name of the curator – Bill Smith. It hadn't taken long to connect him to Martha, his former fiancée. A few phone calls had revealed an address and a local rumor about a mysterious engagement gift that was worth exploring. They figured she was as good a person as any to ask about what had happened to Nate and Bill at the museum.

"Come in," she said, barely looking at them. "How's she cuttin'?"

Ryan looked at Hawke, confused. "Um…"

"You want coffee?" she said sharply.

"Yes, thanks."

"Anyone want something to eat? I can fire up a scoff if you want."

"Not *entirely* sure what a scoff is," Ryan said, peering into a small pot on the stove, "but I think your wallpaper paste's gone off,"

"Wallpaper paste, what the..?" Martha looked at Ryan and squinted. "That's fish and brewis you fool."

Ryan repeated the words like an admonished child. "Fish and brewis?"

"Want some?"

"Um…"

"I'll have a go," Hawke said.

"Me too," Scarlet said.

Lea and Victoria joined Ryan and passed, but Martha served Hawke and Scarlet two bowls of the local tradition – cod and hard tack – and added some

49

scrunchions, a salted pork fat fried until crunchy and sprinkled liberally over the top.

Scarlet looked disappointed when Martha set the pot down and poured herself a coffee. "Don't I get any of those little scrunchy things?"

Martha looked at Scarlet and then over at the scrunchions. "Women don't need no scrunchions. Just sit down and eat what you got."

Ryan smirked as a reprimanded Scarlet lowered herself to the kitchen table and spooned in a mouthful of the fish and brewis.

Martha jabbed the wooden spoon in Ryan's face. "What about you – you sure you don't want none? Scrawny little chicken like you could do with feeding up."

A frowning Ryan peered into the pot once again. "You have to be *joking*."

"Huh?" Martha looked at him accusingly.

With all eyes on Ryan, he had no escape. "I mean you *have* to be joking – of course I want some!"

Martha spooned out another bowl and set it on the table. "It's all yours."

Ryan looked at the food sheepishly. "Thanks."

Lea had chosen to stick with the coffee, which came from an original Atomic coffee machine from the early fifties. She was marvelling at the thing as it creaked and whined when Martha caught her in the corner of her eye.

"Wedding present."

"Ah…"

"Don't worry, it's not gonna blow up or nothing like that."

"No, I'm sure it won't." Lea stepped closer to the machine to highlight the meaning in her words.

"Just that the way you was looking at it made me wonder if it was admiration or horror in your eyes."

Lea smiled. "A bit of both, sorry…"

"George fixed her up a few times over the years and I reckon she'll outlive me – here's your coffee."

Lea took the cup. "Thanks."

"Wait till you try it before you thank me," Martha said flatly.

Lea watched the old woman shuffle across the small kitchen and sit opposite Hawke and Scarlet who were busily tucking into their meals, Ryan with slightly less enthusiasm.

Martha sipped her coffee and let out a long, tired sigh. "So how d'ya like the brewis?"

"Actually, it's rather good," Scarlet said.

"Well, don't sound so surprised!" Martha said, laughing.

Three empty bowls was the real answer Martha was looking for, and she got that a few moments later when everyone was finished, including Ryan.

"Didn't taste like wallpaper paste after all," Ryan said.

Martha turned to Lea. "And how's that coffee?"

"The best I've ever had."

"You wouldn't be bullshitting me now, would you?"

Lea laughed. "No! I mean it."

"And what about you with them ear-rings?" The old woman stared at Victoria.

"Absolutely delightful, thank you."

Martha grunted and nodded. "George's parents got that for us the day we were married."

"How long were you married?" Lea asked.

"Fifty years. He's been gone nearly fifteen years now."

"You must have been very much in love."

Martha nodded. "Before I got married to George I was engaged to another man."

51

They all looked at her but only Lea replied. "What happened?"

"Things didn't work out – just the way it goes sometimes."

"What was his name?"

"You already know his name – his name was Bill Smith, or Billy back in the day."

Now she officially had their undivided attention, but again it was Lea who led the conversation.

"Why didn't it work out?"

"He cheated on me in Korea," Martha said without emotion.

"I'm sorry to hear that."

"Why are you sorry? It was over half a century ago!" She leaned forward in her seat. "You know, when I read about his death it was a bolt from the blue. I hadn't spoken to him since I got his letter when he was in the army."

Martha rubbed her eyes and suppressed a yawn. She glanced at her watch before continuing. "I wondered if I was reading about the same man, but I guess I knew in my heart I was. A sad way for an old man to go out, and I just hope they catch the bastards who did it."

"That's what we're here for," Hawke said bluntly.

Martha looked at him with scepticism in her eyes. "If you say so, young man. If you say so."

"We'll do whatever we can to find his killers," Lea said gently.

Martha's voice got harder. "But you're not here to find his killers, are you? You're looking for something altogether harder to find, if you catch my meaning."

"Well…"

"Ah, it's been so long… what odds?" She closed her eyes for a moment and took a deep breath. "You know, Billy was poor – very poor. He couldn't afford no ring when we got engaged. I remember it like it was yesterday. It was a mausey day all right, and he was so nervous about telling me. I made a big thing about telling him how it didn't matter and I didn't need nothing like that, but then he gave me something else."

Lea leaned closer, gripped by the tale. "What did he give you?"

Martha looked at her sharply. "You must have some idea, or you wouldn't be up here drinking my coffee."

"We're only trying to help," Lea said.

Martha sighed again. She was looking tired. "So now you want to know about what Billy Smith had hidden away in the museum, am I right?"

Hawke nodded. "That would be a good start, yes."

"Then listen up, because I want to go bed and I can't yarn all night like I once could. I'm only going to say this once."

CHAPTER SIX

The Pyrenees Mountains

Álvaro Sala watched with unrestrained delight as the inland taipan slithered through his fingers and glided up around his neck. He felt the smooth head of the world's most venomous snake parting his long lampblack hair and pushing its way around the base of his skull. Moments later it appeared on the other side of his head, nudging through his hair once again like a wicked magician emerging through black velvet stage curtains. It slid back down into his hands and he wondered if the serpent was enjoying this game as much as he was.

Lit only by a narrow crack of light emanating from the entrance to the mountain cave a hundred feet behind him, a devilish grin could just be made out on the Andorran recluse's morbidly thin face.

The man opposite him strained against the tension of the climbing ropes which Sala's loyal thug, the convicted Belgian serial killer Marcus Deprez had used to lash him to the rocks at the back of the cave. High above them was Sala's impressive luxury château, but down here in the cave systems far below was nothing but an eerie whistling wind and the stench of imminent death.

Álvaro grinned. "Tell me, Antonius... did you ever think it would end like this?"

"Threaten me all you like, Álvaro, but we've known each other for long enough to understand why I can't tell you what you want to know."

Sala paused as the taipan made another circuit of his neck. "And we've known each long enough, Antonius, to know what will happen to you if you do not get what your fragile body so badly craves. Now you are here, you face the same fate as I."

Antonius attempted a laugh, but the nearness of his terrible destiny killed it in his dry, constricted throat. "The Oracle was right to ostracize you, Álvaro. I can see that clearly now, and you must surely see it too. Your failure in Ethiopia was quite unforgivable."

Sala's grin faded from his gaunt face as Antonius's words blew gently away on the cave's cold breeze. "I'm very disappointed in you, Antonius. I thought when you accepted my invitation to come here you would bring me better news than this. Now, you force me to act against my own will."

"Be sensible, Álvaro! We both know why I can't tell you what you need to hear. No one goes against the Oracle." Antonius yanked at the chains holding him fast but there was no chance of escape, only the sound of the steel links rattling against the rocks in mockery of his dire situation.

Sala nodded his head thoughtfully. "I suppose you realize by now that I will not simply allow you to perish the normal way."

Antonius's eyes crawled from Sala's face to the snake in his arms. "Yes, I thought that unlikely. Mercy was never in your character, Álvaro."

"Ha! You talk of mercy after you and your brethren tried to consign me to the worst fate imaginable."

"You deserve it."

Sala was silent for a short time as he paced around the cave deep in thought. His most loyal personal security guard, Marcus Deprez, leaned up against part of the rock face and watched in silence as the exchange unfolded, his only animation being to light an unfiltered Gauloises caporal and blow a smoke ring into the cave's cold atmosphere. A heaving, rasping cough followed moments later.

"I deserve it, you say – how curious... In all your years on this planet, Antonius, did you ever find your way to the North?"

Now, goaded by the question, Antonius's deep laugh found its way to the surface at last. "The North? I know the North better than you ever will, Álvaro!"

Sala took a step forward and raised the snake closer to Antonius's face. "You mock me, but you cannot begin to imagine the hatred burning in my heart for your damned Athanatoi. My vengeance will be savage and final."

Now Antonius laughed. "You of all people must surely know how many men have sworn to take their revenge on us, and you must also know they all failed. We are too mighty to be touched by mortals." He paused for effect and smiled smugly at Sala. "You *are* a mortal now, aren't you, Álvaro?"

Sala's face began to twitch with rage and he had to fight hard not to squeeze the snake in his hands, such was the level of anger coursing through his veins and muscles. "Do you know, dear Antonius, how I will destroy the Athanatoi and take my revenge?"

"Enlighten me."

"By exploiting the weak link in your chain."

"And what is that?"

"It's the same weak link that has brought down countless empires... the factions."

Antonius scoffed, but kept his eyes on the writhing taipan. "What are you talking about, Álvaro? Have you finally gone mad?"

"You know what I'm talking about, Antonius. Throughout history the story of conquered peoples has been one of exploiting factions and sects – I believe Philip, the king of the ancient kingdom of Macedon summed it up very well over two thousand years ago when he called it dīvide et īmpera... divide and conquer." He leaned in ever closer to his victim. "Is that right, dear Antonius – you knew the king, didn't you?"

"I have nothing more to say to you, Álvaro."

Sala gave an evaluating nod. "I don't need your words or thoughts, brother. Those days are far behind us. I simply need you to know, before your death, that I will destroy your precious brotherhood – or should I say *cult?* – and that I know how. That I will exploit the sects and when I reach the dark heart of the Athanatoi I will tear it out with my bare hands and burn it."

"You're insane even to contemplate it," Antonius said sharply. "My death at the fangs of that serpent will be as nothing compared to what they will do to you if you dare to challenge them."

Sala paced the cave for a moment and then spoke quietly. "This taipan was caught in the deserts of South Australia, Antonius. Its venom contains a presynaptic neurotoxin that will paralyse you. The next thing you will experience is a terrible difficulty in drawing breath."

"You're wasting *your* breath."

"You will probably die of suffocation first, but there is a possibility that the hemotoxin in the venom – a powerful procoagulant which enters the blood and causes the activation of a clotting cascade – will lead to blood clots forming all over your body. Either way, the pitiful remnants of your life will be characterized by unimaginable agony. This will occur less than half an hour after the envenomation."

"I mean it, Álvaro. If I told you anything we both know my punishment at the hands of the Athanatoi would have me begging for your snake."

"I'm not so sure… Remember, just one bite from this creature will deliver a fatal dose of these neurotoxins, hemotoxins and myotoxins into your bloodstream."

"I care not what your intentions are."

"I tell you only as a courtesy, so you know what fate is waiting for you, lurking like a hideous, grasping shadow-creature at the foot of your bed. Your ancient life will now come to an end, here in this cave. Yes… you will now come face to face with your mortality, just as you never thought would happen, and more than that, you will die the way I want you to, because I hold that power in my hands, literally…"

Antonius looked once again at the snake.

Sala grinned. "A little like Loki."

"Loki… you can teach me nothing about Loki, Álvaro. Believe me."

Sala closed his eyes and spoke as if conjuring the memories from a dream. "After trying to hide from the goddess Skaði by turning himself into a salmon, Loki was finally caught! I thought my inviting you to a spot of salmon fishing in Béarn in order to lure you up here was a particularly amusing touch, don't you think?"

"With every poisonous word that tumbles from your sour lips, you show why the Oracle was right to expel you."

"Talking of poison, as you knew Loki so well you will know what happened next."

"Of course I know what happened next! He was lashed to the rocks beneath a waterfall with the entrails of his own son, Nari, and then killed when Skaði secured a poisonous snake over him and allowed its venom to drip down and kill him. His loving wife, Sigyn remained at his side and caught the venom in a bowl she held at the serpent's dripping fangs. I presume that is what this ludicrous charade is all about!"

"You forgot the best bit – the bit about how when she went to empty the bowl some of the venom would fall into Loki's face and in response, his painful, agonized writhing was so horrendous that it caused earthquakes." Sala stroked the taipan.

"Don't forget that Loki escaped from his chains, fled Ragnarök – the Doom of the Gods – and helped the giant spirits destroy the cosmos."

Sala glanced theatrically over his shoulder for a moment. "I see no sign of Sigyn, Antonius, so this time there will be no escape."

"Will there not? I'm starting to think you're bluffing, Álvaro. You always were all talk."

"Was I now?" Sala gave a low chuckle and ordered Deprez to set up the apparatus. Moments later the Belgian killer was rigging up a bowl above Antonius's head and connecting it to some twine. Then he placed a candle inside a metal lantern, threaded the twine above it and tightened Antonius's chains so he couldn't move an inch.

"You see here a simple device, Antonius," Sala explained coolly. "When Deprez here lights the candle in the lantern, you will have around fifteen minutes to tell me the location of Valhalla, and if you fail to do so the heat of the flame will break the twine and the bowl of poison will pour in your wound, killing you in agony. This way there is much more torment than a simple snakebite would induce and I liked the irony of the bowl being used to kill rather than to save."

"What wound?" Antonius asked, confused.

Sala smiled and snapped his fingers. Deprez padded over to the bound man and pulled out a long hunting knife. The blade flashed dully in the low light as he drew it slowly across Antonius's chest. The soft flesh split open like a ripe fruit, and blood poured keenly from the fresh wound and stained his chest. He suppressed a scream and clenched his jaw hard.

Sala smirked. "That wound."

Antonius stared in horror as Sala then gripped the snake's head and forced an envenomation from its fangs into the stone bowl.

"I will never tell you where Valhalla is! If a creature like you ever got its hands on the power hidden behind its walls the world would be brought to a precipice."

"Fifteen minutes, Antonius, and then you will share a similar fate as your hero, Loki – only no escape for you!"

Sala walked slowly from the cave, leaving Deprez to guard his old friend, but the days of friendship were a long time ago. Too long to imagine. Would Antonius talk? He doubted it, but no matter. Soon he would have the location of Valhalla from another source – his man Smets was seeing to that. He didn't need Antonius to give it to him – he just wanted to force it out of him for sport. That fool in the cave would die whatever happened today and Valhalla would still be his.

If his long life had taught him anything, it was that there was always more than one way to catch a rabbit – even if it was a very fast Irish rabbit that knew how to get away.

CHAPTER SEVEN

Martha poured more coffee and they moved into the front room by the fire. The summer was growing nearly as old as she was now, and she needed a fire at night and she didn't care who knew it.

She slowly looked at their young faces and knew it was time to tell them what they wanted to hear. They had come nearly as far as they had to go, she considered, and if it meant helping them track down Billy's killers and bringing them to justice, then so be it.

"You all wait there, you hear me?"

The young people nodded, and she was satisfied they'd do as she told them. She left the room and walked to the other side of the house where she opened her wardrobe and began pushing her dresses out of the way. This one she hadn't worn since the eighties, and that one for much longer. She smiled at the sight of them all lined up and she guessed the wrinkles on her face proved Mark Twain was right after all. She'd certainly had a good life full of fun, and not all of it wholly approvable.

At the bottom of the wardrobe, beneath a pile of old shoes were some boxes of photographs – a black and white life in two dimensions would be all that was left of her soon, she contemplated without emotion. She opened the box and found what she was looking for – a small engagement ring box, handmade from green velvet with a white silk interior.

She pulled it from the box of photographs and creaked back up to her full height, cursing as she went. Before she rejoined the young, foreign, treasure hunters in the other room, she held her breath and gently opened the tiny box.

She gasped when she saw it again. When was the last time she had seen it – maybe twenty years ago, maybe longer... she had no idea. Yesterdays slipped away like grains of sand when you were her age, she considered, and she had no idea how many had fallen through her fingers since she'd last opened the box.

And yet... it seemed like it had been *literally* yesterday. There it was again, as beautiful and enigmatic as ever. Anyone else would have thought the box contained an antique emerald ring – her mother's – but she knew better than that. She knew that the little ring box also kept another treasure safe from the world.

She smiled and closed the box before joining the others and setting the precious cargo on the tea table in front of the crackling fire. She sipped her coffee and looked at their young faces one by one. She wondered if they would catch up with Billy's killers or not, but she knew whoever those men were, they'd regret if the older Englishman ever got hold of them. It was just something in his eyes.

She opened the box and handed it around, watching the look of surprise on their faces as they witnessed its compelling power for the first time.

"This is incredible," Lea said. "At first it looks like a simple glass bead you can see through but then you realize you can see through whatever's behind it as well." She studied it closely and saw one side was convex and smooth and there was a tiny hook on the flat underside at the back.

"Not everything that's behind it," Martha corrected her. "It don't see through walls or nothing like that. It can only make things right up close to it disappear."

She handed it to the Englishman and he held it to the light and then drew it closer to his eyes for a more detailed look. "Bloody hell! Talk about weird."

Ryan held it next, holding it so Victoria was able to see it as well. "This is outstanding – it seems to be bending light somehow – a technology we've only just started working on!"

Martha nodded. "It was Billy's father who gave them to him. He had a few of them knocking around the place from his father and so on up the line. You know the way it goes. And before you ask, no one knows where they came from. Billy gave me that one right there in place of the ring, just like I told you, and the others found their way into the museum. He stashed them up there because he felt they might have had something to do with the old Mi'kmaq legends. He was part Mi'kmaq, was old Billy and very proud of it."

"What old legends?" Lea asked.

"The Invisible One," Martha said gently. "It's not unique to Mi'kmaq culture – the story comes up many times in traditional tribal folklore all over North America. Sometimes they called him the Hidden One or the Invisible Warrior, but it all amounts to the same thing. Billy told me all about it."

Ryan set his cup down. "It's a fascinating part of the culture, because…"

"Young man, do you want to tell this story or are you going to let me do it?"

Ryan blushed. "Sorry…"

Scarlet gave him a thinly veiled smirk as Martha continued.

"Billy talked to me a bit about it when we were together. These legends vary in their details depending on the culture, but they all add up to the same thing." She paused and cast her watery eyes outside on the dying day. When she spoke next it was as if she were talking to a ghost. "The Cherokee talk about the Nennehi, a race of immortal spirit folk..."

She noticed the others share a subtle glance when she mentioned the word *immortal* to them, but continued without letting on she had seen anything. "The name Nunnehi really means 'those who live anywhere', but..."

"But it's sometimes transliterated as 'those who live eternally'," Ryan said.

Martha gave Ryan another of her stares and that seemed to do the trick.

"I was *going* to say that there are different interpretations of Nunnehi, but yes, Billy told me *immortal* is sometimes one of them. Immortal means something different when you're twenty than when you're my age, believe me... Either way, the word means something that cannot be translated *exactly* into English, if you get my meaning. It means immortal, but not *exactly*, it means ghosts or spirits, but not *exactly*, it means gods, but not *exactly*. You understand?"

They all nodded. It looked like they understood.

"Like any legends in the world, no one knows why these things become such a big part of the culture, but they're important enough to travel down through the generations over centuries, so we can take something from that, I guess."

With the slightest of pauses, Martha turned to Victoria. "It was your partner who died with Billy, right?"

With a short glance at the others, Victoria nodded and finally broke her silence. "Yes, how did you know?"

"I'm nearly ninety, dear. I know just from the lookin'. What was his name?"

"Dr Nate Derby. For some reason he was up here visiting the museum but I really don't know why. In the days before his murder he started talking to me about some strange things."

Martha gave her an oblique look. "Strange things like what?"

"About Norse mythology – about Thor and Thor's Hammer."

Martha nodded and gave a sad smile. "There were rumors, sure."

"What sort of rumors?"

"Listen carefully. Billy only told me this once, and I thought he was crazy. He told me that the Invisible One could have been part of something the Vikings used to talk about. I told him he'd been drinking and he never mentioned it again. He could be crazy like that."

"I don't think he was crazy at all," Victoria said quietly. "I think this is all connected somehow."

"Well, don't look at me," Martha said flatly. "I know squat about the damned Vikings. What about you?" She looked at Ryan.

"A bit, but not too much, sorry."

"Anything will do, Ry," Lea said.

Ryan frowned. "In the context of what we're talking about the main thing would be that invisibility was an important part of the Norse mythological canon so there's an immediate link with the tribal cultures of ancient America. They had many beings who they considered had the power of invisibility, and most of these, of course, were the Aesir gods and goddesses who were key divine figures. These deities such as Thor, Loki, Frigg and Idun all had the power of invisibility. It's possible the Vikings brought the power of invisibility to North America somehow and that's what started the legends."

Lea looked at Ryan sharply, her face suddenly a study of anxiety. "Say those names again, Ry."

"Which ones – Thor and so on?"

"Sure."

"Thor, Loki, and Idun – there were many more, and of course, Idun was the keeper of the sacred apples which imparted eternal youth..."

"I'm hearing that expression an awful lot these days," Scarlet said, sighing.

"None of those Ry," Lea said. "You said another name."

"Was it Frigg, maybe?"

"Frigg... that's the one."

Martha saw a terrible mix of uncertainty and fear color Lea's slim face.

"What is it, dear?"

"What's the matter, Lea?" Hawke asked, gently placing his hand on her shoulder.

"Frigg – that was one of the names in my father's research files."

A short silence fell upon the room, the only sound now was the meditative crackling of the apple-wood fire. Hawke squeezed Lea's shoulder. "I guess we now know for sure that all this is connected with the attack on you in Ireland, in that case."

"I agree," Scarlet said. "This is way too much of a coincidence otherwise."

"And I don't believe in coincidences," Hawke said, frowning.

Lea looked confused and scared. "But what does it all mean?"

Ryan sighed. "That's exactly what we have to find out, but somehow the attack on you in Ireland, the murder of Bill Smith and Nate Derby here in Newfoundland and the attack on us down in Florida are all connected for sure, and the common denominator seems to be invisibility."

"And Thor," Victoria reminded him. "Don't forget Nate talking about Thor's Hammer just before he died and how it could be some kind of Tesla coil."

Martha watched the young man in the Batman t-shirt flinch at the mention of the word Tesla.

"So this is all pointing to Vikings, in other words," Hawke said.

"And if it is," Martha said with a gentle authority, "what you need is one of them experts on Norse mythology. You can take the bead. I won't be needing it for much longer."

All eyes turned to Ryan, but for once his usual confidence had gone. "I think this is going to need someone who knows more than me."

Lea looked at them for a moment, and then pulled out her phone. "I'm pretty sure Rich knows someone – an old friend from university years ago. He studied archaeology before moving into Norse legends. He lives in Iceland. Let me give Rich a call and see if he can get us an address."

"And I'll call the newspapers," Scarlet said. "The world needs to know Ryan Bale doesn't know everything after all."

CHAPTER EIGHT

Iceland

Their private jet touched down on Runway 13 of Keflavik International Airport and taxied through the drizzly half-light to a gate on the north side. After a short conversation en route between Lea and Sir Richard Eden they had made the decision that Hawke, Lea and Victoria would drive into Reykjavík and meet with his old friend, a Dr Gunnar Jónsson, while Ryan and Scarlet stayed with the plane and refuelled ready for whatever came next.

On the flight, Eden had brief them that Vincent Reno had identified the images of the man taken by Ryan back in the Florida Keys. He confirmed his name was indeed Leon Smets, a former French Foreign Legion Warrant Officer thrown out of the service for brutality against junior ranks, including Vincent when he was a raw recruit. The other men were assorted corporals all of whom were now out of the Legion and working as mercenaries alongside Smets.

Vincent, who was making amends with his wife in Marseille, was unable to help them with the shaven-headed woman, but Alex had worked her magic on that score and identified her as one Dasha Vetrov, the younger sister of Maxim Vetrov, the man ECHO had dispatched in the Tomb of Eternity. It looked like she had joined with Smets and whoever was pulling his strings to get her revenge on Hawke and the others. Eden was certain they would both be working for someone else, but for now that person was unidentified. He also thought it significant that she hadn't killed them all when she had the chance in the Florida Keys.

Now, Lea was thinking Reykjavík looked a lot like St John's in Newfoundland – both cities were around the same size and the brightly colored clapboard houses added to the feeling of similarity as their taxi cruised the short distance into Miðbær, the downtown district. This was as far north as civilization got – a first-world state with an advanced economy of fish-processing and metals exports, all tucked away in a country whose north coast skirted the Arctic Circle. As they got closer to the center, she watched the sun skim the horizon out on the Westfjords.

"Nearly two in the morning and the sun's still up."

Hawke opened one eye and looked at her for a second before closing it again. "Fascinating."

"Heathen."

They reached Dr Jónsson's address and Lea told the cab driver to pull over. Victoria paid him in American dollars and he grumbled before trundling away into the midnight sun. Then they walked up the steps to the professor's front door and rang the bell.

"If you weren't the one showing me this, Lea," the middle-aged academic said quietly, "I would think it was all some kind of joke." Gunnar Jónsson stared at the glass bead for a long time, mesmerized by it as it gave the effect of being able to look through his own hand. "Look! I can see the sheepskin rug right through my own hand – like it wasn't even there!"

"Not like it wasn't there," Hawke said. "It's there all right – but it's invisible."

"It's... *amazing.*"

"I felt the same thing back in St. John's when I first held it in my hand, too," Lea said, peering over Jónsson's shoulder at the strange, sparkling bead.

Jónsson looked away from the bead for the first time and fixed his eyes on Lea. "This is an absolutely *huge* discovery, and of course I would do anything to help you, but what exactly is going on? Richard was vague, as usual."

Hawke stepped forward. "We need to know all you know about Norse mythology."

Gunnar laughed. "It has taken me twenty years to know what I know, but I'll do my best."

"You can start with what you think this bead is."

Gunnar looked at them, astonished. "Looking at the hook on the rear, which is obviously designed to fix it to something, it can only be one thing – a small bead from the legendary *Tarnkappe!*"

"The legendary *what* now?" Lea asked.

Gunnar looked up at them one at a time and smiled. "We're going to need some coffee – please, make yourselves comfortable by the fire while I make some and then I will tell you all about it."

Victoria peered around the door and watched Gunnar as he banged and clattered around in his old kitchen in the pursuit of fresh coffee and loftkökur while loudly whistling a bombastic classical tune.

Hawke turned to Lea. "Is this guy for real?"

She nodded and smiled. "Sorry, but yes. Gunnar is one of a kind, for sure. According to Rich, he knows more than anyone on earth about Norse mythology, but if you think you can bundle him around the planet in search of treasure and adventure then think again. He's a great guy and all but he has only one gear, and that's slow."

"Excellent," Hawke said, sighing. "That'll come in handy when we're being chased and shot at... and what is that bloody awful tune he's whistling?"

Victoria looked at Hawke shocked. "Why, it's Wagner of course – Götterdämmerung."

"Eh?"

"Twilight of the Gods, Mr Hawke. He's whistling the opening to it – as Siegfried emerges from the cave."

"Do tell me more," Hawke said sarcastically.

Victoria smirked. "If you had any sort of education you'd realize the significance."

"The significance of what?" said Gunnar.

They turned to see him standing in the door with a tray laden with coffee cups and a shiny tin of biscuits.

"Siegfried," Hawke said, giving Victoria a sly glance.

"Ah – a man of culture!" Gunnar said in his melodic Icelandic accent. "I knew it as soon as I saw you."

"I try my best," Hawke said with another flick of the eyes to the English archaeologist.

Victoria started to speak. "Hang on, you just said..."

Hawke interrupted Victoria before she could finish her sentence. "As I said earlier, Gunnar – we really need your help – so perhaps you could explain for Lea here the significance of Siegfried."

Lea rolled her eyes as she took a coffee and relaxed back in her chair.

"Well, yes of course... Siegfried was in two of Wagner's operas, but Wagner himself took the character straight from German folklore, and that of course derived from the ancient Norse mythology."

"See, Lea?" Hawke said. "I told you."

"Listen, *Josiah*, if you..."

"Please, Gunnar, continue," Hawke said with a wink at the Irishwoman.

"As one of the most legendary heroes of the entire Norse mythological canon, Siegfried, or Sigurd, as we call him, is central to the folklore of all the Scandinavian nations. Here in Iceland we have the famous Völsunga saga, an eight hundred year-old saga featuring him. As I say, he is central to the folklore."

"But," Hawke said, taking a sip of coffee, "and I know Lea will want to know the answer to this question more than anyone – what has this glass bead got to do with Sigurd?"

"It's obvious to anyone who knows the legend, Mr Hawke – and I already told you earlier when I mentioned the Tarnkappe."

"Ah, yes..."

"The Tarnkappe was Sigurd's secret power – the power he used in the Nibelungenlied to help Gunther beat the Queen of Iceland in a javelin-throwing competition."

"Am I on drugs or something?" Lea asked, confused.

Gunnar ignored the comment. "The Tarnkappe gave him the power to win."

"Like some kind of protein shake then?" Lea said.

Gunnar stared at her expressionless for a moment. "No... Sigurd's secret power was the Tarnkappe – the Cloak of Invisibility, and I believe this bead was once part of that cloak – proving once and for all that the legends were more than just myth, and that all of these legendary heroes really existed!"

"You mean Sigurd was real?" Victoria said, astonished.

Gunnar held out the bead. "If this is real, then why not?"

"But if Sigurd was real," Victoria said, her voice hushing to a whisper barely audible over the sound of the crackling fire, "then Thor must be real as well – just what Nate was talking about. Maybe this means that even... Valhalla was real!"

A heavy silence fell over the small room as the implications of Victoria's words sunk in, but then Gunnar broke the tension with a smile and a vigorous shake of the head. "No... no I think that might be taking things a little far. I am ever-cautious and I think now would be as good a time as any to pull back and not jump the gun, as you say."

"But she could be right," Lea said.

"No... really, I must insist." Gunnar set his coffee cup down and scratched his chin absent-mindedly. He pulled off his glasses and polished them with the hem of his jumper. "There's deduction, and extrapolation, and then there's *this*... Just because we have a strange bead which seems to have the power of invisibility, and just because Sigurd had an invisible cloak, doesn't mean we can infer the existence of one of the world's most famous mythological locations. I think this is going too far."

"But just imagine," Victoria said. "Speaking as an archaeologist I can say it would be the greatest discovery of all history."

"Perhaps, but it's wise to be cautious."

"But you're the one who said the bead must belong to some kind Harry Potter cape," Lea said. "If that's not a leap then what is?"

Gunnar smiled. "Yes... I am guilty of that, I admit – but what else could it be? If what you say is true then this bead was found in a small Canadian fishing village and is thousands of years old. Even today this technology is only in its most basic form and nothing as efficient and amazing as this."

"Which is exactly what Ryan told us," Hawke said.

"Whatever civilization produced this bead was far ahead of ours in technological terms."

"And you think it could be evidence of Sigurd's Cloak of Invisibility?" Lea asked.

"Yes, but…" said Gunnar apologetically, "unless you have more information it's very hard for me to give any more assistance."

"Wait!" Hawke said. "Lea – After Smets stole the flash-drive, Alex sent your father's research to your iPhone, yes?"

Lea took out her phone and started to scroll through the research files Alex had re-sent after her flash-drive was stolen in Florida. Gunnar watched in amazement as the text and images flashed by in front of his eyes.

"I've never seen so many references to the old Norse culture," he said. "This is a treasure trove in itself! It seems to be focussed on stories about healing. How did your father get this information?"

Lea shook her head and sighed. "I don't know… yet."

"Wait – go back!"

She looked at the professor and then began to scroll backwards. "What did you see?"

Gunnar gave an innocent grin and almost jumped up and down on the spot with excitement.

"There's something here – but it's written in a very old Runic script."

"I know – I couldn't understand any of it."

"But *I* can read it," Gunnar said. "I've spent my life working on this." His voice became a whisper. "I thought I was the only one…"

"You can translate this?" Lea asked.

Gunnar nodded. "Yes… my understanding of this script is not complete, but almost. Here are my notes."

He handed Lea a scrappy notebook. She leafed through the dog-eared pages and saw endless scrawls of the strange symbols with heavy annotation in Icelandic.

Hawke looked at Gunnar. "So what does it say?"

"It's a reference to Basque raiding parties in Newfoundland."

"Raiding parties?"

Gunnar shook his head and smiled. "We've always known about the connection between Atlantic Canada and the Vikings, and consequently what connects that part of the world with Norse mythology, and we've also always known about the seventeenth century raiding parties from Europe who sailed the Atlantic looking for new lands to plunder, but this is something else!"

"Go on."

Gunnar peered closer at the text on the phone. "This looks like a description of an account given by the raiding party in question. It says that in the case of the Mi'kmaq culture and territory of Newfoundland, one specific raiding party was a Spanish frigate crewed by Basques, and there seems to be an obscure reference to…" Gunnar stopped and looked at the strange script with a furrowed brow. "I think it's referring to something they described as a kind of cloak made of hardened water. They said when they held it to the sky they could still see the clouds. This is clearly the same thing we have here in this room now, only they describe an entire garment made of it!"

"You think the raiding party found this Tarnkappe?" Hawke said.

Gunnar nodded enthusiastically. "Yes, my friend! If this script is right then yes – absolutely!"

"Wait a minute," Lea said. "Most of the research in Dad's files was written in English, and a little was in Irish too, but that weird Runic stuff I presumed he'd copied from somewhere else. If it's mentioning Basque raiding parties in the seventeenth century it couldn't have been written by ancient Norse gods."

Gunnar looked at her with surprise on his face. "No, of course not. This was written by your father. It is signed by him here – Henry Donovan."

Lea felt like the world had stopped spinning. As Gunnar's words sank in, the astonishment she felt grew like a tidal wave until she thought she was going to drown. The implications of his words immediately struck her like an ice-pick. "But... how did Dad know all this? It all sounds so far fetched."

"Not at all! As I say, that part of Newfoundland was raided and looted by the Basques in the 1650s. This is common knowledge. It's perfectly possible that they discovered Sigurd's cloak, left behind by the Vikings centuries earlier, and took it back to their homeland."

"So where exactly did they take it?"

"That's why this script is so important. It says that when they returned to Spain they sold the cloak to a very rich merchant." Gunnar peered at the screen as he made the translation. "A Francisco de la Cosa."

"Never heard of him."

Gunnar carefully finished the script and smiled. "Me neither – he doesn't seem to be an historical figure, but according to the script he was a very rich man and over the years he bought many interesting and exotic items from both raiding parties and legitimate explorers. This says that he kept them in a vault at his castillo in northern Spain, and guess what?"

"Surprise us," Lea said.

Gunnar checked the script one more time. "At the time your father wrote this the castillo was still standing and there's a better than good chance that it's still standing to this day, and I would bet it's still in the hands of the de la Cosa family! Your father seemed to think that they were considered to possess one of the finest private fine art collections in the world."

"So you think they've still got the cloak?"

Gunnar shrugged. "I don't know, but would *you* give something like that away?" He paused for a moment and stared unblinking at the text. "Woah!"

"What's up, Gunnar?" Hawke asked.

"There seems to be an oblique reference here to the Axe of Baldr."

"What's that?"

"Baldr was Thor's brother – another son of Odin and Frigg. A fragment of what is supposed to be his axe is in Sweden today, but most of it is missing. According to this, it claims the axe was reputed to contain an inscription which would lead to Thor's... this can't be right."

"Don't tell me," Hawke said. "Thor's tomb, right?"

"Yes, but perhaps my translation is wrong. Surely they mean *temple*."

"No, Gunnar," Lea sighed. "They surely do *not* mean temple, believe me."

Hawke rubbed his eyes. "Just what the hell do these maniacs want with Thor's tomb? Gunnar, does it say if that raiding party ever got hold of the axe?"

"No, but..."

"But maybe there's a chance," Lea said.

"In other words..." Victoria's words drifted into the crackling fire.

"In other words," Hawke said coolly, "if we want to find the rest of this cloak, and maybe even this axe – and wherever that leads us – then our best shot is Basque country."

"So let's get out of here," Lea said.

"Wait," said Gunnar. "If you're researching Thor and Valhalla you'll need a copy of the Gesta Hammaburgensis ecclesiae pontificum."

Hawke looked at Victoria. "Is he speaking English or Icelandic?"

She rolled her eyes. "It's the Deeds of the Bishop of Hamburg."

"What's Hamburg got to do with it?"

"You'll find out," Gunnar said, and rummaged around on his shelf before handing them a thin document. "Here it is."

Hawke took it from him and glanced at it. "Right... excellent... brilliant. But this is written in Latin."

Gunnar frowned. "I couldn't find one in Icelandic. Read it before you get to Spain because it could be of some use. It describes Thor's temple at Uppsala in great detail and might have some other important clues. If you have any problems, then call me."

"No need for that, Gunnar," Hawke said. "You're coming with us."

CHAPTER NINE

Basque Country

The drive from Bilbao Airport to the Castillo de la Cosa was long and winding, and took them deep into the hills of Gipuzkoa Province. They drove through the town of Urretxu before finally driving north into the mountains where the castle had been nestled away for hundreds of years. Known as the Euskaldunak in their own language, the Basques had lived in the Iberian Peninsula since before the time of agriculture, and since 1978 Basque Country had been an autonomous region in the northwest of Spain.

The castillo was an imposing building of honey-colored stone hidden among dogwood, oak and ash, and a thick grove of hazel trees. Two turrets towered above them as they emerged from the car and walked toward the foreboding entrance in the warm Spanish air.

With no small thanks to an introduction and bribe from Sir Richard Eden, the owner of the property welcomed them warmly and invited them inside. They were shown through to an enormous hall in the center of which was a large table covered in food and wine.

Javier de la Cosa smiled broadly and extended his arms to emphasize his generosity. "Please, you must sample some of our local cuisine before we talk business!"

"That's very kind," Lea said. "But we have so little time."

"Nonsense, you must eat!"

Lea looked at the others.

Hawke shrugged his shoulders, and soon they were all sitting around the table tucking into various Basque dishes like kokotxas, marmitako and pintxos.

"This really is very generous, Señor de la Cosa," Lea said. "But we need to talk – you could be in danger here."

"Danger? Rubbish! My family has defended this castle for seven hundred years."

Ryan closed the notebook full of symbols that the Icelandic professor had given him to study and stared at a dish in the center of the table. "What's *this?*"

Javier peered over his glasses at the dish and smiled. "It's bacalao – a sort of salt cold."

"Salt cod?" Ryan said, recalling Martha's bubbling pots and pans back on Bell Island. "Interesting."

The Spaniard waved a meaty hand at the generous spread. "Try some!"

"Thanks, but I ate in Canada…"

The rest of them tucked in with gusto, and toward the end of the meal, which included plenty of Spanish wine, Javier turned to Hawke and his tone was suddenly all business. "Now – Sir Richard told me you have something of great historical significance that might be of interest to the collection here at the Castillo de la Cosa."

Hawke and Lea shared a glance. "We think so, yes, and we also think you might be able to help us with something as well."

"In that case, I'd better see what you have."

Lea pulled Martha's small ring box from her pocket and gently pushed the lid open as she slid the box across the table.

Javier stared down into the little ring box. His face straightened and for a few tense moments Lea was scared she had somehow lost the precious artefact, but then a broad grin appeared on the tanned face of the Spanish millionaire and he began to nod his head with unmitigated pleasure.

"I see you have in your possession exactly what Sir Richard described." He carefully picked up the small invisible bead and held it between his thumb and forefinger. Its strange, watery appearance sparkled for a moment, yet Hawke could only see the indentations made by the bead as it pressed into Javier's fingers and pushed the blood away from the surface of his fingertips. The object itself was gone from the world.

"What do you think?" Hawke asked. "Is it the same as the ones you have in your collection?"

Javier replaced the bead and clipped the lid shut. "It is exactly the same, yes."

"Can we see the others?" Hawke asked.

"You may see them, yes. As you know, under the terms of Sir Richard's agreement this small and mysterious piece of ancient history is the price of admission." Javier smiled and slid the box into his pocket.

The Spaniard rose from the table and clapped his hands together. "Please, my friends… if you'll follow me I will show you the collection." He lowered his voice to a confidential tone. "Not the public collection, you understand, but the private pieces that only the family see."

He led them away from the grand hall and down a long corridor lined with oil paintings of his predecessors. He stopped at one particularly sombre gentleman wearing a black and red slashed doublet stitched with gold thread. A rakish reticello lace collar framed a vaguely arrogant face, and topping it all off was a broadrimmed black felt hat replete with a turquoise ostrich plume pointing into the vermillion oils of the background.

"Bet he knew his way around a galleon," Lea said.

"Or a bordello," Scarlet whispered from the back of the party.

Javier stopped and looked proudly at the painting. "This is Francisco de la Cosa, my ninth great-grandfather. He was the man who started our family dynasty back in the middle of the seventeenth century."

"He was a treasure hunter?" Victoria said, admiringly.

Scarlet stepped forward. "Someone say treasure?"

Javier looked confused. "No... not really. Francisco was a merchant who made his wealth importing gold and silver from the new world, and also cocoa beans, not to mention ivory and pepper from Africa. He was a very successful man and definitely not a treasure hunter." As he spoke he beamed with pride and then turned to Scarlet and lowered his voice. "And as far as I know, he never visited any bordellos."

Hawke gave Scarlet a disapproving glance as Javier started off once again down the corridor. They turned a corner and began to ascend a narrow stairwell that was built into a tower on the northeast corner of the castillo. "What you are about to see is only available to the family, and even then only my immediate relatives. I hope you realize that this is a great privilege, afforded only by the fact you have brought me this bead."

At the top of the stairwell Javier stopped before a heavy wooden door and took a large iron key from his pocket. He put the key in the lock and looked at each of them in turn. "And even with the bead it still took the incredible persuasive capability of Sir Richard to get you this far."

He turned the key in the lock and pushed open the door.

Inside was darkness, but then he flicked an old light switch and several naked low-watt light bulbs came to life and cast a greasy, orange light over the room. It smelled of dust and neglect.

Hawke followed Javier inside and the others joined him in single file. The room was not impressive but instead redolent of an unused loft filled with family junk. Three narrow windows were shuttered up and several large wooden tea and coffee chests were stacked haphazardly along the far wall.

"So this is where the magic happens?" Scarlet said.

This time, Javier ignored her comment and moved to one of the coffee chests. "In here is what you seek."

He patiently opened the lid and pulled an old hessian sack off the top of the contents. "As you will see – or *not* in this case – the item you desire to see is most impressive."

He moved what looked like an old blunderbuss out of the way and pulled a cloak from the chest, holding it up to them. From their perspective it looked like a simple garment made from some kind of coarse linen, but then Javier draped the cloak over his shoulder. Hawke could hardly believe what he was looking at when the Spaniard disappeared from view leaving only the bottom of his legs visible.

"Oh *wow*," Ryan said, making no attempt to hide his amazement. "I have *got* to get myself one of those babies."

Scarlet gave him a disapproving look. "I dread to think what you would do with it."

"Impressive, no?" Javier said with pride. "As you see, I have only a fragment, but it is still a remarkable thing!"

Hawke studied the cloak without making comment. Javier was still visible to him but in a strange, distorted way. Somehow, Hawke was able to look right through the Spaniard and see the shuttered windows and the tea chests on the far wall, and yet he was still conscious that someone was in front of him.

"It's like you're surrounded by ripples or something," Lea said.

"Exactamente!" Javier cried out. "You see, the beads somehow bend the light around themselves without creating any kind of shadow. They are remarkable… magical! I can tell you my brothers and I had much fun with this cloak when we were children playing here in the castle."

"This is… outstanding!" Gunnar said, taking step closer. "This must be Sigurd's cloak!"

Victoria stared in awe. "This is crazy."

Ryan nodded his head to show his agreement. "But it's not as crazy as it looks. I was reading about this on the plane from Iceland. Modern science has developed a device known as a Rochester Cloak which uses a clever arrangement of lenses to bend the light around an object so that the person viewing the object simply can't see it."

Scarlet sighed.

"What's the matter?" Hawke asked.

"Wherever there's a Ryan, there's a *but* ten seconds later."

Ryan smirked. "*But*… the big elephant in the room is that the Rochester Cloak is not only brand new technology but it isn't anywhere near as effective as what we're all looking at right now. This is just the craziest blend of old and new tech I've ever seen! I mean, look at it – on the one hand we have an old garment made of what looks like animal skin and a very crude linen, and on the other hand we have a cloaking technology frankly decades ahead of current level of scientific knowledge."

Javier slipped off the cloak and handed it to Lea.

"What are these strange markings on the inside?"

Javier shook his head. "I don't know – my father told me they were Runic script but I don't think so. I had them studied by experts and no one knows."

"We'll see about that," Gunnar said taking a closer look.

"Well?" Lea asked.

"I can't read this line here... it is similar to the Runic script in your father's research but different somehow, but this bit is simple..." Gunnar said, suppressing a smile. "It says 'Sigurd'. This is the Tarnkappe and that means..."

"It was more than a myth," Hawke said. "It means Thor's tomb and maybe even Valhalla were real."

Ryan stepped forward and photographed the strange markings. He emailed it back to Alex without delay and then slipped his phone back into his pocket.

Scarlet looked at them both. "And that means gold, right?"

"And what's this?" Ryan said, ignoring her.

"What have you found?" Hawke asked.

Ryan peered into the chest and whistled low and long. "Something that might have just changed everything."

CHAPTER TEN

Hawke and the others watched as Ryan pulled a piece of wood from the chest. It resembled a solid hardwood like oak or ash, and had been smoothed by the passing of countless centuries.

Javier shrugged his shoulders. "Just an old stick."

Ryan gave him a look of disbelief and examined the wood.

"Are you for real? This is no stick!"

"Of course it is!"

Scarlet lowered her voice. "This guy's a real *Basque-et case...*"

"Oh *please*," Lea said.

"What is it, mate?" Hawke said, ignoring them.

"Remember what Gunnar read in Lea's dad's research notes? Well to me this looks like an axe handle that's been split in two down the vertical axis – look here how it has the ridges at the top – this is where the blade would have gone, and this here..." his voice trailed away as he peered more closely at the handle.

"What do you see, Ry?" Lea said.

"It's probably the most precious thing in this entire castle."

Javier looked bemused and shrugged his shoulders. "It's just an old piece of wood, as I say – a stick, a common piece of wood dumped up here by my father no doubt!"

"It's hardly a piece of wood," Ryan said, astonished. "If I'm right, and let's face it I'm never wrong... then what we have here is the missing half of one of the most famous battle-axes in the world – the axe of Baldr!"

Gunnar's eyes widened like saucers. "This is incredible! When I read the reference in the notes I never believed we would really find it."

Hawke turned to the Icelandic scholar. "Didn't you say the other half was in Sweden?

"It's currently in Stockholm," Ryan said as he ran his fingertips over a series of strange lines carved into the handle. "And these here…"

"What?" Lea said. "Those scratches?"

"I don't think they're scratches."

"The inscription mentioned in the research!" Gunnar said

"Right," Ryan continued. "If this is what I think it is, then these markings will correspond perfectly to similar scratch marks on the fragment of the axe in Stockholm, thereby completing the inscription. This is massive!"

"So where was the Stockholm half found?" Victoria asked.

Ryan turned to face them, his face unusually serious. "The axe handle in Stockholm was found at an archaeological dig in the Temple at Uppsala – Thor's temple, right Gunnar?"

The Icelandic scholar nodded enthusiastically.

"Is that good?" Hawke asked expectantly.

Ryan shook his head "Not particularly. Everyone knows there was a center of Norse religious activity at Uppsala."

"I don't," Lea said with a shoulder shrug.

"All right then, everyone who finished school knows."

"Hey! I was dangled out the side of a freaking A380 for this team! I nearly got sucked into a bloody jet engine for this team and you're making fun of my education!"

Gunnar cleared his throat. "Actually the temple was actually located at Gamla Uppsala, which means old Uppsala. Gamla is the Swedish word for *old*, which is why Stockholm's old town is called Gamla stan."

"But they only ever found half of it there?" Hawke asked.

Gunnar nodded. "Yes. The axe in Stockholm is very famous, of course – but now with this new information from your father's research it puts a completely different complexion on it. Imagine if this really could lead us to the location of Thor's tomb – hidden for millennia!"

"But I thought Adam of Bremen said that was in Uppsala?" Lea asked, confused.

"Keep up, Lea," Ryan said. "Remember that our chronicler chap called Adamus Bremensis, or Adam of Bremen, wrote a handy description of the *temple* back in the eleventh century. That's a real place – where the axe of Baldr was found."

"As Gunnar here just said, darling," Scarlet muttered.

Ryan continued. "There have been many successful archaeological digs there and they've found various wooden structures and evidence of ritual sacrifice as well. Adam describes it in some detail right down to how it was 'decked in gold' and that Thor, Wotan and Frikko all had thrones in it."

"I'm liking the bit about 'decked in gold', Ryan," Scarlet said. "Tell me more."

"It's a real place all right but the problem is our old one – what Adam of Bremen was describing and what these excavations have dug up is the *temple* of Uppsala. It's a religious center, like the modern equivalent of a church, but what we're looking for, and what the cryptic message on this axe handle is certainly alluding to is Thor's *tomb* – they're two entirely different things."

"Is Thor's tomb not Valhalla?" Lea asked.

Ryan shook his head. "Doubtful. Valhalla is where Thor would have gone *after* his death. His tomb would be wherever he fell in battle."

"But how can Thor have a tomb" Victoria asked quietly. "He was a mythological figure, wasn't he? I'm still having trouble with all of this."

The others shared a look before Ryan spoke. "No, in a nutshell, he wasn't mythological – or at least we don't think so. We've seen proof of the existence – or at least manifestation – of other gods on earth, like Poseidon, Lei Gong the Chinese thunder god and even Osiris. As for Thor – we have no evidence yet but that's kind of what we're doing now. Sorry to have to break it to you like this."

Victoria was silent for a long time and the others gave her time to process the information. "What do you mean, *evidence?*" she said at last.

"It's a long story but just take our word for it," Lea said with a smile.

"Want a drink?" Scarlet said. "I seem to recall a stash of Rioja down there that's simply begging to be plundered, if that's okay with you, Javier?"

Javier nodded and shrugged his shoulders.

"I think I might, yes…" Victoria said, her voice trailing away.

"So we're one step closer to Thor's tomb," Hawke said.

Javier sighed deeply. "If what you say is true, then I must come with you!"

"We need to know where we're going first," Scarlet said.

Hawke sighed. "We'll need the other half of the axe for that, Cairo."

"So we're off to Stockholm?" Gunnar said, rubbing his hands together gleefully. "I have a good friend there – she'll make us very welcome!" As he spoke, Ryan handed him the handle for him to have a closer study.

"Are there pictures of the axe handle in Stockholm on the internet?" Lea asked. "We could just use those and save a shed load of time."

Ryan shook his head "Nice try but it's no good. There are a couple of pictures but the scratch marks on it are just too weak to be read properly. We're going to need to see the real thing."

Victoria slumped down on a chest. "I'm seeing now that Nate wasn't mad after all – but if he was right and Thor was real, wouldn't that mean his hammer was also real? If it really is some king of Tesla coil thing, it sounds awfully dangerous to me."

Gunnar looked anxious as he weighed the axe handle fragment in his hands.

Ryan shook his head in wonder. "Yes, very dangerous, but this is…"

"A mystery sent by God, young man," Javier said with reverence.

"Or,' Ryan countered, "You could argue that…"

His words were cut short by the sound of a terrific explosion emanating from somewhere far beneath them in the bottom of the castillo.

"What on earth was that?" Javier asked, his face a picture of confusion and fear.

"Sounds like we have company," Hawke said, unsurprised.

Scarlet nodded. "I agree – but how did they know we, or *that*," she said, indicating the cloak in Lea's hands, "were here?"

"Presuming they're looking for the cloak," Lea said. "Could be the axe they're after. It's front and center in Dad's research after all and they have the flash-drive."

A second explosion and this time they felt the entire tower shake beneath their feet.

"All questions for later,' Hawke said, cocking his SIG. "Now it's time for action."

CHAPTER ELEVEN

San Juan, Puerto Rico

Zhang Xiaoli, known to the Chinese Ministry of State Security as Agent Dragonfly, and to the Western intelligence agencies as Lexi Zhang, watched the man enter the bar. Obscured behind a pair of Gucci sunglasses and slumped down in her seat in order to use the menu for cover, she was in no danger of being seen by the man unless she wanted to be seen.

She lit a cigarette and sucked in the smoke. The curve of her lips formed a soft cushion around the tip of the filter and she winced as she drew the smoke down. She hated filtered cigarettes. Passing over the cellulose acetate of the filter imparted a slightly plastic quality to the taste of the smoke, but they were all she could find. No matter, it was time for business.

Having decided the man was alone, she sauntered across the room and stood beside him at the bar. She looked at him casually out of the corner of her eye. He was wearing a dishevelled linen jacket and had a slightly crumpled Panama hat at a jaunty angle on his head. Soft, purple bags around his eyes told her he still wasn't sleeping at night without the assistance of his faithful Ambitropin.

"I'll have another rum," she said to the barman coolly, and turned to the man beside her. "What will you have, Señor Arocha?"

Arocha looked at her with tired eyes and barely any movement of the head. He was a year from retirement in the Cuban Dirección de Inteligencia. What Arocha didn't know about the region wasn't worth knowing, and it just so happened he was in debt to Lexi Zhang.

"I'll have a beer," he said flatly.

They waited in silence as the barman organized their drinks. It was a little before sunset and the atmosphere of the small bar was relaxed but even with the gentle whir of the wooden ceiling fans above their heads the humidity wasn't pulling any punches. Lexi wondered how long this was going to take. The thing about Miguel Arocha was you never could tell what sort of mood he was in and how generous he was feeling.

The man at the bar gave them their drinks and Arocha paid with a folded bill, casually waving his change away. The CDI was obviously picking up the tab, Lexi thought, and they walked to a corner table without further acknowledgement of each other.

They reached the table and took a seat. On the small table between them was an unlit candle in a bottle and a torn menu that looked like it had seen better days. In Lexi's opinion the whole place needed an intimate date with a wrecking ball and a couple of bulldozers, but Arocha seemed to fit right in.

Lexi looked at the menu. "How romantic."

Arocha glanced briefly over his shoulder before speaking. Lexi thought he looked like he was expecting someone, but too many years in the business had warped both their perceptions for the worse.

"What do you want?" he asked at last.

Straight to the point, she thought. Obviously he was in a generous mood tonight, and not going to play around with her. For that, at least, she could be grateful.

"Repayment for that job I did for you in Santo Domingo last year."

The man nodded. "You're calling it in."

93

Lexi raised her glass and took more of the cheap rum. "Yes."

Arocha rested his elbows on the tabletop and began gently drumming his fingertips on the scarred wood. He was starting to look vaguely nervous, she considered. "Name it."

Lexi ran her finger around the rim of the glass and made it sing for a moment – B flat, she thought. Two men with serious tattoos turned to see what had made the noise, but turned their backs when they saw she was sitting with Arocha. Obviously this was his local. "Word has it there's an island in the Caribbean that isn't exactly on the tourist trail."

A heavy sigh from the Cuban. Life looked like it was getting on top of him. "There are so many islands in the Caribbean, Agent Dragonfly."

She nodded and sipped the rum. "Do you know what I'm talking about or not?"

A long pause and then a brief nod. "Perhaps."

"I'm talking about an island owned by a private consortium headed by an English politician. A maverick archaeologist named Sir Richard Eden."

"In that case, I know what you're talking about, but not many do. Its location is really only known by a few intelligence agencies and maybe some local fishermen. Why do you want to know about it? I can hardly believe a tiny island all the way out here is causing the Chinese Government any difficulties."

"I have my reasons, Arocha."

Another businesslike nod from the Cuban. Lexi thought he looked like he had gained at least twenty pounds since their last meeting.

"And if I tell you, we're even?"

"Of course. That's the deal."

"You're going to cause trouble down here?"

94

"What makes you say that?"

"I heard a rumor about an assassination getting played out somewhere in my little sea." He gestured with his hand out the window of the bar at the vast ocean on the far side of the road.

She smirked and winked at him. "You mind your business and I'll mind mine. I won't cause any trouble for you, I promise."

"Your promises are of very little value to me, Xiaoli," Arocha said with genuine disappointment. "In a few months I will be out of this business. The most stressful thing in my life will be deciding which fishing rod to use."

"Give a man a fish, Miguel, and you feed him for a day, but teach him how to fish and you put a trawlerman out of business."

Arocha suppressed a laugh, and pulled the label off his beer. He drew a pencil from his shirt pocket and Lexi watched with feigned disinterest as the Cuban scribbled down the information she had crossed the world to secure. "I like the old things in life, Xiaoli... pencils over pens, typewriters over computers..."

Lexi smiled as she took the piece of paper from Arocha. "We have a saying in China, Miguel. The palest ink is better than the strongest memory."

*

Outside the bar Lexi wasted no time in calling a cab and ordering the driver to take her down to the Cangrejo Arriba district. One glance at the information Arocha had given her told her that she was going to need to take a short flight to a neighboring island and from there get hold of a small boat. Anything less might risk Eden and his team discovering what she was up to and that would

ROB JONES

be the end of the mission. Arocha had also given her the name of intel agent by the name of Raoul who might know more.

The cab driver had started to ask questions about what looked like the very heavy tool bag she was carrying, but a hundred dollar bill made him look the other way, and moments after watching Arocha waddle into a side street she was on her way.

As the battered Chevrolet made its way around the north side of the Laguna Los Corozos, she repeated the mantra to herself over and over: All is fair in love and war, all is fair in love war...

All is fair in love and war.

She knew in her heart she should have done this a long time ago, even if it meant the sort of betrayal and deceit she was now ready to engage in. She knew she could never be forgiven for doing what she was about to do. She knew she would make enemies for life who would stop at nothing to track her down and kill her, but she had no choice.

She simply told herself that there was no other way. She went over the scenario in her head once again. They would kill her family if she did not redeem herself in the eyes of the Ministry. She had wasted the opportunity to deliver the Map of Immortality to the Chinese authorities and now they would kill everyone she loved if she did not make amends in the ultimate way: she had to kill Sir Richard Eden, and anyone else who got in her way. Only then could she achieve the redemption she needed to make things right again. Deception and redemption... betrayal and murder... darkness and light.

Was she capable of doing such a thing? She knew in her heart she was. She had done far worse, and she wasn't afraid of making an enemy out of Joe Hawke. She knew taking Hawke out of the game was simply a

96

case of exploiting the feelings he had for her. Like all men he was weak and she would play him like a violin if she had to, all the way until his last breath.

That last thought made her pause for a moment and she considered who she would have to take out on Elysium in order to get to Eden. How many would be there? She had no idea. Lea? Scarlet – she might be a challenge... and then maybe even Hawke.

With a bit of luck, she considered, most of the ECHO team would be off on one of their wild goose chases in some far-flung corner of the world, leaving Eden alone and unprotected. Sure, he had some moves – he was a former Paras officer after all – but he was getting on in life and no match for a world-class assassin in the prime of her life. Perhaps Raoul would know who was on the island tonight.

She turned to glance over her shoulder and watched dreamily as the setting sun illuminated the skyscrapers of San Juan. A moment later it sank into the Atlantic and a purple twilight began to cross from the eastern sky ahead of them. She could see why Eden had chosen this part of the world for his hideout – isolated from the rest of the planet but still close enough to get to America or Europe in just a few hours by jet.

To say she felt on top of her game was an understatement. She would plow through dozens of armed guards if it meant achieving her objectives and neutralizing the English politician. She flattered herself that she was probably only one of a handful of people in the world capable of storming the island without aerial backup, and with a bit of luck, Eden himself would know it too in a very short time.

Now, as the taxi cruised the final few miles to the airport, she did what she had done so many times before – she started to build in her mind an outline of how she was going to execute her mission. She had completed similar jobs often enough to know how it would play out, but in one way this was totally unique. There would be no going back after this one.

She glanced at her watch. It would all be over sooner than she knew it.

CHAPTER TWELVE

Hawke went to the door and peered around the arch into the stairwell. The sound of men shouting and hurried footsteps echoed up the steps of the castillo's tower.

"Sounds like our friends from Florida, all right," he said. "They're speaking French."

"But how could they possibly know we're here?" Scarlet asked again.

"Like I said – maybe something in Dad's research," Lea said. "They must have gone up one side of my flash drive and down the other ten times by now."

Gunnar looked like Lea had slapped his face. "I was convinced *I* was the only one who knew how to read the script…"

Hawke gave him a look of consolation. "It doesn't look that way now, Gunnar… sorry."

Gunnar's crestfallen expression was wiped from his face by the sound of the men's screams as they stormed their way further up the tower's winding, stone steps. They sounded like a pack of wild animals.

"Guys," Ryan said. "I hate to break up the debate here, but we have an undetermined quantity of heavily armed Belgian psychopaths running toward us and I'm thinking they'll be here in less than twenty seconds."

Victoria gawped at Ryan and blinked. "Oh gosh…"

"He makes a solid point," Scarlet said.

"So let's get the hell out of here then!" Ryan added with emotion.

"Sounds like a capital idea to me," Victoria said, peering anxiously over Hawke's shoulder and looking down the stairwell. "They're already too close for comfort."

Hawke turned to Javier. "Are the shutters on those windows nailed down?"

Javier shook his head. "No."

"Excellent."

"There's no need – we're five storeys up."

"Ah…"

Hawke looked at the door. "What's this wood?"

"The strongest Spanish cedar!"

"Strong enough to keep them busy for a while, in other words." He slammed it shut. "Give me the key, Javier!"

Javier handed him the key and the Englishman locked the heavy door. "They'll waste a lot of ammo trying to get through this and that will give us some time to work out a way out of here."

"Perhaps we can use this to our advantage?" Javier said, taking the cloak back from Lea. "Below the two windows on the right is a drop all the way to the outer courtyard but there is a narrow battlement below the window on the right that leads to a parapet walk. From there we can make our way to the roof of the old chapel and descend to the inner courtyard."

Hawke opened the shutter and looked at the route Javier had just described. It all seemed straight-forward enough and beyond the north wall of the castle was a large olive grove they could use for cover.

Outside the room they heard the men reach the top of the stairs and began pounding on the door. After a few seconds of rethinking the problem they heard the obvious next step as dozens of bullets smashed into the heavy cedar door.

"Right," Scarlet said, cocking her gun. "Ladies first, and that means you, Ryan."

"Hey!"

"You object?" she asked.

"Are you kidding?"

A second later Ryan was following Victoria through the window, then Scarlet climbed out. Lea was next and then Hawke turned to Gunnar and Javier.

"Right you two – out now!"

"Absolutely not!" the Spaniard said with wounded pride. "I go last! My family has defended the castle for seven centuries from people like this!"

Hawke yielded and turned to Gunnar. "Come on – out!" Gunnar made his way quickly to toward the window, axe handle in his grip, but Javier was undeterred and draped the cloak over his shoulders, vanishing from sight.

Outside the window Ryan jogged back from the parapet walk. "It's an easy trip to the chapel roof and... wait a minute – where's Javier?"

"Playing the Predator again," Hawke said.

"What?"

Hawke sighed. "All right Gunnar, out you go!"

"What about Javier?"

"He's going next"

"No!" protested the Spaniard. "I will surprise them when they enter the room and shoot them with the blunderbuss!"

Hawke rolled his eyes. "Javier, these men have automatic machine pistols. An invisible cloak and a three hundred year-old gun won't save you if they spray the entire room with lead, which I predict they will do about five seconds after blasting their way through the door."

"You think?" Javier said with regret creeping into his voice.

"Yes!"

"All right then on this *one* occasion," Javier said, holding his finger up to Hawke to underline the point. "I will retreat, but only so I can kill them later with the blunderbuss!"

Hawke fought hard not to look at Javier like he was a total fool, and agreed he could kill them later with the blunderbuss, but only if there *was* a later, and that meant getting out of here as fast as possible.

But then the door finally burst open and a man stormed in with a Heckler & Koch MP7, raking full metal jackets all over the room. Hawke watched in horror as the rounds drilled mercilessly through Gunnar Jónsson's chest and throat. He dropped the axe handle and fell on top of it a second later, stone-cold dead.

The gunman turned the weapon on Hawke but the Englishman grabbed the gun's muzzle and pushed down hard. The man squeezed the trigger in response, firing off dozens of rounds into the floor, but Hawke spun him around and aimed the weapon at the open door, taking out the second man at the top of the stairs and giving them a few more seconds.

"Out now!" he screamed at Javier.

"Never! Defend or die!" Javier snatched up the blunderbuss and ran toward the stairs. As he reached the door one of the men lobbed a grenade into the small room. Hawke picked it up and dived out of the window, using a shoulder roll to propel himself up with his own momentum back to his feet where he hurled the grenade over the battlement.

It exploded before it hit the ground and as the fireball fell down to the courtyard in a smear of black smoke and fire, he turned to see Javier was climbing through the window.

"What happened to defend or die?" Hawke said.

"There are more of them than I thought!"

Javier began to clamber through the window. He was still wearing the cloak. It was draped over his back so from Hawke's perspective he was perfectly visible, but to the gunmen who now were rushing back into the room the Spaniard would be invisible. That, at least, was something they would hardly be expecting.

"Hurry up, Javier!" Hawke said, the frustration growing in his voice. "We don't have much longer."

"Lo sé!" Javier said, but it was too late.

No sooner had he uttered these words when the men were in the room once again, guns raised and ready to fire.

Javier seemed calm, knowing the cloak made him invisible to the men, but he had made a terrible miscalculation. As soon as the gunmen re-entered the room they saw the open window and looking right through the Spaniard as if he weren't there they immediately caught sight of the Englishman helping him and opened fire.

Hawke watched in horror as the bullets ripped through the cloak and blasted into poor Javier's back. Blood ran from his mouth, just inches from Hawke's face, and then the fatally wounded man released his grip on the coquina casing of the window and fell backwards into the room. He collapsed in a wheezing heap alongside Gunnar's dead body which was still smoking from the terrible wounds inflicted on him earlier.

Hawke knew there was nothing he could do as the enemy swarmed further into the room, firing their guns and rushing the open window.

"Get moving!" Hawke shouted at the others.

Lea led everyone along the parapet walk while Scarlet kept up the rear, walking backwards to cover Hawke as he hid at the side of the open window, pushed back flat against the wall.

"We've got to get that axe!" he shouted.

A gunman appeared – the same who had murdered Javier – and leaned out of the window with his submachine gun a few inches ahead of him.

Hawke grabbed the muzzle of the gun and yanked it forward, raising his right hand and driving it into the man's surprised face at the same time. A crunch of broken nose bones followed a split second later before he pulled the man out of the window, wrenching his gun off him as he fell outside.

Taking his gun, Hawke fired into the room once again forcing the men back, but when he turned to run the man outside on the battlement was now on his feet, arms extended and lunging toward him.

Hawke swung at him, turning his hips as he went to put as much momentum into the punch as possible. Striking the man in the jaw he drove him backwards to the wall where he teetered uneasily for a moment before lashing out at Hawke.

The Englishman dodged the punch and fired a second back at the man, catching him in the face and smashing his cheekbone into shards. He brought his left hand up and plowed his knuckles hard into the man's eye socket, creating another terrible crunching sound and filling the cavity with blood.

Behind him the gunmen were at the window again, aiming their weapons at Hawke, so he grabbed the disoriented man and spun him around, using him as a human shield. Holding him up to cover himself from the onslaught, Hawke raised his gun and fired back, driving them back once more. He knew he had to get the axe handle and cloak – they hadn't even had time to grab an image of the markings on the axe yet.

He hauled the half-dead man to the wall and pushed him over on his way back to the window. His bloodcurdling screams filled the Spanish twilight but it was all over in a second when he landed with a squelchy smack on the cobblestone courtyard hundreds of feet below.

With the man's gun in his hands, Hawke used the window casing as cover as he pointed the muzzle of the weapon into the aperture and sprayed the room with hot lead. Knowing that there was only one narrow exit in the room, he knew this was the definition of shooting fish in a barrel, and it was no less than they deserved after murdering Gunnar and Javier in cold-blood. Plus, the Cloak of Invisibility and the axe handle fragment were still inside.

He kept firing. Some of the men got through the door, others hid behind the chests, while others were now dead. Hawke knew his magazine would be empty any second, but he waited until all of his friends were out of sight and across the chapel roof before retreating. So heavily outgunned he knew there was nothing he could do now to save the cloak and axe from falling into the enemy's hands but he was also a big believer in the saying *live to fight another day.*

He stepped backwards along the parapet walk firing his gun in short bursts to keep the men pinned down in the room and stop them firing at him, but when he heard the familiar *click click click* of an empty magazine he turned on his heels and ran for his life.

Within seconds the men had worked out what was going on and one of them leaned out of the window and fired a ferocious burst of fire at him.

The bullets bit at his heels as he sprinted across the chapel roof, smashing the tiles into shards and dust in his wake and slowly getting closer to him. With seconds to spare he reached the edge of the roof and leaped into the air – a suicidal move for most people but he knew his limits were beyond those of most people thanks to his parkour training.

He sailed through the Spanish evening for a few seconds, a least fifty feet above the courtyard but just out of the gunmen's firing line. The flight came to a rapid end when he smashed into a wall opposite the chapel, only just gripping hold of the top of it. The enraged screams of the men behind him grew louder as he lowered himself carefully down the wall and dropped the last few feet to the courtyard where the others were waiting for him by an archway in the outer wall.

"Glad you could make it," Scarlet said, glancing at her watch.

"Bad news I'm afraid... they killed Gunnar and Javier and now they have the cloak and the axe."

"Excellent," Scarlet said. "Maybe we should have sent you out first with Victoria and Ryan and left me to do the hard stuff?"

Victoria covered her mouth with her hand. "Those men *killed* them?"

Hawke nodded and placed a heavy hand on her shoulder. "I'm sorry."

"I... I can't believe it!"

"I'm sorry, but we don't have long," he said. "They're right behind me. We need to get into that olive orchard right now and use it for cover. When I was on the chapel roof I saw there's a road at the northern end of the orchard so we'll head there."

"That's your plan?" Ryan said.

Hawke shrugged his shoulders. "Sure –why not?"

"We have a car around the front!"

At that point the men's shouting grew even louder and they heard more gunshots.

"You think those guys haven't got that covered? There's a small army of them!"

"I see your point."

"So we're going into the orchard, right?"

"It's better than a poke in the eye with a sharp stick, I suppose."

"Gee, *thanks*. Get on the blower to Eden," Hawke said, still scanning the tops of the castillo's crenelated walls for any sign of the men. "Tell him Javier and Gunnar are dead and whoever murdered them not only has Lea's flash-drive but also the cloak of invisibility and the axe."

"Can't you tell him?" Lea said.

"Why me?" Hawke said. "I'm the new guy!"

"I don't want to break it to him…"

Scarlet sighed. "Give the phone to me, you big baby!" She snatched the phone and made the call as they made their way deep into the olive trees. They lost the men more easily than they thought, but Hawke knew their escape was probably a lot more to do with the fact that whoever the gunmen were they now had a nice, new invisibility cloak and a mysterious axe handle, which was probably what they were there for in the first place. Chasing half a dozen people around an olive orchard would be nothing more than a waste of their time and resources.

"What now?" Lea asked as they reached the road.

Hawke glanced at Victoria. She looked like she needed a very strong drink.

"We hitch a ride into town."

Lea stood on the side of the road doing her best interpretation of a lost lamb for half an hour before an old Mitsubishi Fuso flatbed creaked and rattled around the corner. One of its headlights was flickering and it looked a little worse for wear, but a lift was a lift, Hawke thought.

An old man wound down the window and leaned halfway out, grinning at Lea.

"Necesitas ayuda?"

Lea smiled. "If that means you can offer five people a lift into town, then the answer's yes!"

Before the man knew what was happening, Hawke and the others scrambled out from behind the olive trees and down the stony bank to the road.

"Hey!" the man said in English. "What is this, some kind of robbery?"

"Don't be silly now, darling," Scarlet said, climbing into the cab. "We just need a short ride into town. Now you be a good chap and drive us, will you?"

The man started to object, but then he noticed that most of them were carrying side arms, and the tall Englishman was even carrying a submachine gun slung over his shoulder.

"My truck is your truck!" he said with a nervous smile.

CHAPTER THIRTEEN

Elysium

After Scarlet rang off, Eden was in shock about the news of Gunnar's death. He had known him for many years and couldn't believe what had happened. He felt a wave of hatred rise in him but knew how thoughts of vengeance clouded judgement, so put it out of his mind to concentrate on the mission. Revenge could come later.

In the meantime, he looked at the images of the cloak they had sent. Losing the cloak to the enemy was a major blow, but something told him the axe handle might be of more use. Either way, he agreed with Hawke that whoever the assailants were they must have used information on Lea's stolen flash-drive to get the location of the Castillo de la Cosa. That meant Lea's father had known a lot more about all of this than they did, but now wasn't the time to go down that particular rabbit hole.

Now was the time to get Alex and Ryan working together on Gunnar Jónsson's notebook, which luckily he'd lent to Ryan before his murder. Now the Icelandic scholar was dead, there was no way to decode the Runic script on the axe handle unless they cracked the code themselves. They had little to go on – the Icelandic scrawl in the notebooks and Gunnar's translation of the symbols on the cloak as 'Sigurd', but Eden knew this was enough for Alex to get started on.

They put Ryan's pictures of Gunnar's notebook and the cloak up on the plasma screen in the main room alongside the original script written by Lea's father. It was projected with almost cinematic scale and impressiveness.

"So what do you think?" Eden asked the young American woman. "Gunnar told us this part says 'Sigurd', but the rest is down to us, and by us, I mean you."

Alex squinted at the images and tipped her head to one side as she lost herself in the study of the strange, scratchy lines. "It's going to be tough, for sure, but I think I can use what's been translated so far by Gunnar to try and translate the script – which seems more like some kind of Pre-Runic system to me."

"Which is exactly what Mr Bale said."

"Right... and he's not often wrong."

"Annoying but true," Eden said with a rare smile.

Alex returned the smile but it quickly faded when she immersed herself back in the study of the script. "I'm going to need some time to crack this little baby, Rich." She looked more closely at the images of Gunnar's notebook. "It's so unlike anything we've ever seen before."

"It's vital we decode them, Alex. When the team catch up with that axe handle and join it to the one in Sweden the inscriptions could lead us to Thor's tomb. Why these maniacs are so desperate to get into that tomb we don't know, but we need to beat them to it."

"Got it, but looking at this..." She took a step forward and pointed at a couple of places along the strange markings. "I'm just saying these notes are all over the place and look like they're missing important elements... and while the script is obviously *similar* to Runic it obviously isn't, so that's another big deal right there. I wish Ryan had had time to get a picture of the axe as well. Damn it!"

"All right – well get started with what we have for now. In the meantime I have a call to make to Diego Velasco and then hopefully I'll have something to give the team."

"Who's he?"

"An old friend of mine."

"You think he can help us with what's going on?"

"I've no doubt of it. He's the Spanish Minister of the Interior."

*

Half an hour later, Hawke disconnected the call and turned to Lea and Scarlet. Eden had just called him back with the information he'd gleaned from his conversation with Diego Velasco. Now, the three of them were in a hotel room in San Sebastián on the northern coast of Spain. Ryan, who had argued strongly in favour of making the truck driver take them all the way to Biarritz, was with Victoria downstairs in the bar. After the deaths of Gunnar and Javier the English archaeologist had decided it was time for a strong drink or three.

"And?" Scarlet said impatiently.

Hawke looked at her. "Turns out Rich just happens to be old fishing buddies with the Spanish Minister of the Interior."

"Oh sure, I met Diego once," Lea said matter-of-factly. "Funny guy after a few sherries."

Hawke looked at her for a few seconds, speechless, and then continued. "*Anyway*, according to this Diego bloke, the man we're after could well be an individual named Álvaro Sala. He's an Andorran national with a past that's proving very difficult to shine any light on, but the good news is that the French and Spanish authorities have been watching him for some time in connection with some pretty serious drugs trafficking."

"So how does this help us?" Lea said.

"It helps us because they just happen to know where his little hidey hole is – he's the fortuitous owner of a château in the Andorran Pyrenees. It would certainly explain how he was able to mobilize men to assault Javier's castle so fast."

"So we're off to Andorra?" Scarlet said.

"Looks that way, but there's one more thing. Apparently one of Sala's associates is a creature named Marcus Deprez. He's a convicted serial killer who escaped from a high security prison on the outskirts of Brussels. He's a nasty piece of work so keep an eye out for him."

"I'm worried about Victoria," Lea said. "Things look like they're going to get nasty and I'm not sure she's up to it."

"Not much we can do about it though," Scarlet said. "Poor little rosebud."

"Maybe," Hawke said, frowning. "Anyway, we need to make a call to Reaper. He's lives near here, right Cairo?"

Scarlet nodded. "Sure, Marseille."

"Great then get on the blower. We've only got half an hour until our date with some rotors."

"Eden's organized a chopper?" Scarlet asked.

Hawke nodded.

Lea looked at him. "What's wrong with the jet?"

"Andorra la Vella hasn't got an airport."

*

Courtesy of Eden's connection with the Spanish Interior Minister and a bribe which the senior politician had described to Lea as "greasier than usual" they had managed to get hold of an Aérospatiale Puma which Diego Velasco had personally ordered to fly to them from its base in Zaragoza over the border into Andorra. It was with them around an hour later and they took off into the east immediately.

With a cruising speed of two hundred and fifty kilometers per hour, the twin-engined transport chopper didn't take long to leave Spanish airspace and head toward Andorra along the French side of the Pyrenees. After battling their way through his wife Monique, their call to Vincent Reno in Marseille had been a success and he had arranged to meet them at the coordinates in Andorra. He knew the area well from rock-climbing and his knowledge of Smets would be invaluable, not to mention the extra muscle he could deliver.

They flew back into Spain for brief time at Bagnères-de-Luchon before finally crossing into the landlocked principality of Andorra at Os de Civís. Hawke gazed down at the world's sixth smallest country – a tiny microstate no more than fifteen miles across at its widest point whose most famous export was tobacco.

He had tried to catch some sleep on the short flight to refresh himself and rebuild some energy – he'd taken a slow whisky after take off and even asked Ryan to give him some facts about Andorra, but nothing had worked and he had remained wide-eyed all the way.

The four tonne helicopter now flew over Andorra la Vella – it was the country's capital but with a population of just over twenty thousand people it was no more than a large town by most British or American standards. It was night now, but the lights lining its ancient, winding streets far below offered a glimpse of a different kind of lifestyle – slower and more peaceful. Ryan's statistic about its people having one of the world's greatest longevities surfaced in his mind, proving not only that a diet of Mediterranean vegetables and red wine was good for you, but also that some of Ryan's waffle always got through in the end.

They knew from Velasco's surveillance that Sala's château was situated in the mountain range to the north of the capital, on the northern slopes of the Pic de Casamanya, a mountain just under ten thousand feet in altitude. From the basic schematics Velasco was able to provide to them, it looked like an impressive structure, built by a French count in the eleventh century on the site of a much more ancient fortification.

Its location was strategic – constructed with the specific goal of regulating access to the valley leading to Andorra la Vella and monitoring all those travelling between the capital and France. Ryan relayed these facts with fascination but all Hawke heard was trouble – specifically how hard it would be to storm such a place, even with a modern weapon of war like the Puma.

Not long after these thoughts, he was jolted back to reality by the chopper rapidly descending into a narrow valley and the pilot telling them through the headsets that they were approaching the target destination.

"Right, this is the plan," Hawke said, getting straight down to business. "Me, Lea, Scarlet and Vincent are going to storm the château, retrieve the flash-drive, the cloak and axe, and then do whatever damage we can to Sala and his goons. Ryan and Victoria are staying with the chopper when it goes down to El Serrat."

"Sounds fine with me," Victoria said. "I don't think I'd be much good with a submachine gun."

Scarlet looked at her sceptically. "I don't think I'd trust you with a spud gun, darling, never mind a submachine gun. Mind you... if it came down to you or

Mr University Challenge here I think you'd get my vote."

"Hey!" Ryan said, but enjoying the reference. "You're only jealous because going to the University of Hard Shags doesn't qualify you for entry to that extremely prestigious game show."

"Oh *please*, is that the best you can come up with?" Scarlet said as the Puma touched down. Outside the window they saw the silhouette of Vincent Reno standing isolated on the mountainside. Marseille was closer to Andorra than San Sebastián and he had arrived well before them.

"At this point in time, yes," Ryan replied. "But I can do better with preparation. I have so much to work with after all."

Hawke shared a grin with Lea as the team readied their weapons and jumped out of the chopper one by one. Despite the month, the high altitude had chilled the night and their breath was visible as they ran out from under the downdraft of the rotors and made their way toward Vincent. He was standing on a goat track leading to the château.

With instructions to wait in the town of El Serrat, the Puma turned and flew away down the valley. The reverberations of its four mighty blades faded into eerie echoes and the chopper vanished from sight.

"Bonsoir, mes amis!" Vincent said, cigarette hanging off his bottom lip. The moonlight caught the silver stubble on his chin, but his shaved head was hidden beneath a black beanie hat. He glanced at his watch. "I thought perhaps you had decided to do some sight-seeing first."

"Funny," Hawke said, but grateful to see his old friend. They shook hands and Vincent turned his attention to the château. "All quiet here so far."

"Then let's get our stuff back!" Hawke said.

"And see if those bastards have got any Scotch up there," Scarlet added, a look of genuine concern on her face.

Lea frowned. "Seriously guys… if these really are the same people behind the attacks in Ireland, and maybe even Dad's murder, then we have to be careful. There's something about these men I just have a very bad feeling about. I don't think the man behind this is the same as the others."

"What are you talking about?" Hawke asked, glancing from Lea to the château perched on the cliffs high above them. Slowly the clouds broke to reveal a full moon hovering ominously above one of the turrets.

Lea shrugged. "Like I said, I don't know. It was just something about the way they acted in Ireland when they caught me at the cottage, and again on the yacht in Florida. Maybe it's just because the whole connection it all has with my father is freaking me out, but it's something I can't shake off."

Hawke nodded and ignored Scarlet's eye-rolling behind Lea's back. "I understand, but you have to put that out of your mind now. This is a simple retrieval mission…"

"Joe's right," Vincent said. "Don't let them steal your focus."

Hawke turned and pointed up at the château. "We're going to get your Dad's research away from them so they can't use it and maybe get some answers, all right?"

Scarlet shouldered her gun and began marching up the track. "Like to the question – where is the drinks cabinet?" she called out over her shoulder.

Hawke, Lea and Vincent caught up with her and made their way toward the base of the château. From this high up they were able to look down at the valley below all the way to El Serrat.

Hawke considered the awesome mountain vista and saw the advantages to the location at once, and not just for the original French counts. The place was perfectly situated for any search of the Basque region, which is exactly why the mysterious Álvaro Sala must have chosen it as his headquarters, but now it was time to break that particular party up.

Ahead of them was a gatehouse. Hawke studied it and frowned. His mind began to fill with various strategies they could use to storm the building.

"What's the problem?" Scarlet asked.

"I was just thinking about what sort of charge we'd need to get through those gates. They look pretty substantial."

"We don't need any bloody explosives when we have this," Scarlet said, holding up her fist.

CHAPTER FOURTEEN

Château Sala, Andorra

Scarlet tapped on the gate as cool as ice. A security guard opened a small wicket gate which was around head height and squinted at her in the darkness.

"Què vols?" he said gruffly in Catalan.

"I seem to have lost my way," Scarlet said, doing all but fluttering her eyelashes.

The guard switched on a powerful electric light above the gatehouse and leaned closer to the small opening for a better look. He liked what he saw, and made no effort to hide his leering, stubbly grin.

"Estàs sol, anglesa?" His eyes swivelled quickly as he scanned to see if the woman was on her own. Thanks to the others hiding up against the curve of the wall, it looked like she was.

"I really just need a telephone."

He peered around the sides of the wicket gate once again and then slammed it in her face.

"Oh *excellent*," Lea whispered. "I see your charm worked just like usual."

Scarlet scowled. "Well maybe we wouldn't even be here if you hadn't been so bloody secretive about those research files!"

"No – wait," Hawke said. "He's opening the gate."

The heavy gate swung open and the man nodded his head with satisfaction as Scarlet stepped through and drew nearer to him. He seemed less amused when she pulled a gun on him and pressed its muzzle into his sweaty neck.

"Take me to your leader, Vaquero."

Before she had finished the sentence Hawke, Lea and Vincent stepped out of the shadows and emerged into the broad inner courtyard of the château.

"Good evening, sir!" Lea said, walking past the guard.

The man moved forward slowly, not lifting his anxious eyes from the gun which Scarlet was now pointing at his crown jewels. As they passed the end of the gatehouse their captive made a bid for freedom, diving inside on the floor and slamming his hand down on a button fixed to the bottom of the desk. Seconds later an alarm boomed all over the château.

"Oh, *sod* it!" Scarlet said, booting the man across his face and instantly knocking him unconscious, but it was too late. Searchlights were activated and moments later Sala's goons were running all over the château, armed and ready for action.

They headed for the cover of some bushes which were growing up against the north side of the main building. Inside their shadows, Hawke saw a wooden door tucked away a few yards further down the wall. Outside in the yard several armed men were now congregating and starting their search in an attempt to track them down.

Hawke aimed his gun at the door's lock. "Time for us to exit stage right, I think."

"Just get the bloody thing open," Scarlet said. "They're getting closer."

"I count at least ten," said Vincent.

Hawke fired once and blew the ageing mechanism from its housing. Immediately the men knew their location and began to run over to the door, screaming orders in Catalan and waving their guns and flashlights in all directions. Somewhere in the distance behind them Hawke heard the unmistakable sound of two or three Alsations barking wildly.

They ran inside and slammed the door shut behind them. They were in a small, damp hall with a corridor leading away to the east and a circular staircase of white plaster and stone leading both up and down.

Hawke saw a heavy chest against the wall. It was filled with old boots and walking sticks but before he could touch it Scarlet had already wedged it against the door.

"That should keep the tosspots busy for a while," she said, dusting her hands off.

The second she said it, they heard someone trying the door, and then after a few more orders were barked in Catalan, the men outside began ventilating the door with their submachine guns. Dozens of bullets ripped through the old wood, blasting the panels to shards. Moonlight poured in through the holes until all that was left was a shredded mullion in the shape of a cross.

"Time for another one of our exits, don't you think?" Lea said.

But it was too late. Suddenly, the small space was crawling with Sala's men, the barrels of their guns flashing in the moonlight as they poured into the hall. Hawke jumped into the fray, smashing the butt of his pistol into the lead man's face and breaking his jaw.

Lea winced when she heard the cracking sound and then she, Scarlet and Vincent piled in behind Hawke and started to get their hands dirty.

Hawke grappled with another man – a tall individual with wild, staring eyes and greasy black hair. Whoever he was, he was good and knew more than a few moves. For a second he got the better of the Englishman, wrapping his arm around his neck and choking him, but then Hawke managed to force him backwards until he lost his footing and fell back against the chest.

The man released his grip to try and get his balance back and stop his fall, and in that second Hawke rammed his fist up into his jaw. Then he brought his other hand around in a classic haymaker, wildly swinging a second clenched fist down hard into the bridge of the man's nose. Another terrible cracking sound as the nose gave way, and then Hawke finished the job by yanking an old Tassel loafer from the top of the pile in the chest and striking the man hard around the side of the head with its heel, instantly knocking him unconscious.

One of the men saw him get knocked out. "Deprez!"

The other men glanced over but fought on – obviously Hawke had taken out their leader, and a moment later he recognized the name. The man he had just knocked out was the serial killer Eden had warned them about.

Vincent was grappling with a man on the floor, each armed with a hunting knife and trying to cut the other man's throat. It was a fight to the death, but the Frenchman was never in any doubt who would win. His superior strength prevailed as he forced his heavy arm down against the man's weaker arm muscles and killed him on the stone floor.

Across the room Scarlet was elbowing a man in the face. He staggered backwards giving the former SAS officer time to plant a hefty spinning heel kick in his groin. He groaned loudly and moved his hands down instinctively to protect himself, at which point she aimed an axe kick with lethal accuracy at his face and knocked him off his feet. He landed with a smack on the stone floor and Scarlet muttered something about him being lucky that she hadn't debagged him instead.

Lea ended her struggle with the last man by planting her knee in his groin and introducing the butt of her Glock to his face at the same time. He staggered back and the Irishwoman finished the point by sweeping her boot behind his ankles and hooking him off his feet. He tipped back and fell down the steps into the darkness.

"That's them done and dusted," Scarlet said, wiping the dirt and blood from her hands. "Now for Sala."

"And that bastard, Smets," Vincent said. "He treated me like shit in the Legion, and now he pays for it, hein?"

They ran up the steps to the upper levels of the château. From the scarce information Velasco had given to Eden, they knew Sala's private apartments were on the top floor, and deciding to start there was the obvious choice to make.

At the top of the steps they went through an archway and found themselves staring down a long corridor with a marble floor and an impressive vaulted ceiling. They made their way along the corridor, checking the various rooms they passed for any signs of Sala or his study. They knew the alarm would have alerted him some time ago to the presence of intruders, and it wouldn't take him long to work out who was behind the intrusion.

At the end of the corridor they were faced with a choice of two final rooms. On the left was what looked like a library of some sort – walls of books stretching from floor to ceiling and a handful of expensive leather chairs dotted around some reading tables. The whole scene was lit by dim, amber lamps fixed to the walls.

"In there?" Lea asked.

Before Hawke could reply gunmen opened fire on them from the other room. They dived for cover inside the library, Hawke and Lea on one side of the door and Scarlet and Vincent on the other. Vincent fired back with a vengeance, shielding Scarlet from the incoming rounds.

"I never knew you cared, Vincent," she said. "But I fight my own battles."

She leaned around him and shot one of the men in the throat. He fell back, pointlessly gasping for air as blood pumped from his severed carotid arteries and sprayed out into the room. He collapsed in a heap on the floor while another man took cover behind an expansive desk, firing back single-burst shots at them, blasting splinters out of the doorframe and tearing holes in the floorboards at their feet.

Taking cover behind Hawke's broad back, Lea squinted and fired a single shot at the man's leg which she could see through the knee hole in the desk. She struck the tibia and the man screamed in agony as the bone shattered. As he fell to the floor gripping his leg with his hands, Lea fired a second shot and ended his life.

Hawke looked at her. "Get out the wrong side of bed this morning?"

"He was begging for it."

They crossed the corridor and entered the room. Looking around they saw instantly it must be Sala's study. The large desk the man had tried to use for cover was covered in old scrolls, and large maps of the ancient world adorned the apple-white plaster walls. Above them was an impressive gilded ceiling with a painting of a god holding a thunderbolt.

"Thor," Hawke said.

"And is that what I think it is?" Scarlet said, pointing her gun at the long piece of wood on the desk.

"Bloody hell," Hawke said. "I think it just might be!"

He leaned forward and picked it up. It was without a doubt the same strange split piece of wood they had first seen back in Javier's secret loft chamber. He weighed it in his hands and looked carefully at the intricate carvings. "I think this is our lost little baby all right – here, take a look."

He handed it to Lea and her eyes wandered over the severed symbols. "This is it, no doubt about it, but no sign of the cloak. Wait... did you hear that?"

"What?" Scarlet's eyes darted to the door but there was no one there.

Vincent turned and readied his knife. "What did you hear?"

"Nothing," Lea said, returning her gaze to the handle. "I just thought I heard..."

And then, without any warning, the ground beneath their feet gave way and they began their descent into darkness.

CHAPTER FIFTEEN

They fell down the chute for several seconds, mercifully falling at a slight incline which slowed their fall. The walls of the tunnel were smooth and obviously carved by man.

Before any of them had a chance to speak or even scream, they hit the bottom – a soft fall because of a thick layer of straw on the floor. They got their bearings back and began to look around their new home. It looked like a natural cavern in the shape of a tear-drop and they could see no way out other than the way they had just arrived.

They looked up the gently inclining tunnel and saw the gilded ceiling of Sala's study – the face of Thor looking down on them, with disapproving menace.

Scarlet stood up and began to dust herself down. "Oh, well this is just another fine mess you two have got me into. I'm going to start calling you Laurel and Hardy, I think."

Vincent got to his feet and gave an appreciative nod. "Ah, a comedy classic."

"Hey, that's not fair, Cairo," Hawke said. "Lea looks nothing like Oliver Hardy."

Lea slapped his shoulder. "Hey! She meant *you* were Hardy, right?"

Scarlet pursed her lips. "You're making my point for me now."

"What are you talking about?" Lea said, getting to her feet and squaring up to her.

"Well, just then when you slapped Joe," said Scarlet. "You may as well have knocked his bowler hat off or pinched his nose."

Lea put her hands on her hips "Nose pinching was the Three Stooges, ya eejit."

"Was it?" Scarlet asked.

"Yes it bloody was!" Lea said. She turned to Hawke. "Was it?"

Hawke sighed as he got to his feet. "Yes."

"I told you!" Lea said, jabbing Scarlet in the arm. "And that would make you Zippo!"

Hawke sighed again. "It was Zeppo, not Zippo! And he was in the Marx Brothers not a Stooge."

"Was he?"

Hawke and Vincent nodded simultaneously.

"Are we *really* having this conversation?" Scarlet said, raising her hands in the air with disbelief.

"Wait," Lea said. "So who was Zippo with – the Stooges?"

"Oh my God!" Scarlet said, tipping her head back and sighing deeply. Looking up at the trapdoor she froze. "Ah…"

Hawke and Lea stopped talking and looked at her. "What is it?"

"We have company!" Scarlet said, and pointed at the trapdoor.

They stared up at the circular aperture, at least thirty feet above them, and saw the figures of two men appear on the rim.

"Holy craparola!" Lea said as she glanced at them.

Scarlet sighed. "Seconded."

"I knew I should have ignored your phone call," said the Frenchman with a sigh.

One of the men was wearing a herringbone suit with an open-necked black shirt, and stood casually with one hand in his pocket. He wore rimless glasses and had long, black hair that hung forward as he peered over into the pit, but the feature that really stood out was that he was holding a golden straw-coloured snake in his hands.

They'd never seen the man with long hair before, but they recognized the man beside him immediately. He was the creature behind the vicious attack on Victoria's beach house back in the Florida Keys who had snatched Lea and the flash drive. Worse, he was the man who had led the assault on the castillo in the Basque Country and murdered Javier and Gunnar before fleeing with the cloak of invisibility and the axe handle. Now, he was standing above them with a KRISS Vector submachine gun gripped in his hands.

The man with long hair gave them a grim smile. "Ah – bona nit, my friends. Please, don't get up." He laughed at his own joke and gently caressed the snake.

Hawke knew they were totally vulnerable. With a weapon like the KRISS, the ape on the right could turn all three of them into Swiss cheese in half a second and there was nowhere to run.

"Who are you?" Hawke shouted.

"I am Álvaro Sala, and this is Leon Smets. I believe you had the pleasure of his company in Florida."

The goon with the KRISS gave them a mocking grin and bowed his head. Now Hawke saw the grenade tattoo once again, and so did Vincent.

"You bastard, Smets!" Vincent yelled.

Leon Smets leaned over the pit and grinned as a look of recognition crossed his face. "Wait – Legionnaire Deuxieme Classe Reno? Could that be you?"

"Why don't you come down and find out?" Vincent said. "I owe you something."

"Why don't you shut your mouth?" Smets said.

127

Sala hushed Smets and took a step closer. "I am to presume from your presence here that you successfully overcame my men... Tell me, what happened to Deprez?"

"If you mean the baboon downstairs," Hawke shouted up, "I gave him the boot."

Sala looked at Hawke with cold, emotionless eyes. "You are very funny considering your death is only moments away."

"Oh yeah?" Lea shouted. "So what are you going to do about this then?" She waved the axe handle in the air. "If you want your little clue back you're going to have to come down here and get it, ya loser!"

Sala smiled. "I think not. We have already taken several photographs of the handle, so you are more than welcome to keep it for yourself. Perhaps you can use it to try and defend yourselves!" He let out a low chuckle.

Lea turned to Hawke and Scarlet and lowered her voice. "Defend ourselves against what, guys?"

Hawke shrugged his shoulders.

"That's very kind of you," Scarlet shouted back. "But how can an axe handle defend us against your breath?"

"You will see this is no laughing matter, but now I must go." Sala gently rubbed his lips, lost in the moment. "When I find what I seek, the world you know will be destroyed forever. Everything you think you know about humanity will be smashed on the rocks of the epiphany I will bring to you all..." he paused and drew a long, deep breath. "I have few regrets in my long life, Lea Donovan. One is not being able to watch you die in this snake pit, and the other is not being chosen to kill your father."

Lea's blood ran cold, but before she could find any words, Álvaro Sala dropped the snake into the pit and ordered Smets to close the trapdoors.

The snake hit the straw and lashed out with a violent hiss. Hawke and the others jumped out of its way and kept a concerned eye on it as Smets continued to shut the doors.

Now with one door closed, all they could see were each other's outlines. Then, as Smets hauled up the other half of the trapdoor and secured the bolts, total darkness fell upon them.

"Joe?"

Hawke heard Lea's voice in the dark, small and scared. "It's okay."

"What did he mean by that?"

"He was just winding you up," Scarlet said. "He's obviously a total tossrag."

Hawke knew it was more than that, and by the sound of her voice, so did Lea, but now was not the time. "Listen, I presume you have a lighter about your person, Cairo?"

"C'est une bonne idée," Vincent said. "I can hear that damned snake moving around in the straw."

Scarlet's reply came a second later when Hawke heard the rotation of a sparkwheel and Scarlet's face was suddenly in front of him, amber in the glow of the tiny butane flame. "Bien sûr," she said with a cat-like glance at Vincent.

"I knew I could rely on you."

"Just call me Zippo," she said, looking at Lea with a smug grin.

"Like Zippo the clown or Zippo the climbing monkey?" Lea said.

"All right, let's just get on," said Hawke, interrupting Scarlet's reply before it left her lips. "We need to find a way…"

His words were stopped by a strange grating noise which had begun to fill the small cavern.

"What the hell is that?" Scarlet asked.

Vincent frowned. "Sounds like metal scraping against rock."

"No – something's moving," Scarlet said.

Lea stared at the floor. "She's right! The floor's moving."

Hawke realized they were right – the floor was moving. It was almost imperceptible, but slowly he was moving closer to the wall behind him. Worse, he realized Vincent and Scarlet seemed to be moving away from him and Lea at the same time.

"Get this straw out of the way!" he shouted, and began to kick the straw matting away with his boot.

The others did the same but soon wished they hadn't. Beneath the straw was a metal grated floor that was divided in two and joined in the center. Now, the two halves were retracting toward their separate sides of the cavern, and beneath the grating was a deep pit of snakes sliding over one another in a mass of hissing, slithering tangles.

"Oh – it's my lifelong dream!" Scarlet's words were heavy with sarcasm.

"So when the grated floor is fully retracted," Lea said slowly, "we've got nowhere to go but down. Have I got this right?"

Hawke looked grim. "Yes."

The snake Sala had dropped into the cavern slid down over the edge of the grating and joined the others.

"Not digging this one, Joe," Lea said.

"I'm not exactly cock-a-hoop over it, either."

Vincent frowned. "Translation, please."

"He says let's get the fuck out of here," Scarlet said.

The floor continued to slide back into the walls. Now, Hawke and Lea were divided from Scarlet and Vincent by almost a yard.

Hawke strained his eyes around the dimly lit cavern. If the grated floor was retracting like this then it must mean the walls weren't particularly thick. Sala's goons wouldn't have been able to carve the retraction slits into them otherwise, and that gave him hope.

"This isn't a natural cavern," he said. "This whole thing is man-made."

"You think?" Lea said. "Looks pretty realistic to me."

"Looks realistic, sure, but looks can be deceiving."

Scarlet sighed. "Ain't that the truth."

"I noticed it on the way down – the chute was obviously man-made, and I think all of this is too."

The floor continued to push back. Now they were on ledges just a few inches wide.

"These grates can't be rolling back into solid rock," Hawke continued. "Also, think about where we are – we fell thirty feet from Sala's study but that was on the top floor. This can't be the bedrock. This whole place is artificial and if you ask me these walls are fake. It's just some hideous theater where Sala can watch his victims die."

As he spoke, he turned on the ledge and pulled out his gun. He aimed it at the rock above Scarlet's head and fired.

She ducked and the bullet blasted a hole through the rock.

"Thanks for the warning, darling!"

"My pleasure, Cairo."

"But it worked!" said Lea.

"So get shooting!" Hawke screamed.

They got busy emptying their magazines into the rock face, which they quickly realized was as Hawke had surmised – totally fake and built out of some kind of plaster. Seconds later the holes were big enough to climb through, and they made their way out of the pit with seconds to spare as the floor fully retracted with a heavy thud.

They were now standing on opposite sides of Sala's killing room and saw it was just as Hawke had described – nothing more than a set made for killing people. It was housed inside what looked like the furnace room.

"That was a close one," Lea said.

"You can say that again," Scarlet said. "Just as well we sent Ryan down with Victoria or there'd be a shortage of Huggies in Andorra for the next week and half."

Vincent frowned. "Why don't you talk in English?!"

"It's not worth translating, Vincent," Hawke said, scowling at Scarlet.

"So what now?" Lea said.

Hawke clenched his jaw. "We need to get this axe back to base because it looks like Sala has a head start on us."

He scanned the room and saw two doors. One led to a set of metal steps going up to the house, but the other opened out onto stone steps carved out of rock.

"That's is the real bedrock down there," Hawke said. "Not like Sala's theater. I say we see where this takes us – we have no idea how many men he's left up in the main house."

They made their way down the steps and quickly found themselves in a series of tunnels carved into the rock deep at the base of the château.

"Your Zippo is required again, Cairo."

Scarlet fired her lighter up and joined Hawke at the front.

"Thanks."

"Don't mention it. We have to get out of here, darlings and it's this way! I see light!"

Scarlet led the way in the gloom using only her lighter for illumination, and they made their way along the carved rock tunnel until reaching another small cavern, only this time it was the real thing. Ahead of them they saw the unmistakable sight of moonlight in a narrow fissure in the rock face outside. Hawke estimated they were halfway between Sala's morbidly theatrical snake pit and freedom.

"I think we're almost there," he said.

But then they turned the corner and a terrible vision of torture and suffering met their eyes.

"What the hell is that?" Scarlet said, horrified.

Vincent recoiled in shock.

Hawke looked at the far wall in the cavern and saw what had once been a man was now strung up on the slimy rock face. They moved slowly over to him and by the light of Scarlet's Zippo they were able now to see something that horrified all of them. It was obviously a human skeleton, but pieces of flesh were hanging from parts of the frame here and there, and what looked like a desiccated heart was snagged on the bottom of a badly deteriorated rib cage. In a hideous kind of grim mockery, there were still two shoes on its feet and above its head was a strange apparatus involving a bowl and a burned out candle was in a lantern on a nearby table.

"That's not nice at all," Lea said, covering her mouth.

Vincent made the sign of the cross. "Mon dieu..."

Hawke leaned in closer, the terrifying decayed corpse flickering in the warm glow of the lighter flame. "You know what I'm thinking?"

"That at least he died with his boots on?" Scarlet said.

Hawke gave her a look. "No, funnily enough I was *not* thinking that."

"Then do enlighten us."

Lea spoke next, her voice trembling in the damp cave. "I think I know what you're thinking, Joe."

"Oh, someone just tell me!" Scarlet said.

Lea spoke next. "That what's left of this guy has more than a passing resemblance to what old Maxim Vetrov ended up looking like."

Hawke nodded grimly.

That is exactly what he was thinking.

"And what do we make of that?" Scarlet said. "That we're looking at the corpse of someone who tried to take the elixir?"

Hawke shook his head. "I'm not sure of anything anymore. All I know is we need to get the other half of this axe before Álvaro Sala gets his grubby hands on it. If this is how he treats people now, just imagine what he'll do when he gets hold of whatever power's lurking in Thor's tomb. His hammer alone could have unimaginable powers."

And with that sobering thought, they made their way out onto the mountainside and called the chopper up from El Serrat.

CHAPTER SIXTEEN

Stockholm

After clearing customs at Bromma Stockholm Airport the ECHO team, plus Vincent and Victoria jumped into a hired Toyota HiLux and drove east to the city as fast as they could. It was a little before morning rush hour and Hawke was surprised by the easy flow of the traffic as they left Kungsholmen and crossed the bridge by the famous Town Hall on their way into central Stockholm.

Joe Hawke slowed the HiLux and looked suspiciously along the Centralbron which snaked away to the south. It divided the main island of Gamla stan, or Old Town, and the small 'Knights' Islet' known to locals as Riddarholmen. He knew there was little chance of finding Sala in a city of this size, but there was a good chance he was somewhere in the vicinity of the history museum.

They passed the Sheraton on Tegelbacken and spent a tense few moments at some red lights opposite the Aftonbladet tabloid newspaper building. The view to their right overlooked the harbor, and was framed by the famous Riddarholm Church, the burial place of the Swedish monarchs.

Beyond that the impressive prospect of Södermalm stretched up into the clear Scandinavian sky. Closer to their truck, a young woman opened up a small café on the ground floor of the Aftonbladet building and set out some chairs and tables, promising another day of cinnamon buns and fika to an unsuspecting citizenry. It was a beautiful scene, but after letting Sala and the repulsive Smets slip through their fingers back in Andorra, Hawke was more on-edge than usual.

The lights turned green and he rolled the HiLux gently forward in the traffic until he was a few yards from the rear bumper of a metropolitan bus trundling east on Fredsgatan. The bus stopped outside a department store and Hawke overtook it and emerged from the side street into Gustav Adolfs torg, a smart public square named after Gustav II, the 17th king who established Sweden as a major European power after winning the Thirty Years War. Hawke glanced momentarily at the statue of the old king, high on his horse and pointing his sword imperiously at the kungliga, or Royal Palace at the other end of the Norrbro bridge.

"Hope all this still standing when we fly out," Scarlet mused.

They drove around the square's roundabout, passing the Ministry of Foreign Affairs and the Royal Opera building before making their way along Strömgatan and passing into Östermalm. This was Stockholm's answer to London's Mayfair or New York's SoHo, and boasted the most expensive property prices in the whole of Sweden. It was also where the Swedish History Museum was located, and after parking up in a side street to the south of the museum, Hawke and the others emerged into the Stockholm summer drizzle and crossed the street.

They headed toward the entrance, a modest affair beneath a sign which read HISTORISKA MUSEET when they heard the sound of a single gunshot and then a woman's desperate scream.

Hawke looked at the others. "We're too late!"

Scarlet unceremoniously yanked a gun from her jacket. "So let's get in there, Tonto!"

They slipped through the entrance and quickly worked out the scream had come from the Viking History section. No one was surprised about that, and they ran there as fast as they could in stark contrast to the hundreds of members of the public who were running for the exits.

A security alarm began to trill loudly down all of the corridors and outside Hawke heard the faint and familiar sound of police sirens. "Things are about to get lively here – we have to hurry."

They ran up a flight of stairs and along another short corridor before reaching the Viking History section, but when they got there what they saw chilled them. A man in a museum uniform was lying dead on the floor and another man was holding a terrified woman in a similar uniform hostage with a knife at her throat. Marcus Deprez and Dasha Vetrov were standing behind him. Hawke could still see the gash on his temple where he had struck him with the shoe back in Andorra.

"Where's your organ grinder?" Hawke asked, noticing no sign of either Sala or Smets.

"No closer," Deprez said. "Or my man here will tear open her throat."

Victoria took a step back and gasped in horror, but Ryan put his hand on her shoulder to calm her. "Take it easy – it's just a bluff."

Dasha blew a large purple bubble. It popped in her mouth and then she spat the wad of gum on the polished tiled floor before sliding a fresh piece in her mouth. She spoke in rapid Russian.

"She says," Deprez drawled, "that you killed her brother and she will torture you to death for it."

Hawke didn't reply, but carefully weighed the situation up. Deprez was standing next to a display of

Viking weapons, specifically a large stainless steel and glass case holding axe handles.

"Tell her it's a date," Hawke said.

Deprez said nothing but pulled a gun from his pocket and put the butt of the weapon through the top of the case. He smashed the glass into hundreds of razor-sharp shards. "You let me leave with this or we'll kill her."

He put his hand in the case and pulled out the other fragment of the Axe of Baldr. It was without a doubt the other half of the one Ryan had in the bag slung over his shoulder.

"Just let the woman go and we'll talk," Hawke said.

"I know who you are – Hawke and Donovan… When you're dead I will shit on your graves," Deprez hissed.

"Shit on your graves!" repeated the goon holding the knife.

Dasha laughed and blew another bubble with the gum in her mouth.

"Language, please!" Scarlet said, feigning disgust. "There are ladies present, not to mention Ryan."

"I'm standing right here and still she says it," Ryan said, deflated.

Deprez focussed on Hawke. "Drop your weapons."

Hawke and the others did as they were told. He crouched slowly and put his gun on the floor before standing back up with his hands raised in the air. The next thing he knew, the goon was staggering back from the woman with a knife in his neck. Hawke turned and saw Scarlet had thrown the knife she kept on her belt.

Deprez and Dasha had the axe and turned on their heels and ran while the hostage screamed and scampered away. Lea and Vincent took off after them while Hawke stormed forward and drove a tightly clenched fist into the wounded goon's stomach.

The man wheezed hard and doubled over, giving Hawke time to bring up his knee and grab the back of the man's head at the same time. Driving his knee up and pulling his head down simultaneously, he tested the hypothesis about immovable objects and unstoppable forces. The conclusion came in the form of a severe crunching sound as his nose splattered all over his face and showered Hawke's knee in a thick coating of blood.

Hawke pulled the man's head back up by the ears and slammed his fist into his broken face, once again hitting the nose. The goon howled in pain as he stumbled back a few steps, but Hawke had finished playing and after propelling a well-aimed kick into the Belgian thug's groin he ended the game with another savage roundhouse punch to his lower jaw. He sent him flying back into one of the display cases where he landed with smack and slid to the floor unconscious in a shower of broken glass and antique pottery.

Hawke watched with amusement as the dust settled and an old Viking chamber pot slid onto his head.

"That'll teach him to be a potty mouth," Scarlet said, pulling her knife from his neck and wiping it clean on his shoulder.

Hawke ignored it, and reloaded his gun. Further down the exhibition room Vincent and Deprez were out of sight but Lea was fighting with Dasha.

Hawke, Scarlet and Ryan ran towards her with a confused Victoria a step behind, but it turned out there was no need for the heroics. Before they got anywhere near the fight, Lea had snatched up one of the many fine examples of Dane Axes and incapacitated the Russian woman with it, swinging the light, carbon steel blade in a sweeping arc at her stomach.

Dasha Vetrov leaped back to avoid being cut in half, giving Lea time to bring the other end of the heavy oak haft across into her face at speed, breaking her jaw and knocking her out. She collapsed on the floor in a heap and Lea leaned casually on the axe's long, wooden handle. "And you stay there too, ya grubby little pox!"

Hawke arched an eyebrow as he stared at the unconscious woman. "I see she didn't make the cut."

Lea rolled her eyes. "Is that the best you can some up with?"

"Well, axe a silly question and…"

"Just stop it. Right. Now."

"Gotcha – come on, it's time to split."

"I mean it, Joe. You're just not funny. We've been through this before."

"Just because she couldn't handle your charms, don't take it out on me."

"Cut it out," she said with a sideways glance.

"Sorry – ah! Now you see the fun we can have, at last!"

Their banter was cut short by the sound of gunfire in the next room, and they ran forward to find Vincent Reno bleeding out on the floor. Deprez had shot him and he was down.

Victoria screamed and covered her mouth in shock.

"Jesus!" Scarlet said, kneeling beside the Frenchman. "We need an ambulance!"

Lea pulled out her phone and it was then Hawke saw Deprez, lurking at the rear of the room beside the fire exit. He could easily have exploited the disarray to escape but instead he raised his gun and aimed at a disoriented Victoria.

Before Hawke could even call out, Deprez fired the weapon.

Ryan, who was closest to Victoria reacted in a heartbeat, spinning around and pushing her out of the way. She hit the floor hard but Ryan got hit harder – the bullet smashed into his upper arm and spun him around like a Matryoshka doll.

"No!" Lea cried, running forward to help her former husband, but before she could take another step Deprez laughed and sprayed the room with more submachine gun fire. Most of the rounds drilled into the far wall but at least one must have struck the fire extinguisher attached to the wall beside the other exit.

The bullet tore through the stainless steel casing of the extinguisher and as the cylinder depressurized it dispersed its contents with startling rapidity through the bullet hole. A thick jet of nitrogen and potassium bicarbonate instantly filled the small space and brought further pandemonium to the scene of the double shooting.

Before the room was lost in the fog, Hawke saw Ryan collapse to the floor and grip his upper arm in agony. He charged across the room and grabbed Ryan by his ankles, hauling him backwards along the floor until they were in the clearer air of the main room.

"He's been shot," he shouted at Victoria. "Do what you can."

Hawke looked up into the chaos and watched with a sense of desperate anger and frustration as Deprez snatched up the axe handle and sprinted from the room, a morbid smile on his face.

Hawke thought fast. "Lea, Vincent and Ryan need tourniquets right now, so do that and wait here until the paramedics arrive. Scarlet and I are going to get that bloody axe handle back!"

Scarlet cocked her weapon. "Finally, Hawke asks me on a date!"

Hawke gave her a weary glance but there was no time for talk. Without another word the two of them took off

141

after Marcus Deprez and the other half of the broken axe handle.

With the lives of Ryan Bale and Vincent Reno hanging in the balance, Hawke was very clear in his mind about what had to happen next.

CHAPTER SEVENTEEN

By the time they hit the fire exits the day had turned nasty. Black clouds were moving at some speed across the city, so low they almost scraped the tops of some of the higher buildings, and they were dumping a heavy, cold rain over everything.

Hawke and Scarlet scanned the road for any signs of Deprez but for a few seconds all they saw was empty, parked cars and lots of rain. Then, Scarlet saw him. "Over there in the Saab!"

Hawke followed her hand. She was pointing to an old, sky blue Saab 900 into which a soaked Marcus Deprez was climbing with great agility. The engine roared to life and its headlights illuminated the rain streaking in front of the car. Seconds later the Belgian serial killer was spinning the wheel around and driving the car out onto the road.

"Quick!" Hawke shouted.

"To the Batmobile!" Scarlet yelled.

Hawke gave her a look of disapproval and opened the locks of the HiLux with the car remote. Cairo Sloane took gallows humor to new heights – it was just how she handled the tough stuff. She'd never told him about her younger days, but he guessed that was where it all came from. Either way, now was hardly the time to ask her.

They climbed inside the truck and seconds later they were strapped in and ready to go. Hawke fired up the powerful 3.4 litre V6 and with the help of the power steering, he moved the heavy vehicle out of the parking space with ease and speed and they were soon on their way.

"Any sign of the repulsive little shit?" Scarlet said, peering through the windshield as the wipers cleared the deluge from their view.

"He's just gone down there," Hawke said calmly, checking his mirror for local law enforcement. He indicated a sharp right turn, which Deprez took so fast and tight he smashed into a litter bin, spraying its contents all over the junction. A man in a Wigens linen cap who was walking a nonchalant Vallhund across the road expressed serious Scandinavian disapproval as the cans and bottles and newspapers tumbled out across his path.

"He didn't even get a fist wave!" Scarlet said.

"I suspect he thinks violence isn't the answer."

"And quite right too," she replied as she checked her gun.

Looking ahead they saw the Saab was accelerating and putting more distance between them. Hawke wanted to go faster but this road was busy with pedestrians and he didn't want to put any of them in hospital, or worse. Clearly Marcus Deprez didn't share his concerns.

"What the hell's he doing now?" Scarlet asked.

Hawke saw that Deprez was turning in his seat. A moment later he was leaning out of the driver's side and aiming a gun at them. It looked like he was keeping the car steady with his other hand, but Hawke saw danger ahead. The Saab began to swerve dangerously as it snaked up the road.

"Look out, Cairo!" Hawke shouted. He pulled the wheel to the right and the HiLux skidded out of its lane. It was worth the risk. Deprez's bullet missed and smashed into the trunk of one of the many linden trees lining the street.

"That was lucky!" Scarlet said.

"What can I say?" Hawke said with a crooked grin. "I'm faster than a speeding bullet."

Scarlet rolled her eyes and shook her head in despair. "Tell me, Joe, how do you fit your enormous ego inside that tiny mind?"

Hawke didn't hear the barb. Instead, he was now focussing on bringing the HiLux back into the correct lane while at the same time trying to ensure the insane Belgian killer in front of them wasn't any luckier next time.

But he was. Deprez fired another two shots, the first striking the front fender of the truck with a metallic *plink* and ricocheting off into the air. The second plowed into the center of the windshield with a crunchy smacking sound.

A massive spider-fracture instantly exploded in the glass, leaving Hawke's view of the street badly impaired, but he didn't have to wait long for a solution. Before he could open his mouth Scarlet had started to kick the glass out of its frame.

He gave a brief smile as he watched Cairo Sloane handle the situation so coolly, and it reminded him a little of that night back in Geneva when he had watched Lea do exactly the same move.

With the windshield now spinning around on the road behind them, Hawke could once again see his target. Deprez was now back inside the Saab and in full control, speeding the old car towards a small intersection lined with high, old nineteenth century buildings.

The lights at the intersection were red, but this didn't seem to concern Deprez who raced through them leaving a trail of destruction in his wake. Two cars smashed into one another in an attempt to avoid a collision with the speeding Saab. A third swerved away and braked sharply but the driver wasn't quick enough to stop the car from mounting the kerb and plowing into the display window of a Cantonese restaurant.

With an angry Chinese chef screaming and waving a meat cleaver on the sidewalk behind them, Hawke guided the HiLux deftly through the broken glass and dented bumpers of the accident and accelerated once again in a bid to close the gap between him and Deprez. Without that fragment of the axe handle they would never be able to find the location of Thor's tomb, so this was a race he couldn't afford to lose.

Staring ahead, he saw Deprez was now trying to get around a bus. The Belgian's patience ran out fast, and he resolved the situation by driving up onto the sidewalk and smashing through the terrace tables of a small café. With the bus now between him and Hawke he pulled back in sharply and disappeared from view.

"I don't think he likes Stockholm very much," Scarlet said.

"I don't think he likes *people* very much."

Now they were on Narvavägen, a tree-lined boulevard channelling much of Östermalm south to Djurgården, a large island in the center of the city covered in beautiful parkland.

"Where's the numbnuts going?" Hawke asked.

"Nowhere clever," Scarlet said, glancing at her iPhone. "According to the map, that's an island with only one way on or off, at least by car."

"So he's driven into a dead end?"

"Maybe, but a bloody big dead end. We can still lose him – plus it looks like there's a foot-bridge back to the mainland at the other end of the island if he really gets desperate."

Hawke drove the HiLux over the Djurgårdsbron, the three lane bridge which connected the island to

Östermalm and slowed as a tram glided past down the middle of the road. He could still see Deprez and the old Saab, but he was accelerating away and trying to use the tram for cover.

"He's heading up there," Hawke said, pointing up a gentle incline in the road ahead of them. He accelerated as they passed the Nordic Museum, a vast building in the Danish renaissance style which resembled a cathedral more than a museum housing the country's cultural history.

Deprez followed the incline around to the right and then suddenly accelerated out of view on the other side of the hill's brow. Hawke floored the throttle and the mighty HiLux soon made the top of the rise, only just in time to see the Saab skidding around to the right and disappearing into a side street.

"Don't lose him, Joe!"

"I was just considering stopping for a latte but now you've said that I'll speed up."

Hawke took the corner at speed and was confronted by a crowd of angry and confused people waving their fists at Deprez's blue Saab. He slowed and weaved through them. The road twisted around to the left and Hawke increased power to the engine in another bid to close the gap between them and the Belgian.

Hawke kept his eyes fixed on the Saab. "Any idea where he's going, Cairo?"

"Looks like there are a couple of amusement parks on the island," Scarlet said, checking her phone.

"What a shame we never packed a lunch."

"You're *so* funny, but...ooh – there's an Abba Museum here!" Scarlet said in shock.

"I think we have more important things to worry about right now."

147

"I know *that*, Joe. I must remember to tell Ryan, that's all."

Hawke gave her a look and they got back to business.

Deprez raced past the entrance to the Gröna Lund Amusement Park and continued further along the enormous island. Gröna Lund Amusement Park was built on the south-western tip of the island back in the 1880s by a German named Jacob Schultheiss. It was the oldest amusement park in Sweden with well over a million visitors per year.

"Doesn't look like he's going in there today," Hawke said.

"Bugger – I was looking forward to that."

Hawke continued his pursuit of the man as he drove over the tramlines in the center of the road and watched up ahead as Deprez then braked hard and brought the old Saab to a sharp stop not far from the entrance to the Funland Amusement Park, a newer and smaller park further along the southern coast of the island. He clambered out the car and slipped into the crowd, still carrying the axe handle.

"Looks like you're going to get your day at the fair after all," said Hawke.

Scarlet pointed her phone at the Saab. "Yes! He's going into Funland!"

"And trying to lose us in the crowd," Hawke said, sighing. Everywhere he looked he saw men, women and children milling about in their raincoats, many carrying umbrellas. He gave an appreciative nod – he liked people who weren't afraid of a bit of weather.

Scarlet checked her gun once more and slid it inside her holster out of sight. "He's obviously rattled or he'd never have come in here in the first place."

Hawke shook his head. "It's not that. He knows this city about as well as we do – he's lost and looking for any way out he can get."

"He's got a way out, all right," she said, tapping the gun under her jacket.

They leaped from the HiLux and sprinted into the bustling crowd. Deprez crossed a large car park and disappeared into some trees up ahead.

Hawke and Scarlet followed closely, doing their best not to panic the people around them.

Looking ahead they saw Deprez was now moving into the main part of the park.

Hawke didn't know how many of those were repeat-visitors, but he guessed not many of those present today would be in a hurry to return to Funland.

They watched as the serial killer pushed his way through the crowd, weaving deeper into the park as he went. The axe handle fragment under his arm was attracting a few looks here and there, but thankfully his gun seemed to be out of sight – more for his benefit than anything else. People screaming and pointing at him was hardly conducive to a successful escape.

Deprez moved deeper into the park and was now in a street lined with small wooden houses. They were decorated with flashing light bulbs and promised all the fun of the fair, but the Belgian had something else on his mind: evasion. He scanned the area for an escape route and saw his chance – a building with a wooden fascia and the words Kärleks Tunneln – the tunnel of love.

"Why's he going in there?" Scarlet asked.

"Maybe he's trying to give you a hint."

A withering glance came his way but he never saw it. He was too busy focussing on the hunt. They moved through the crowd and went inside the Tunnel of Love.

In the darkness, Scarlet pulled her weapon and moved the slider to put a bullet in the chamber. "I hope they don't have to rename this place the Tunnel of Blood after we're finished."

Hawke hoped so too, and the two of them moved into the darkness.

CHAPTER EIGHTEEN

Hawke strained his eyes in the darkness to see Marcus Deprez. The little train that took people around the tunnel was obviously at another stage of the ride, so Hawke and Scarlet climbed down onto the tracks and began to move forward on foot, passing beneath an enormous red love heart which served as the start of the ride.

"Where the hell is the bastard?"

A bright muzzle-flash in the darkness ahead and the sound of a bullet smacking into the wooden panels behind him was his answer.

Scarlet ducked for cover. "You had to ask, didn't you?"

Suddenly a faint red glow emanated from bulbs hidden somewhere above them and they caught a glimpse of Deprez as he rounded a bend and slipped out of sight further ahead in the tunnel.

"There he is!" Hawke said.

They moved ahead and found themselves in a long tunnel of moulded plastic designed to look like they were in a cave deep underground. As they progressed, fairytale music began to play. Designed to be cute, it took on a sinister and eerie feel under the circumstances.

Further along now, they passed little models of Animatronic elves waving cheerily at them from a landscape of miniature waterfalls and fairy lights.

"This place is giving me the creeps," Scarlet said. "Tunnel of Terror, more like."

"Just be grateful he never ran into the Fun House," Hawke said.

Now they passed another Animatronic scene of tiny people making brightly-colored cakes in a little kitchen. The figurines spoke to each other in Swedish, and canned laughter ensued, but their amazement was shattered by the sound of another gunshot.

The bullet traced past them and blew the head off one of the smiling elves, reducing it to a cloud of dust. The headless elf continued to wave happily as Hawke fired back. He heard a moan of pain.

"I think you got him!"

They heard another gunshot, but this time it was followed by the unmistakable sound of people screaming. Hawke and Scarlet knew those screams meant their man had caught up with the ride and was trying to clear the tunnel.

They reached the exit of the tunnel which was now a chaotic space of terrified people and confused park security. One look at Hawke and Scarlet and their guns sent another wave of fear through the crowd, but they had no time to explain. Looking over the people they saw Deprez limping away from the ride and heading toward the edge of the park. Hawke had obviously hit him in the leg.

The wounded Belgian moved past a small fountain before turning and firing blindly in their direction. The bullets could have hit anyone, including a number of children, but luckily they missed and struck the metal support struts of the rollercoaster. Another eruption of fear convulsed through the day-trippers and they scrambled in a dozen directions looking for cover.

Deprez cursed and returned to his escape, going as fast as his limp would allow. With the axe handle in his other hand he resembled a caveman as he tried to drag himself to the safety of the shadows.

"He's not going on that thing, is he?" Scarlet pointed to the Skräcken, an inverted roller coaster from which people were strapped into their seats and dangled beneath the rail. "Did his parents not love him enough as a kid, or what?"

"No, I don't think so – to either question… I think he's heading in there because it's on the outside of the park and the easiest way out." Hawke pointed to the House of Horrors.

"You've *got* to be joking!"

"No – and there he goes!"

They reached the House of Horrors, a building designed to look like a broken-down, haunted house. It was on the southern edge of the park overlooking a number of boats moored at Waldemarsviken, a small bay off the coast of Djurgården and the smaller island of Beckholmen to the west.

Scarlet looked at Hawke. "Not scared are you?"

Hawke gave her a look but made no reply.

Ordinarily the experience would have been a busy affair with people enjoying the horror, but after Deprez's intervention with his gun, the ride was now deserted as the people scrambled and cowered outside, waiting nervously for the police to show up.

Hawke and Scarlet moved into yet more darkness, only this time cheery elves and cake shops had been replaced with mannequins covered in blood and decapitated heads hanging from meat hooks.

A burst of gunfire emanated from the top of a stairwell and they gave chase, knowing they were closing in on a badly injured man. He would be even more deranged and irrational than usual.

The sound of heavily reverbed moaning and screams filled the house, booming from speakers tucked away out of sight. All of it was designed to terrify those who had entered the House of Horrors, but Marcus Deprez was providing enough terror all on his own.

With Hawke in the lead, gun raised and ready to fire, they moved down the stairs and drew closer to their target. This part of the horror experience was designed to look like some kind of abandoned asylum, with white tiled walls smeared in blood. Most of it was the fake, theatrical kind, but Hawke realized halfway down the steps that some of it was real and had been left by the wounded Deprez as he'd limped down the steps.

In the basement of the house now, they were surrounded by more scenes of horror and the noise of the screams and moans over the sound system seemed louder now. It would have unsettled most people, but Hawke and Scarlet weren't most people so they pushed on undeterred.

Suddenly the dark space was filled with bright daylight as Deprez smashed open a fired door and staggered out the back of the building. Hawke and Scarlet squinted as their eyes adjusted to the surprise change in light levels, but were soon after their man.

They found themselves in a narrow side street running parallel to the east side of the amusement park. It was a green, leafy space with a few cars parked here and there, and the rain had relented now to the same light drizzle they had experienced when they had arrived at the history museum.

"Where did he go?" Scarlet asked, searching both ends of the street.

"Judging from the blood, I'd say that way." Hawke pointed at the south end of the street toward the boats moored in Waldemarsviken marina. Splashes of blood were smeared here and there on the concrete leading down toward the water.

They ran to the end of the street and quickly reached the waterline. Following the blood, they realized that Deprez had gone aboard what looked like some kind of tourist paddle boat.

"Quick!" Hawke said. "He's cut the mooring ropes!"

The boat's engines started up and it began to move forward in the sound. Hawke and Scarlet jumped from the jetty to the boat's wooden stern and were welcomed aboard by a burst of gunfire from Deprez's pistol.

They dived for cover and then returned fire at the wounded man blasting the wheelhouse windows to shards. Deprez dodged the bullets and fired back blindly like a man possessed, but he was caught like a trapped pig and he knew it. Whatever plans he thought he had of escaping off the island on a boat had gone badly wrong and now it was time to pay for the error in judgement.

In a panic now, the Belgian fired a shot through the front window of the wheelhouse and clambered away from his pursuers toward the front of the ship.

Hawke and Scarlet drove him forward with their superior firepower until he had run out of space and had nowhere to run.

"Get back!" he screamed at them, waving his gun.

"Just drop the weapon, Deprez!" Hawke shouted, his gun aimed at the Belgian's head. "You can't take us both down before one of us takes you out and you know it."

"Do as he says," Scarlet said. "The last time I shot someone on the bow of a ship it was the President of the United States so don't think I'd think twice about wasting a round on little crap like you."

Deprez tossed his gun to the ground but pulled a knife and held the blade to the axe handle. "Come any closer and I'll cut these precious carvings off the handle, then no one finds the tomb!"

Scarlet glanced at Hawke, but the Englishman didn't bat an eyelid. "Put the axe down, Deprez. I'll kill you before you can move that blade an inch."

Deprez called his bluff, and pushed the blade into the handle, but Hawke was true to his word, firing at the man's chest. He struck him in the heart and sent him staggering backwards with a look of confused terror spreading across his face.

He tottered backwards over the rail at the stem of the bow, his arms flailing wildly in a last vain attempt to save his life, but it was too late.

Scarlet raised her gun and fired at him, striking him dead-center in the forehead and powering him over the ship into the dark water of the sound. He landed with a tremendous splash and began to float away from the shore.

"Where did you learn to shoot a moving target like that, Cairo?" Hawke said, strolling to the starboard side aft lazarette. He picked up a mooring hook and walked back to the bow.

"In a fairground,' she said with a wink as Hawke pulled the floating axe handle through the water toward the boat. A few yards beyond it, Marcus Deprez's body bobbed up and down in the wake of a long, glass-roofed sightseeing boat. Some of the people aboard pointed in horror at the corpse and others whipped out their phones to film the scene as Scarlet proudly extended her middle finger at them, accompanied by a polite smile and bow of the head.

Hawke rolled his eyes as he manipulated the hook in the water, dragging the ancient relic closer to the paddle boat. "We've got to get back to the others," he said, finally hefting the ancient axe handle from the water.

"Ryan needs to get to work on this thing – presuming he's all right that is."

As he finished speaking he looked up to see Deprez's corpse getting sucked into the blades at the back of the tourist boat. A terrible grinding sound ensued and then the water turned a deep crimson color as it filled with the dead man's blood.

"That's for Vincent and Ryan," Hawke said without emotion, and then turned to leave.

CHAPTER NINETEEN

Elysium

Her mind was now focussed on nothing but the fateful mission ahead of her.

Lexi Zhang slid her hand along the pipe guard railing as she skipped down the steps and made her way to the wheelhouse. From the crow's nest of the small trawler she had studied the silhouette of the small island known to a tiny elite as Elysium, but now they were closing in and it was time to shut down the engines.

Federico had been fishing these waters for most of his life and had nodded casually when she showed him the coordinates. "Isla privada..." he had said with a nonchalant shrug of the shoulders.

"Si," she had said. "Don't worry about." She checked the fisherman's tired eyes to see if he had understood her broken Castilian. It was all she had, and no matter how many subjunctives she mangled it was better than poor Federico's English. After deciding his Mandarin was probably even worse, she made another sentence in her Spanish.

"Veinte minutos," he said in reply with an apologetic smile.

He lit up an ancient-looking pipe and leaned against the rickety navigation panel as he blew the cloud of sweet-smelling tobacco into the hot air. He resumed the story about how he had inherited his father's gambling debts and not for the first time Lexi wondered if she shouldn't just shoot him and give him to the sharks, but that wouldn't be fair she thought. Not on the sharks, at any rate.

She decided to get some fresh air and stepped out onto the deck. Slowly the old boat creaked forward in the water and drew her ever closer to her mission. She wondered if she should check the weapons again, but she'd already done it more times than she could remember. This wasn't like her, but then this wasn't like a regular mission.

Now, Lexi swayed softly with the gentle rocking of the boat as it drifted a mile off-shore in the darkness of night. There was a calm stillness to the ocean she had loved since she was a small child and this was about as smooth as things got. Here in what sailors called the intertropical convergence zone the trades could drop away and leave a sailing boat lost at sea for what might be as good as eternity.

She looked up into the sky and noted the full moon. A mistake on her part, but not one that would stop her doing her business tonight. A little way to the moon's left, Jupiter hung silently in the sky. She stared at the tiny cream disc until the motion of the boat began to make her feel uneasy. It was time to go.

As the engines puttered to silence, Lexi paid Federico the second half of his fee. He took hold of the heavy brown envelope with a sweaty hand and peered inside. Smirking and nodding with satisfaction, he unfastened a small rowing boat at the rear of the trawler and pushed it into the water.

He held its mooring rope tightly in his hands. "This is where we part company," he said in Spanish.

Lexi understood and climbed into the small boat with her tool bag over her shoulder. A few seconds later she was rowing gently to the high cliffs on the west coast of the island, and Federico started up his engines and steered the boat back to port. Now she was on her own.

The island rose up before her, its craggy tropical cliffs looming higher than she'd expected – but this was the last place anyone would attempt an insertion on Elysium and so that was the plan.

When she was fifty feet from the shore she used one of the oars to test the depth of the water and it was just as she expected – knee high and an inviting twenty degrees. She retracted the oars and secured them in the rowlocks before pulling her bag of tricks from beneath the sternsheets and shouldering it. Then, she stepped into the ocean and walked silently to the shore in the moonlight, dragging the boat behind her with the mooring rope.

After securing the boat to a lonely coconut palm in the breaker zone, she took a deep breath and tilted her head back to survey the cliffs towering above her. Then she pulled on a pair of crag gloves and began to ascend the sharp, vertical rocks. Also as she had expected, this was the sort of classic volcanic cliff that was so common to this part of the world, and especially on a former volcanic island such as Elysium.

She struggled onwards and upwards, the heavy weight of the weapons in her bag pulling on her back all the way. She used a heel hook to get some pressure on a hold, and then a few yards from the top she gripped what she thought was a secure arête, but then it broke loose and she swung wildly to her left. She hung on for her life with one hand as the treacherous piece of cliff tumbled the few hundred feet to the beach below and smashed into the moonlit surf.

Lexi strained to keep her grip as she swung her right hand up and grabbed hold of another small ridge. She balanced her bodyweight and used a move known to climbers as a *gaston* where she pushed her thumb down into a crag and forced her elbow out in order to push herself upwards just enough to reach a more secure hold. She sighed with relief. She was too high to bail out now, she thought, and kept on going.

Finally she crawled onto the top of the cliff and took a second to get her breath back. Looking behind her, she was able to make out the faint silhouette of Federico's boat as he steamed toward the horizon. Ahead of her Elysium stretched out, majestic and tranquil. From one of the highest points on the island she was able to survey everything. She put a night-vision monocular to her eye and began to study the facts.

Directly below her, on the eastern slopes of her conquered mountain, she saw what looked like the western perimeter of the ECHO complex. Standard fare, she thought without emotion – it looked like a razorwire fence, clearly electrified by the solar-powered chargers and insulators she could see – and by the looks of the photodetectors and mirrors she thought she could spy a laser tripwire alarm just inside the perimeter fence as well. She expected nothing less.

I wonder, she contemplated with interest, *exactly what Richard Eden keeps hidden away in this place?*

She made her way down the slope, weaving in and out of the tropical undergrowth. In places it was so thick she was forced to hack her way clear with a machete. At times like this, she thought, was it all worth it? What was it that drove her onward through the night like this, so far from her family and the comfort of home? Ah yes, she thought... *I remember now.*

But she wasn't here to reminisce. She brought her attention back to the mission. This was about settling old scores and righting old wrongs. Ever since Joe Hawke had run into her life again back in Hong Kong she knew this day was inevitable. It was just the way things were with her and sometimes she felt like she couldn't stop herself even if she wanted to.

At the bottom of the mountain she stopped again and refocussed. Her mind was buzzing with a mix of adrenalin and dopamine as she went through her mission plan once again – it was always like this... When the hunt was getting hot and the victims' end drawing closer, only this time there were so many differences. This time there could be no going back, and she knew it. For a second, she felt her heart waver – was she really going to go through with this?

Yes, she said, newly determined and pushing all doubt from her mind. She was a highly trained assassin and this mission was a cakewalk, not to mention the new life she would have after it. Her mission objective was sitting down there somewhere in a secret, luxury compound in this paradise, and it was time to reintroduce them all to the Dragonfly.

CHAPTER TWENTY

Hawke stared suspiciously out of the window of the hotel and across the harbor to the north. After retrieving the axe handle from the newly dispatched Marcus Deprez they had booked into the Hilton Hotel Stockholm Slussen on Guldgränd on the north shore of the island of Södermalm.

Known to Stockholmares simply as "Söder", it was one of the busiest districts in the whole of Scandinavia. Once a slum, now a gentrified, bohemian quarter full of expensive, minimalist coffee shops and dense traffic, all Hawke knew about the place was that they weren't safe here.

Deprez was out of the game, having retired permanently from being a bastard back on the south coast of Djurgården, but Álvaro Sala and his chief goon, the hit man from Brussels Leon Smets were still out there somewhere, and now they would be wasting no time searching for the axe handle. It was their only way to reach Thor's tomb and he was sure a man like Sala wouldn't give up until he was dead.

Even worse news was Vincent Reno. When the paramedics had arrived he'd been in a bad way and they'd rushed him to Södersjukhuset, a large hospital not far from the museum where he had been shot by Deprez. According to the latest reports he hadn't regained consciousness on the way to the hospital and was now undergoing an emergency life-saving operation.

According to the paramedics, Ryan had been much luckier than Vincent and the bullet had just missed his humerus. The speeding lead projectile had instead torn through his bicep. It was painful, but some Alvedons and a lot of bandages had reduced the burning sensation and there would be no permanent damage.

"Are you okay, Joe?" Lea asked.

Hawke nodded sullenly.

"What happened to Deprez?" she asked.

"He's definitely not playing any more," Hawke said.

"He seemed pretty cut up about it, actually," Scarlet said, lighting a cigarette. She blew a cloud of smoke out of the window and shook her head in confusion. "Is it obligatory to have a bicycle and a beard in this town, or what?"

"Eh?" Hawke looked up, distracted.

"Nothing, and can we get a sodding balcony next time so I can smoke without setting the buggering alarms off?"

"Yeah, let me make a note," Lea said. "Because *that's* the most important thing we have to think about at the moment."

"All right, we need to focus," said Hawke, turning to face the others. He stopped when he saw Scarlet at the drinks cabinet and rolled his eyes. "Really, at this time of the day?"

A gentle clink of ice cubes and a sip of the vodka followed before her response. "I'm on Caribbean time, darling."

"It *is* a little early," Victoria said, a look of serious concern on her face as she glanced at her watch.

Scarlet stared at the woman until she looked away and then took another sip.

"Why is it that you can always find a time-zone to justify it?" Ryan said.

She winked and lit a cigarette. "What can I say? It improves my aim."

Victoria frowned. "Perhaps a coffee would be more appropriate?"

Scarlet raised an eyebrow but made no reply, restricting her response to another drag on the cigarette before leaning out the window and blowing a second cloud of the hot, blue smoke into the air.

Ryan watched her for a moment and shook his head with a sigh. "You must be responsible for more carbon monoxide pollution than Shanghai."

"Are you trying to be funny, *boy?* It's just that if you are could you signal it in advance so I know when to laugh."

"I'm surprised you're not personally named in the Kyoto Protocol."

"All right, let's get on," Hawke said, cracking a much-needed Åbro from the fridge.

"I thought it was too early?" Scarlet said.

"I just went to Caribbean time," he said with a scowl, and then joined Ryan and Victoria at the desk.

As soon as they had checked into the room Ryan had joined the two halves of Baldr's axe handle together and began his research into the strange markings. Now, the reformed dropout was doing what he did best, hammering information into a laptop, slowed only by the bandage on his wounded arm.

"What's the latest?" Hawke asked.

Ryan sighed. "If you place the two halves of the split axe together then what looks like almost meaningless scratches in the wood suddenly becomes a pretty obvious inscription. The glyphs created by joining the fragments are clearly the same strange ancient symbols Dr Donovan had in his research files."

"And have you worked out what any of it means?" Hawke asked.

"It's hard to say. Even using the deciphering matrix in Gunnar's notes and working on what he already translated back in Iceland, it's far from clear. From what I can make out, it seems to resemble a line from Old Norse poetry. That was always written in Runic inscriptions and was an important way the culture passed stories of their gods to the next generation."

"Go on."

"We know much of that old poetry was big on alliteration, and we can see evidence of this here on the axe handle because the same symbols recur at the beginnings of some of the words."

Lea stared at the carved symbols. "And you can use that to make sense of all this?"

"Yes and no. Old Norse poetry is broken into two categories – the Eddaic and the Skaldic."

"What makes them different?" Hawke asked.

"The former were always anonymous and rather simple – a bit like Scarlet here – while the latter had an identified author and were generally more complex in their meter. The oldest example of Skaldic can be found on the Karlevi Runestone, a very famous runestone on the island of Öland off the coast of Småland in the south of Sweden."

"Sorry, could you say that again, Ryan," Scarlet said, pretending to wake up and yawn. "I nodded off."

"The point," Ryan emphasized with a look in Scarlet's direction, "is that while what I'm looking at here on this axe handle is vaguely redolent of both, it is also clearly neither."

Hawke sighed. "What about Alex?"

"I emailed her pictures of the reunited axe handle a while ago so now she has everything we have and they're working on it back on Elysium. So far we've come up with a partial translation of the first half of the inscription, which as far as I can tell is a simple reference to Midgard, or Middle Earth."

Scarlet laughed. "So we're hunting bloody Orcs now?"

"Of course not."

"I wouldn't say no to hunting Hobbits," she said. "They're really bloody annoying."

"We're *not* hunting Orcs or Hobbits," Ryan said. "As I say, Midgard simply means Middle Earth in Swedish. It's from the Old Norse Miðgarðr if you have to know."

"I really *don't* have to know."

"Midgard is one of Norse mythology's nine worlds, and just happens to be the only one that normal, mortal men can actually see because the other eight are all invisible."

"Oh, great – we're back to invisibility!"

"So while Thor's temple is in Uppsala, which is not so far from here, it's looking like his tomb is in Midgard."

Hawke nodded, pleased that some progress was being made at last. "And how do we get to this place?"

"According to legend, Midgard is directly above the realm of Niflheim, which means the world of darkness."

Scarlet sighed. "Sounds really cosy – do go on."

"Niflheim is one of the two fundamental primordial realms in Norse legend, the other being Muspelheim, the realm of fire. Midgard itself is surrounded by a sea where Jörmungandr, the World Serpent is said to dwell."

"And why, *boy*, are you regaling us with this?"

"Because Jörmungandr is the serpent that killed Thor, or *will* kill Thor to be exact but I don't want to get into that because it might make your brain explode, Cairo. The fact is that after Jörmungandr emerges from the ocean and poisons the sky, he and Thor fight and Thor kills him, but not before the serpent injects its venom into Thor. Thor then takes nine paces and dies, and that is where he's buried, of course. I'm all about the tombs, baby."

"It's all sounding like a nightmare," Victoria said. "As a trained archaeologist I can hardly believe what I'm actually hearing."

Hawke smiled. "We need a location, mate."

Ryan looked at Hawke and pushed the glasses back up the bridge of his nose. "If it's Midgard, then we're talking somewhere in Lapland, without a doubt."

Hawke nodded. "That's vague, but better than nothing."

"A bit like Ryan himself," Scarlet said quietly.

Ryan lifted his head and looked at Scarlet but all he could see was her hand draped over the back of the leather sofa. "It's not as easy as you looking for a shag, Cairo. This takes time and intelligence."

"No one calls me Cairo any more."

"I'm sure no one calls you anymore full-stop, but that's another story."

"Oh, the kitten has claws."

"Do they always fight like this?" Victoria said.

"Pack it in you two," Lea said.

"All right," Hawke said. "Get Alex on Skype and let's see if she has anything new."

Ryan made the call while Scarlet swooped on the minibar and cracked open some more Swedish vodka. She took it neat and fast to the horror of Victoria Hamilton-Talbot who, after an admonishing glance at her Cartier wristwatch, had opted for a cup of tea instead.

Moments later they were looking at Alex on the screen.

"Any news?" Lea asked.

"Oh yeah," the American said with confidence.

Hawke thought she looked distracted, and his mind immediately leaped to what she had said about her legs. He had seen one man die in the most horrible of ways after consuming the elixir, and now he had more concerns after seeing the remains of the dead man in the Pyrenees Mountains. To say he was worried about having given it to Alex to help her legs was an understatement. They had run tests on it in the lab, but its properties still eluded them. Yes, it had brought Lea back to life in Ethiopia, so Alex had been brave, and had taken a tiny, almost homeopathic quantity of the water. Days later she had begun to feel sensation in her legs again, but then she had started to complain of pain in them.

"Are you okay, Alex?" he asked.

On the tiny screen, she casually shrugged her shoulders. "Sure, why not?"

"Just asking. Go on."

"I think I might have cracked the inscription."

"This is amazing news!" Lea said.

"It wasn't particularly hard, actually. As you probably know we already worked out the Midgard bit, but there's much more. The symbols are hard to make out, but when we cleaned them up a tad it was much easier. I started with the symbol that resembles the Norse Rune for earth and then I got to thinking if the familiarity this symbol shares with the Rune for journey, it might indicate a tunnel."

Ryan looked at everyone earnestly. "I was *literally* about to work that out myself as well."

"Sure you were," Lea said.

"I *was!*"

"If you say so," Scarlet said. "Anything else, *Alex?*"

"As a matter of fact, yes. This symbol here is almost identical to the Runic script for lake. I was thinking

169

we're looking for an underground system near a lake somewhere, and that's when I worked out the last two symbols – one was for a cauldron and the other for the crest of a hill."

"Excellent," Scarlet said. "I'll tell the pilot to fly to a hill crest near a lake with a cauldron on the top of it, somewhere near Mordor."

Ryan rolled his eyes. "Let her have it, Alex, *please*."

"Sure," Alex said, laughing. "I searched references to cauldrons and hill-crests and it wasn't long before I found what I was looking for – Kebnekaise."

A look of recognition dawned on Victoria's face, but Lea spoke next. "Which is?"

"The highest mountain in Sweden," Alex replied. "It means cauldron crest in Sami, the language of the Sami people in Lapland. If you ask me – and you did – then I'm saying go to the lake at the base of Kebnekaise and start looking for a tunnel."

"That's great work, Alex," Scarlet said, turning to face Ryan. "Now I know why you're on the team."

Ryan got up from his chair and cracked open a beer. "If I'm so useless," he said, "how come I'm the only one who's thought about Ragnarök."

"Ragna-what?"

"The great battle at the end of the world that kills all the gods, including Thor."

"I thought Thor was already dead?" Scarlet said.

"Well..."

"We're going to his sodding tomb, aren't we? He must be dead!"

Ryan sipped his beer. "Ragnarök was a way the Norse myths foretold the end of the world, and to them that meant submersion under water. I bring it up because I'm starting to hear Thor's tomb and underwater tunnels in the same sentence."

"Thanks for cheering us up," Hawke said.

"He's right though," said Victoria. "Nate spoke to me about this as well. No one knows the significance of Ragnarök, but it's where all the myths and legends come together. Loki finally breaks free from his chains, Thor will fight the World Serpent... everything."

"I'm not digging the future tense here guys," Lea said nervously. "I thought all this stuff happened millions of years in the past?"

"It did," Ryan said. "And it didn't."

"Someone get me another Absolut," Scarlet said. "Immediately."

Victoria glanced at her watch again. "Goodness, you really do drink rather a lot, don't you?"

Scarlet went to reply, but Hawke stopped her before the first word left her lips. "All right," he said. "We can talk about Ragnarök later but right now we've got the advantage over Sala so let's not waste it. We know what we're looking for and where to start searching. Ryan, start looking into the most obvious places a tunnel could be hidden in the vicinity Alex has described."

"Got it."

"Lea, get on the phone to Eden. We need the jet fuelled and ready to fly to Lapland as soon as possible."

"On it."

"What about me?" Scarlet asked.

"Stop being a tit to Ryan."

As Lea made the call, Hawke turned and gazed out of the window once more. His eyes fell on another tourist boat as it trundled from one side of the lake to the other, everyone on board totally oblivious to the threat looming over them. In his heart there was always hope, but Ryan's talk of Ragnarök had begun to set his nerves on edge and with Vincent unconscious in hospital they were a man down.

He finished his beer and set the bottle on the table. It was time to unearth Thor's tomb.

CHAPTER TWENTY-ONE

Swedish Lapland

Kiruna was Sweden's most northerly town, nestled on the eastern slopes of Haukavaara Hill between the Kalix and Torne rivers. This place was deep in Lapland, nearly a hundred miles north of the Arctic Circle, even further north than Reykjavik, and that meant short, breezy summers and winters that were a serious test of human endurance. From the end of May until mid-July, the sun never set up here, and this meant that from early mid-December until New Year's Day it never rose either, plunging the entire population into a three week-long night.

The flight had been sombre. Hawke, like everyone else on board had thoughts crushing down on his mind. Vincent Reno was still unconscious, and now the mysterious spectre of Ragnarök was jostling for space alongside golden oldies like the men who had murdered his wife, Liz. With every sleepless night that passed, her death moved one day further away from his present-day life, but the pain never receded. The anguish he felt was kept alive by the thought of her killers getting away with their crimes and waking up to a new day every day to draw breath and live life while Liz was in her grave.

Their names were etched on his mind indelibly. James Matheson and Alfredo Lazaro. The former was no less than the British Foreign Secretary – mighty, distant and while easily found he was totally untouchable. The latter was a Cuban assassin known as the Spider. He moved in the world's filthiest shadows and Hawke didn't have the first idea how to track him down. One day, he swore, both men would pay the ultimate price for their crimes.

Glancing at Lea on the seat beside him, he saw she too was being tortured by something. Her brow was furrowed and she was staring with dry, unblinking eyes into the glass of whisky in her lap.

"Are you okay?" he asked quietly.

"It's about my Dad," Lea said. She sounded even more worried than she looked.

"I know how tough this must all be."

"Why the hell was he writing in that weird script, Joe? What did he know that he never told me?"

Hawke knew he had to tread carefully. He knew no more about this than anyone else, and it would be the easiest thing in the world to say the wrong thing and upset her or worse still worry her unnecessarily. "I can't answer that, Lea. All I can say is whatever the reason is, we'll find out, but you need to ask yourself if you really want to know."

She looked at him with anxious eyes. "What do you mean?"

He gave a shallow shrug. "I don't know... it's just that everything we've uncovered so far seems to drag us further down the rabbit hole, that's all."

"And I'm Alice, is that what you're saying?"

Hawke smiled. "I think you might be, but you're not alone." He squeezed her hand in his and clenched his teeth. He hated seeing her like this, but he knew she wouldn't stop until she knew the truth not only about her father's death, but about his life, too.

Lea glanced out of the window before replying. "I just wish I knew what was going on, Joe. I've been racking my mind, worrying about so much... I could just about get my head around the fact Dad was researching something to do with Norse mythology. The fact he worked as a doctor and devoted his life to helping people made it easier to understand why he'd been looking into ideas surrounding Mengloth – she was the goddess of healing, you know?"

Hawke nodded. "I do, but only thanks to your ex-husband."

Lea gave a polite smile. "And what was the other one – Eir – the goddess of medicine or something. And there's Frigg as well – now I know she was Odin's wife and the mother of Thor, but it doesn't make any of this more cogent up here, you know?" She tapped her temple with her index finger.

"I know."

"I was freaked out enough that Dad was involved in this all *before*, but at least it all made some kind of sense. Maybe he'd discovered something to do with those goddesses that would help people – I don't know, but now... there's no reason why Dad should be able to write in that script, Joe. I thought he'd found it, or copied it – not that he'd written in it! Gunnar called it the script of the gods!"

Hawke put his arm around her shoulders and gave a comforting squeeze. He had no idea why Dr. Henry Donovan was able to write in that strange, ancient script and even less how he knew about the raiding parties and their mysterious, ancient loot. Maybe it was simply that he had somehow taught himself how to do it to facilitate his research, or perhaps the real reason was something neither of them wanted to contemplate.

He yawned and snatched a glance out of the window. The flight had been a tense one, but a breath-taking display of the northern lights illuminated the sky and reminded them what they were fighting for. Now the

175

tops of some high-drifting cirrus were a bright green color. It was calm up here, he thought, but the kind of calm that came before a storm.

*

Lea looked with a vague interest from the window as the private jet descended through a bank of heavy stratocumulus. The engines were reduced to idle now, and the flaps fully extended. They would be on the ground in minutes.

But what they would find there worried her more than ever. She knew Hawke was trying to help, but he couldn't begin to understand what she was really feeling. She had been on so many missions like this she had lost count of them all, but this one was different. Like her last journey to Ireland, this one felt personal. It *was* personal, she supposed – instead of simply hunting down ancient relics and seeking a long-obscured truth about the world, she was now faced with the unsettling prospect that her father was somehow involved.

Now, as she gazed down at the bleak landscape of Swedish Lapland – the zone where taiga slowly turned to tundra, her mind turned inwards to face the terrible fact that maybe her father really was part of this after all. How else could he have known how to write in the ancient pre-Runic script?

Her thoughts grew darker still. If he *had* been involved with the mysterious Athanatoi, what was the nature of the relationship? Did it involve her? Why had he never told anyone about the truth? It felt like her mind was on fire, and when she finally alighted on the subject of his death, it all got too much. Had he really been killed by the Athanatoi? Who was the man in black?

Her thoughts were disrupted by the squeal of the tires on the tarmac of Kiruna Airport and the roar of the reverse thrusters. Seconds later they were walking through the modest airport and stepping out into a chilly Lapland evening.

"Is this supposed to be summer?" Scarlet said with a sneer.

They climbed into a hired truck – another HiLux as specified by Hawke – and wasted no time in driving west along the 870 toward Kebnekaise. The drive was peaceful and offered a rare moment of relaxation to the team. They had been on the go since landing in the Florida Keys but despite their fatigue they knew the stakes were too high to risk taking their foot off the pedal now.

Outside, the Swedish taiga drifted past in a gentle blur of olive greens and sepia brown, and above them a pure blue Arctic sky poured the day's last sunshine into the hired car and added to the soporific feeling induced by the long, straight road. Pure lakes coasted past them as they pushed on along pine-flanked roads in pursuit of the truth, whatever it may be.

Far on the southern horizon Scarlet saw a lone property, surrounded by a jumble of outbuildings and what looked like a barn.

"Can't believe anyone would live out here," she said dismissively. "You'd have to be bloody certifiable." As she spoke she slapped at a mosquito that had somehow slipped into the car.

"I don't know about that," Hawke said. "It kind of appeals to me in a strange way. I thought the same thing back in Iceland."

"But then you're certifiable," Scarlet said. "So that sort of proves my point."

Hawke turned briefly to Lea, keeping his eyes on the road. "What about you?"

"What about me?"

"You like it up here?"

"Are you kidding? I'd go bloody crazy in a place like this."

"Ah," Hawke said, and pressed on.

*

They reached the base of Kebnekaise in late evening, although the position of the sun made it feel much earlier. In the tranquil, fading sunlight they unpacked their weapons, climbing rope and flashlights from the trunk of the HiLux and for a few moments took in the landscape.

So this was the legendary Midgard – the Middle Earth where Thor had fought the World Serpent and died after killing him. Today, it was a ragged range of dark mountains rising from a plain of stubby brown and yellow grass and pitted marshland, but there was still something genuinely awesome about the place. Running along the horizon to the southeast was a line of birch and poplar trees, and scattered around in patches running away to the west were wild strawberries and cloudberries. They would grow thicker in the boreal forest a few hundred meters to their right, but these were some strays.

"So that's our peak right there," Ryan said, twisting a map around and placing a compass against it. "If my orienteering skills are correct, and of course they are, we have only a short hike until we reach the base of our mountain and then it's not much further from there to the lake in question!"

"Your orienteering skills are not correct," Hawke said, taking the map and twisting it around in Ryan's hands before pointing at the horizon. "*That* way is north, not over there."

Ryan looked sheepishly at the former SBS man for a second but moved along with a grin and a shrug of the shoulders. "Ah…"

"It's absolutely fantastic!" Victoria said, changing the subject. She moved closer to the mountains, utterly spellbound. "I had no idea."

"Come on, let's get on with it," Scarlet said. "I doubt there's a decent bar anywhere around here so the sooner we get back to Kiruna the better, even if it was about as lively as a morgue there."

They picked up their kit and stepped off of the road and into the taiga. Hawke was immediately reminded of old times, not just of the SBS and their punishing training programs but of his childhood too – like the time they went hiking on Dartmoor and he and his sister played hide and seek around Birch Tor. Those days seemed impossibly far away now and when he recalled them it almost felt as if he were imagining someone else's childhood and not his own.

"Whatcha thinking about?"

He turned and saw Lea had caught up with him and linked her arm through his.

He smiled, looked over at the sun and replied: "I was just thinking about how much I'd like a cold beer."

"Don't! You sound like Scarlet Bloody Sloane. I swear if she ever gets shot she's going to bleed vodka."

"I doubt that would happen."

"Which bit?"

"Getting shot, of course… because she'd *definitely* bleed vodka."

To the west, the sun momentarily dipped behind the ridgeline and lit the tops of the mountains and the light clouds a faint pink color. High above and behind them they saw a few pale stars sparkling in the east, and the air took on a decidedly chilly feel despite the late summer month. This was about as isolated as Europe got – cool, distant and far from life.

"It's bloody freezing around these parts," Ryan said with a shiver.

"Don't be such a baby," Scarlet said.

"I agree with Ryan," Victoria said, with a sideways glance at Scarlet. "It *is* rather chilly here, but then one would expect that at this latitude."

"Yes, I suppose *one* would," Scarlet said.

Hawke and Lea shared a private smile, and they pushed on.

By the time they arrived at the canyon at the base of the mountain the sun had sunk ever lower and darkened the ridgeline of the mountain ranges around them. Up here, the latitude was so high that the time before sunset – what photographers called the golden hour – could last for much longer than sixty minutes, and that was the case tonight. It felt like it had been sunset for hours by the time they finally reached the rocks that they had been seeking, and there, stretching out beyond them in the purple, dusky haze, was the lake.

Hawke stepped up. "Right, here's where we have to get out hands dirty. If Alex and Ryan are right, somewhere around the shoreline of this lake is a concealed entrance to a tunnel. You only have to look at the place to know it probably hasn't been touched for thousands of years, so let's get looking."

They worked their way around the shoreline, the ridges of the Kebnekaise massif looming above their heads as they went. Twilight lasted forever up here, so they had light to work with even if it was subdued, but it was over an hour before they found what they were looking for.

"You think this is it?" Lea asked.

Hawke took a step back and nodded his head. "Our best chance yet."

He was looking at a jumble of rocks, some up to ten feet high, that to the casual observer looked random, but he thought otherwise. A large flat rock at the front looked like it had been placed there a very long time ago with the specific intention of concealing something.

"Let's get it out the way then," he said flatly.

"It must weigh ten tons!" Ryan said.

Hawke grinned. "Which is why I've brought along a decent quantity of military-grade C-4 in my picnic basket."

Hawke pulled the explosive from his backpack and weighed it in his hand.

"Oh my goodness!" Victoria said, taking a step back.

"Don't panic, darling," Scarlet said. "It's not dangerous until we detonate it with a shockwave."

Hawke took a few seconds to evaluate the best areas to place the explosives, and then inserted the blasting caps. He dusted his hands down.

"You really like this bit, don't you?" Lea said.

"Well…"

Ryan rolled his eyes.

They took cover and Hawke detonated the C-4. The explosion was heavy and loud, and blasted the thin upper end of the flat rock to oblivion. When the dust settled Hawke was the first to his feet and after briefly checking his work he gave the others the order to come up the embankment and join him with the equipment.

It was time to go inside the mountain.

*

Álvaro Sala lowered the binoculars and handed them to Leon Smets who was standing a yard to his left. Although they were wrapped in kid leather gloves, he rubbed his hands together for warmth. It was much warmer in Andorra at this time of year, but that wouldn't stop him taking what was rightfully his.

Less than a kilometer to the west the Donovan girl and her friends had recently disappeared into a ravine on the south slopes of the Kebnekaise massif. It looked like they were planning an ascent via the eastern route, but not to any real altitude since their equipment was limited.

Tracking down their aircraft to Bromma airport hadn't been the hardest challenge of his life, and tracking it on live radar was a simple facility on any handheld device. Perhaps they should have switched off their transponder, but such things were frowned upon by the authorities and would have generated an enormous security response.

Either way, he and the surviving members of his team had landed at Kiruna less than twenty minutes after the ECHO Gulfstream, and now not only would they lead them directly to the tomb and the location of Thor's Hammer, but they would also pay for killing Deprez and putting Dasha Vetrov on life support.

Now, a hefty explosion rang out down the valley to the south and sent clouds of willow grouse and grey herons bursting into the air.

"They're going inside the mountain," Smets said. He spat on the gorse and sniffed deeply.

Sala gave him a look of disgust. "Of course they are, but they still have no idea what they're looking for."

Smets smirked and nodded his head in agreement.

"If they're like everyone else then they probably think they're looking for a hammer."

"Or a Tesla Coil, perhaps?" Smets said, his face breaking into a malevolent smirk.

"Or a Tesla Coil... Ha!" Sala laughed and shook his head in disbelief before turning back from the ridge. He walked back toward the line of pick-up trucks parked up roughly at the eastern edge of the range.

Yes, perhaps they thought they were looking for a Tesla Coil, but whatever it was they were seeking they wouldn't live to find out the truth, and even if they did they wouldn't live long enough to enjoy it.

Sala shouted at the men hanging around smoking cigarettes. "Into the trucks! We're going inside the Kebnekaise!"

CHAPTER TWENTY-TWO

Hawke led the team into the cave, and if they thought outside was cold, it was nothing compared to in here. The cramped cavern was icy and damp and their breath bloomed out before them with each exhalation.

"Place is like a bloody meat freezer."

"It's a cave inside the Arctic Circle, Cairo. What did you expect?"

"I meant Scandinavia."

"Now that's just offensive," Lea said.

Ryan sighed. "Ladies, if it's going to be handbags at dawn can it at least wait until we've found the tomb?"

Lea and Scarlet turned and faced him. "What was that, Ryan?" they said in perfect unison.

Ryan looked at them both, noting the expression on their faces. "I was just saying that we have a lot of work to do and thank mercy you're both here to help."

They shuffled deeper inside until reaching a narrow split in the floor of the tunnel which disappeared into darkness and didn't exactly look like it promised safe passage.

Ryan peered over the edge and squinted. "Anyone got a glow-stick?"

Hawke fired one up and dropped it into the crack. They watched it tumble down, striking the sides of the shaft as it went. It hit the bottom with a gently thumping sound and a cloud of powdery dust puffed out around it.

"Mind the gap," Scarlet said.

Hawke raised an eyebrow. "Looks like our next stop."

They dropped rappel lines over the rocky ledge and began to descend into the abyss with Hawke in the lead, another glow stick in his hand.

He hit the bottom and after releasing himself from the line he gave the others the signal to come down.

"This is all terribly exciting," Victoria said, eliciting an eye-roll from Scarlet.

They started down the vertical surface of the rock-face, working their way down into the depths of the vast mountain above them. Victoria was last, helped down by Scarlet, and when she touched down on the cavern floor they were all ready for the next stage.

At the far end of this lower cave was another tunnel partially obscured by series of impressive stalagmites and stalactites.

Scarlet stared at them as she released her rappel line and checked her pistol.

"Yes, Cairo," Ryan said, glancing at her. "They do look phallic, don't they?"

She sighed. "I was thinking they were vaguely redolent of a set of jaws but if yours looks like any of those then I pity the poor borscht woman."

"Her name's Maria," Ryan said with a disapproving sideways glance.

They moved cautiously through the cave and then through what Scarlet had described as a set of jaws until they found themselves staring into a twisting, ever-narrowing tunnel. The frozen darkness of the place was not something Lea would forget in a hurry, and for a second she wondered if her father had ever been down here.

No, she told herself. Stop being so stupid. Okay, so she now knew her father was mixed up in all of this somehow, but she couldn't let her thoughts run away with themselves like this. Her thoughts ran fast, after all, and usually to the darkest of places. It was hard sometimes to pull them back... like taming so many horses. Whatever her father had known about all of this, how could he ever possibly have been down in this place?

She joined Hawke at the front and looked at his face as he moved fearlessly into the darkness. His strong profile and unshaven jaw were now lit an eerie green in the light of the glow-stick.

He turned to her. "What is it?"

"You just look kind of spooky," she said with a quick smile.

"Do I?"

"Chemiluminescence will do that for a man," Ryan said from behind her. "Even a rugged daredevil like Hawke here."

"I wonder what you would look like with a glow stick up your arse, Ryan?" Scarlet said, tipping her head back and pretending to visualize the spectacle.

"I'd like to see you try!" Ryan said. "No wait, that didn't come out right."

"Look at the walls!" Victoria said quietly. She ran her hand along the rock. "The carving at the entrance looked manual, but these tramlines here suggest some sort of machinery."

"Machinery?" Ryan asked. "Are you sure?"

Victoria took a step back from the wall and nodded. "Almost certain – in fact the lower part here looks like it's constituted of rectilinear stone blocks cut to size by high-precision cutting tools."

Hawke frowned. "Modern stuff?"

"Sounds mad but yes," Victoria said.

"Ryan?"

Ryan weighed it up. "The temple complex at Pumapunku in Bolivia has attracted a lot of conspiracy theories for the same reason – high-precision engineering of stonework around fifteen hundred years old that many people say must have been done by a higher intelligence. The thing is the theories are highly questionable because the stone there is a mix of red sandstone and andesite, both of which are conducive to precision carving by hand."

"But this isn't sandstone," Victoria said. "This is granite."

Ryan tipped his head to one side and stared at the tunnel wall for a moment, silent and perplexed. "Granite... yes. Odd."

They descended the declining tunnel until they reached the inner chamber. Immediately the atmosphere changed and they felt the temperature drop again.

"This must be it!" Ryan said.

"It can't be," Victoria said in a whisper. Her eyes crawled over the cavern, lit low by the flickering glow sticks. "Thor's tomb?"

"Got it in one," Hawke said. "Now let's see where the old boy's hiding out."

Ryan clicked his teeth and shook his head gently. "Blasphemous mockery of the gods is not a good idea, Joe."

Hawke said nothing as they progressed into the tomb complex, but Lea was starting to think Ryan might have a point. The place reminded her of what she had seen in Kefalonia when they'd discovered the vault of Poseidon. Ancient motifs were carved into the chamber walls, there were faded renderings of Thor on the floor tiles and a bewildering array of weapons was stacked up in piles wherever she looked. Yet this place seemed different from Poseidon's tomb. It felt more military.

She heard Scarlet whisper a few feet behind her. "Take look at this place!"

"I've never seen anything like it," Victoria said, running her hands over the smooth, painted walls. "Apart from some deterioration in the paint pigments it's like they just finished it yesterday."

They saw Thor's sarcophagus and moved toward it, their flashlights illuminating the dust they'd kicked up as they walked through the frozen chamber.

Lea's breath formed into a thick cloud in front of her face. "It's all very similar to the Poseidon tomb. That's bothering me."

"It definitely raises a few questions," said Hawke. "Not only were none of these legends supposed to exist in the first place, but their mythologies all grew up thousands of miles apart from each other."

The sarcophagus was a similar shape and size to Poseidon's, but it didn't stop there – leaning against the base of the pedestal was a stone shield covered in carved letters – the same letters they had seen back in Kefalonia.

"Looks like Thor went on holiday to Greece," Hawke said.

"Or maybe Poseidon took a visit up here to see the northern lights or something like that?" Scarlet said, lowering her voice in the sombre atmosphere.

"Or *something* like that," Lea said, turning over the shield with the tip of her boot. It clattered to the floor with startling volume in the icy silence of the tomb.

Hawke frowned. "I don't think it was just Poseidon who came here – don't forget this is pretty much where the NSA found Medusa's head back in the sixties. Why am I getting the feeling we're just not getting something about all of this?"

"Beats me," Scarlet said with a sigh. She shone her flashlight over the sarcophagus for a second and then swept the beam around the chamber. It illuminated rows of swords and axes. "We're certainly not getting any bloody treasure out of it, that's for sure. I mean look at this place – it's like an ancient arsenal but where's the loot?"

"Yes, but *look* at all these weapons!" Ryan said. "I've never seen so many swords in all my life."

"Leave them alone, boy," Scarlet said. "They're not Fisher Price."

"And check this out!" Ryan said, lifting a leather belt studded with gold and emeralds from the floor. He blew the dust off it and strapped it around his waist.

Scarlet raised an eyebrow. "What is this – professional wrestling?"

"Get lost, Scarlet."

"What would your wrestling name be? What about Big Mummy?"

"Leave it, Cairo," Hawke said. He turned to Ryan. "It's not a wrestling belt, obviously – but what is it?"

A look of recognition spread on Victoria's face a second before Ryan spoke. "I know! It's the megingjörð."

Ryan beamed, barely able to contain himself. "I know!"

Scarlet sighed. "Well that clears that up. Shall we move on and look for some gold?"

"Just wait where you are, Cairo." Hawke looked at Ryan and Victoria. "In English please, for the rest of us."

"Sorry!" Ryan said with excitement. "This is Thor's magical power-belt, the megingjörð!"

"Then take it off, Ryan!" Lea said.

"Yeah, better stop pissing about, mate."

"One hates to be a clock-watcher," Victoria said, pointing at the sarcophagus. "But oughtn't we get on and take a look in that thing or not?"

Lea saw Hawke glance at her and then at the others. "That's what we do, so… yeah."

It took longer than they thought to prise the lid off the sarcophagus, even with the climbing ropes and crow bars they had brought with them from the plane's hold. After tying off the massive, stone lid and making sure it was secure, they took a tentative step forward toward the gaping black hole in front of them.

"Well…" Lea said with a casual resigned tone usually reserved for the most banal of observations. "That's Thor's corpse, all right."

"Thank God it's so cold in here," Hawke said quietly. "Or it might have *thawed* out by now."

Lea laughed, but Scarlet was less amused. "Oh *please*," she said. "That was *not* funny in the least."

"I thought it was," Lea said.

"You'd laugh at anything. You married Ryan after all."

Lea ignored her and joined Hawke as he leaned over the edge of the sarcophagus with a flashlight in his hand. There was certainly a mummified corpse inside but more interesting than that was the unmistakable shape of what could only be a hammer, a heavy, square anvil of a thing on a thick wooden handle. Beside it was a rolled-up scroll of parchment which Hawke gently picked up and looked at under the green light of the glow stick.

"Bloody hell!" Hawke said. "Check this out."

With the greatest of care, he broke open the wax seal with a gentle snap and unfurled the scroll. "Lea – take a picture of this thing right now. We don't want a repeat of the castillo."

Lea snapped an image of the unfurled scroll. It was covered in spidery letters that made zero sense to her, but she recognized some of them from what she had seen on the axe handle so she was confident Alex and Ryan could get something out of it.

She slipped her phone back inside her pocket and peered inside the sarcophagus, looking once again at the hammer. She'd read about the Mighty Hammer of Thor many times since flying out of Elysium, and could hardly believe she was actually looking at it. It looked small just like any regular war hammer, but some said it could level mountains. She glanced up at the cavern roof and hoped nothing like that was going to happen today.

Hawke smiled. "I think this might be just what we're looking for!"

"But unfortunately it is also what *I* am looking for."

Lea spun around and saw a silhouette looming in the entrance to the tunnel. A flickering torch was backlighting the mystery figure, and then to her right she saw another silhouette emerge from the damp gloom. Then a third, a fourth and a fifth as armed gunmen scrambled into the tomb.

Álvaro Sala stepped into the gleam of the glow sticks. He was wearing a black roll neck, dark blue navy camo trousers and a pair of chunky black boots and had one hand casually in a pocket as if he were perusing antiques.

"Sala!"

"We meet again" he said.

"Oh, *please*," Scarlet muttered.

Sala moved into the center of the tomb, a crazed sparkle in his eyes. "You managed to make more trouble for me in Stockholm after extricating yourselves from the snake pit back at my château. I'm impressed. Even the great Viking chieftain Ragnar Lodbrok lost his life when he was thrown into a snake pit, and yet you survived."

Lea took a step forward. "Go to hell!"

"Many would say I am already in hell. But I digress – I have been waiting for this moment a long time. Drop your weapons."

Lea looked at the man. His long hair was tied back in a tight pony tail and he looked drawn and sick. A few paces behind him was Leon Smets, the man they had fought back in Andorra, the man who had pulled the trap door and sent them falling into Sala's vile snake pit.

Sala looked at each one of them, his eyes lingering on Victoria Hamilton-Talbot for just a second too long, Lea thought. He started to speak to her but was stopped when Hawke broke the silence.

"What do you want, Sala?" he asked with palpable disgust.

Lea glanced once more at the hammer.

Sala's response was wordless but clear to everyone. He held out his arm, pointed at the old scroll and made the "give me" gesture with his right hand.

Lea frowned. "You don't want the hammer?"

"A hammer is a hammer. Give me the scroll."

Hawke looked at him with hatred and Lea hoped he wasn't about to do anything stupid. They were outnumbered and trapped in a mountain's cave complex high up in the Arctic Circle. To say no one would hear them scream was an understatement.

But he didn't. Instead, the Englishman reluctantly lowered the scroll to the dusty floor and kicked it across the tiles. It came to a stop at Sala's steel toecap boots, and without taking his eyes off Hawke, the Andorran stooped down to pick it up.

His eyes sparkled with delight and he nodded his head with self-importance as his eyes crawled all over the ancient text. "This is the final piece of the puzzle. You have no idea how long I have been seeking the treasures this poem will lead me to!"

VALHALLA GOLD

"I thought you were trying to find Thor's Hammer, Sala!" Lea said. "It's right here!"

Sala stepped closer and turned slowly to face Lea. "Yes, I see the resemblance at once... you are certainly Henry's daughter."

Lea looked shocked at the casual, first name reference to her father. "What are you talking about? What did you mean when you talked about killing him back in Andorra?"

Sala grinned. "It's true I never knew him, but in a way... I knew *of* him, and for a very long time indeed. We had certain things in common."

"My father would have nothing in common with a snake like you, Sala!"

"Oh, really?"

"Yes, really! My father was a healer – he spent his life helping people. He wasn't like you. I've seen your idea of helping people."

Sala's hand held the rolled-up parchment tighter, like a baton. "Your father was a fool. He wanted the treasures of the healing goddesses so he could use them to save humankind. This is why he sought the Hammer so tirelessly, and this is why he was killed. I, however seek a different kind of treasure – every weapon ever used by the gods!"

Now Lea understood what all this was about. Weapons and war. "And that's what your little scroll is for?"

"The scroll will lead me to my destiny, yes!"

Scarlet snorted. "I'm starting to wonder if madness is contagious."

Sala ignored her, but ordered Smets and some men forward.

"Get your hands up. It's time to prove your mortality – especially you, Donovan. You led me quite the merry

193

dance all over Ireland... and yet you still brought me here to my destiny. A shame you will not be alive to see me fulfil it." He turned to Smets. "Take them down that tunnel and shoot them dead."

The Belgian mercenary laughed as he marched them to their execution. Lea turned to look over her shoulder as they left the tomb, and saw Sala mumbling to himself as he stared at the scroll once more, totally ignoring the hammer in the sarcophagus.

CHAPTER TWENTY-THREE

At the head of the group with his hands raised, Joe Hawke searched the narrow tunnel for anything he could use as a weapon. He knew the others were counting on him – Lea, Scarlet, Ryan and now Victoria. For one reason or another, he felt responsible for all of them and the idea of leading them to their deaths in Thor's tomb complex, of all places, was just unthinkable.

If it came down to the wire, they could turn on Smets and attack him mob-handed but it would have to be soon while they were still in an enclosed area, and… he knew not all of them would make it. Smets would mow some of them down with that machine pistol before the survivors could take him out. It wasn't much of a plan.

He looked at Ryan, who was beside him. Judging from his facial expression he was also beside himself – with fear. With Thor's tomb rapidly receding behind them, Hawke looked down and saw Ryan had the answer around his waist.

"Hey!" Hawke whispered.

"What?"

"You're still wearing it."

"Wearing what?"

"Thor's jock strap or whatever the hell you said it was."

Ryan looked at him, confused. "Sorry – I'm wearing Thor's jock strap?"

Hawke nodded his head at Ryan's waist. "That thing!"

A glorious epiphany seemed to spread across the young hacker's face. "Ah! You mean the megingjörð – Thor's power-belt!"

"That's the one, mate. What does it do, exactly?"

"According to Norse legend, it increased Thor's godly power many times."

"But you don't have any godly power," Scarlet whispered over his shoulder. "What if all it does when you wear it is increase how annoying you are?"

"Thanks for your input, Cairo," Hawke said, "but we're out of options. This is our only chance now."

Ryan frowned. "Sorry, but what exactly do you expect me to do?"

"I expect you to slam our host into the middle of next week."

"Me? I can't fight!"

"He's right, Joe," Scarlet said. "I've seen toddlers punch with more anger and determination."

"What," Ryan replied, raising his voice. "After you stole their sweets?"

"Hey! Shut up and keep moving!" It was Smets. He cocked his gun and shoulder-barged his way past Lea and Victoria. He leaned into Ryan and lowered his voice to a gravelly whisper. "I hear anyone else say a word I'll shoot you in the stomach and let you bleed out for hours. That includes you, Batman," he said, tugging disrespectfully on Ryan's t-shirt.

Ryan saw his moment and lashed out with his right hand, striking Smets's arm out of the way and hitting his chest. Ordinarily Hawke would expect a man like Smets to take the punch and return fire in a second, but instead he flew through the air like a paper plane and crashed into the rock-face wall with a mighty thud.

Ryan looked at his hand in wonder. "Wow."

"Don't get too excited," Scarlet said. "It's the magic jock-strap, not you... *Batman*."

Smets shook his head from side to side in a bid to regain his composure, and raised the MP7 shakily in front of him, firing off a wild burst wherever the muzzle pointed. Bullets raked all over the far wall of the cave, bursting clouds of ancient plaster and chips of stone fragments flew all over the place.

"We have to get out of here!" Lea shouted.

Victoria frowned as she looked at Smets. "But the only way out is back through the main tomb with Sala and his goons."

"Then that's where we're going – run!" Hawke shouted.

The wounded Smets fired blindly at them as they raced from the cavern, but he quickly got to his feet and gave chase. Now they were caught between Smets behind them and Sala and his other goons in Thor's tomb.

"Good plan," Scarlet said.

Ahead of them, they saw the tomb, and with it Sala and his men who were in the process of moving out. He obviously had what he'd come for and now the place was worthless to him.

"Kill them!" Sala screamed, and his men opened fire.

"What now?" Lea asked.

Before Hawke could reply, Smets fired at them again from behind. Everyone dived for cover and Smets scrambled closer, firing more shots until the magazine was empty. He hurried to reload with a new magazine but the few seconds it took was enough for Hawke to make his move.

In the chaos, he sprinted through the arch which formed the boundary between the tomb and the tunnel and grabbed a sword from the floor. Swinging it into

Smets's stomach, the Belgian doubled over in agony and Hawke brought up his boot and smashed it into his face. Smets flew back with the force of the kick and stumbling over a pile of old pottery he lost his footing and crashed into the side of the sarcophagus.

With Sala's other men still firing on them, Lea grabbed Smets by the belt and using his own momentum against him she finished his journey by spinning him around to use as a human shield. Hawke watched as she crouched behind the Belgian's body as it was filled full of holes by Sala's men.

With Smets dead, Hawke made a bid for the sarcophagus, but Sala and his men fought back hard, spraying the room with lead and making everyone dive for cover once again. The Andorran maniacally laughed with the submachine gun chattering away in his hands, empty jackets spitting out of the extractor.

Chaos now reigned in the chamber as the fighting increased, then Sala ordered a retreat and his men fired flash-bangs into the tomb. The noise of their detonation was deafening, but things got worse when they deployed the smoke grenades. Not only were they disoriented by the flash-bangs, but now the room began to fill with a noxious zinc chloride smoke composition.

"Cover your mouths!" Hawke yelled.

Victoria screamed as the room began to fill with the thick smoke and everyone lost each other in the pandemonium.

*

As the smoke cleared in the freezing air of the chamber, Lea strained in the gloom to try and find her friends. She snatched up a flashlight and shone it hurriedly around the room, its bright beam shining in the smoke like a car's headlight lighting up a heavy fog. All around her she could hear the sound of screams, gunshots and fighting. It was total chaos and she knew one mistake would mean spending the rest of her life here in the caves.

She felt what she presumed was a bullet trace past her head and her thoughts were confirmed a millisecond later when she heard it smash into the wall behind her. A shower of shattered tile exploded behind her ear and she felt some of the shards strike the back of her head. That was too close, she thought, and ran for the cover of the sarcophagus.

With the smoke much thinner now, she was able to see Hawke across the other side of the chamber. He was fighting with one of the goons in hand-to-hand combat and it looked like the former SBS man was getting the better of him.

Nearer the entrance, she saw Scarlet fighting with another man but it looked like another unfair fight as the former SAS officer disarmed him and spun the folding stock of his submachine up into his groin with eye-watering speed and accuracy.

The man's screams were cut short by Scarlet firing a burst of bullets into his chest which exploded and knocked him back into the rocky wall.

Another flash-bang exploded close to Ryan and blasted him back against the rock, blowing Thor's belt clean off him. He clambered to his feet uneasily and tried to make his way back to the safety of the others but as he staggered backwards, he was met by a shadow looming out of the darkness. Lea and the others stared in horror as they saw who it was.

Leon Smets had risen from the dead.

"How the hell..?" Hawke mumbled, numb with disbelief.

ROB JONES

"Sala must have given him something to bring him back," Lea said. "Like you did for me."

"Ryan, look out!" Hawke shouted, but it was too late. Smets knocked Ryan out with the butt of his machine pistol and the young man's limp body fell to the dusty floor.

"I'll kill you for that!" Lea screamed.

"Not unless you can get to him before me," Hawke said.

Smets, whose tanned face was now a pale, greasy white complexion, hauled Ryan to his feet and waggled a knife blade haphazardly in front of his throat. "Get back or you know what happens next."

Sala laughed as they made their way to the rappel lines, this time using Ryan as the human shield.

Smets secured Ryan to the harness on the end of the rappel lines and when the job was done he tugged on them, giving the signal to winch the unconscious cargo to the upper level of the cave complex.

Lea looked on in disbelief as she watched Ryan disappear up into the vertical shaft alongside Sala, Smets and the handful of surviving gunmen, but there was nothing they could do while they held a knife to his throat.

Hawke punched the wall. "Damn it!"

"No time for that," Scarlet said. "Let's get after them!"

But before they reached the rappel lines, Sala cut them and they tumbled into useless pools of black nylon at the base of the shaft.

"What now?" Victoria asked. "I can't climb!"

Hawke sighed and looked at Scarlet. "Race you to the top?"

"Fifty quid."

The two of them free-climbed up the rock-face, hauling the rappel lines behind them in their wake, and when they reached the top they secured them and tossed them back down for Lea and Victoria to climb up.

Then they made their way along the tunnel they had used earlier until finally seeing the faint shimmer of natural daylight up ahead once again, even if it was weakened by the Scandinavian dusk.

Lea reached the opening fissure in the base of the mountain just in time to see Smets fire an RPG into their HiLux. It exploded in an enormous fireball and lit the otherwise silent twilight in a surreal white and orange after-glow. Seconds later various parts of their vehicle – doors, wing mirrors and the tailgate, clattered back to the damp gorse with muffled thuds.

On the road behind the burning wreck of their truck, Sala's crew were moving out. They watched stranded and helpless as the three black vehicles snaked their way toward the main road with their special cargo of Thor's mysterious scroll and Ryan Bale.

Things had looked better for the ECHO team.

CHAPTER TWENTY-FOUR

It didn't take Lexi Zhang long to clear the electric fence. Anticipating such a security device she pulled out a simple rubber mat from her bag and draped it over the top of the top rung of the electrified razorwire. Totally avoiding the nine thousand volt shock she slipped effortlessly over the top and, leaving the mat in place for a potential egress, she sprinted toward her target.

As she approached some of the outbuildings, her mind turned to the specifics of the operation she was about to execute. She supposed this place would be impossible to infiltrate if the full compliment of security were here, but she knew that was not the case.

The intel she had gathered after her meeting with Arocha had cost a lot of money, but reliable stuff always came at a premium. Her source, a Cuban double-agent-turned-car salesman named Raoul, had told her that most of the ECHO team had left the island. He didn't know to where or why. He said only that they had boarded a private jet and flown north.

According to Raoul, there were sometimes as many ten or twelve people on the small island, but tonight that number was reduced to three or four. He couldn't be sure – no one could. Elysium was as private as it got and information like his was expensive for a reason.

Lexi had paid Raoul handsomely for his information and given the matter a great deal of thought. Who were the four? Eden, certainly, and she presumed the American woman whose father was currently rumored to be considering a run for the American Presidency –

Alex Reeve. But who were the other two? She had no way of knowing, but a part of her hoped neither of them was Hawke. Ryan Bale on the other hand... not only would that be easy, but so much *fun*.

Through the outer-perimeter now, she set off an unseen alarm and the whole place lit up like the Trafalgar Square Christmas tree. A shrill, ear-piercing klaxon blared out across the island and informed the world and his wife that Elysium had an intruder. She cursed herself for being so stupid but had no time to dwell on it.

A door in the western end of the complex slammed open and a man began to fire at her. She didn't recognize him, but knew she had to get out of here at once. She sprinted across the wide lawn and dived into a bank of flowering Jamaican Firebirds. The man screamed after her and fired twice more before using his free hand to manually redirect the searchlight into the edge of the garden.

"I know you're in there!" he shouted.

He sounded English, she thought. She wondered if maybe it was another old friend of Hawke's from back in the day. On further reflection it was a distinct possibility, but now the man was moving closer, using the low garden wall as cover. She had no time for ponderous reflections about Hawke's old Commando friends.

With her weapons bag dragging behind her, she crawled through the dirt on her elbows and knees until she reached the other side of the shrubs. Now she was looking at another wide lawn lit an eerie bluish white by the full moon almost directly overhead.

She heard the man fumbling around as he ran into the bushes right behind her. He certainly was fearless – she had to give him that. She considered returning fire, but there was no way she could get a clear shot at him in all this undergrowth so she scratched the idea and decided to make a break for it across the lawn. This way she would be a little closer to the main complex and her ultimate target – Sir Richard Eden himself.

"You can run but you can't hide!" the man shouted. "This is a very small island!"

She pounded across the lawn just as the man broke through the first embankment of shrubs. He wasted no time in firing at her and she heard the shot as it flew past her and tore through the foliage of a mature Arabian jasmine.

"I'll give Eden one thing…" she said to herself as she pushed her way through the bushes. "He certainly knows how to grow a garden."

Another shot whistled past her head and this time she heard the man laughing behind her. "This is too easy! You're not even going to fire back?"

You'll know it when I do, she whispered to herself, and emerged from the final bank of jasmine and bougainvillea. She took half a second to get her bearings and realized she had been chased off course more than she thought and was now further back from the complex and somewhere to its southwest.

Keeping an eye on the man as she moved back around to the complex was hard. He was obviously well-trained and she could see why Eden had hired him. But she was better. For one thing, he had allowed her to occupy the higher ground, and that was a rookie mistake he would pay for with his life.

She moved stealthily through the heavy jungle on the southern perimeter of the compound. As she descended back down to sea level she gave up her advantage over the man, but she also got closer to her target – it was a simple trade off that she had no choice but to make.

Now, she was just a few yards from the southern wall of one of the outbuildings. A cursory glance at the architecture showed her that it was all but impossible to free-climb, but that was why she had brought her bag of tricks. Yes, it had slowed her down when she was being chased by the guard, but its contents were critical to the success of the mission. It was another one of those trade-offs.

Aware that she no longer knew the location of the guard, she unzipped the bag fast and silently. She pulled out a five meter length of kernmantle climbing rope which she had already connected to a small grappling hook. After a quick glance to her left and right she deftly threw the rope over the wall.

She tugged on the rope to ensure the hook was properly snagged under the ledge of the concrete coping, and then she began her ascent. She knew this was as exposed as she was going to get – halfway up a white-painted wall in the moonlight – and wanted this section of the mission over as fast as possible.

She heard a noise and flicked her eyes up to see what she had dreaded. It was the man and he was standing on the top of the wall with a gun in his hand.

"I heard the hook," was all he said, and then he raised his gun.

She saw the amused grin on his face, lit ghostly white by the pale light of the moon, and knew she had only a second to react.

"The name's Ben, by the way," the man said. "I'd say pleased to meet you but there's no point as now you have to die."

Lexi Zhang thought differently. In a heartbeat she whipped her gun from her shoulder and fired at the man. It was devastatingly fast.

He looked down and ran his hands over his stomach, a look of disbelief growing on his lean, strong face.

"I'm Lexi, by the way," she said coolly. "I'd say pleased to meet you but there's no point as now you're dead."

The man slumped to his knees and fell back against an air-conditioning duct, but Lexi was already gone, sprinting along the rest of the wall before leaping over a small courtyard and landing like a cat on the ridge cap of a gable roof. She walked carefully down a steep roof valley until she was at the gutter and then she hung over the side and lowered herself gently past the fascia and into the inner courtyard of the compound.

One down, she thought... but how many more to go until she was face to face with Sir Richard Eden?

CHAPTER TWENTY-FIVE

Alex Reeve pushed her hair back behind her ears and rubbed her eyes. It had been a long day, and by the look of the faces on her friends in the Arctic Circle they were feeling the same thing. They had called her on Skype a few moments ago to give the sombre news that Ryan Bale had been snatched from Thor's tomb along with the scroll they'd found in the sarcophagus. This was a massive blow and things felt like they were beginning to spin out of control.

As if that weren't bad enough, Ben Ridgeley had dropped off the radar a while ago in response to an intruder alert on the island, and she had felt a strange weakness in her legs again which she was now certain had something to do with the way the elixir worked. She knew she could tell none of this to Hawke and the others. There was nothing they could do about any of it and it would only distract them from their mission in Scandinavia. They had to focus on rescuing Ryan and stopping Sala.

Luckily, Lea had photographed the scroll on her iPhone before Sala and Smets had taken it, and she'd emailed it to Alex back on Elysium. Since retrieving it, she had made it her priority and had been studying it closely.

"We don't have a lot of time, Alex." Hawke said, glancing down at his watch. "Sala and his Foreign Legion mercs are going to make use of Ryan and force him to decode the scroll. He could be in a lot of trouble if we don't catch up with him soon."

"You think they'll torture him for his knowledge?"

"They're not going to massage it out of him," Scarlet said matter-of-factly.

Hawke nodded grimly. "In a way it's a good thing. If they need to use him to unlock the rest of this riddle, they'll keep him alive. If not…" he paused for a moment, but continued before anyone else could speak. "What have you got so far?"

"A lot, I think. The scroll contained a poem and it isn't hard to translate using Gunnar's research. It's definitely an ode to Thor's death – there are lots of references to the World Serpent biting and envenomating him and others to the nine steps he took before crashing to the ground and dying. This is pretty much in line with the legend, but there's also a reference in here to how he would surely go to Valhalla, the Hall of the Slain."

"But you'd expect that, right?" Lea said.

Alex nodded. "Yes. According to Norse mythology all brave warriors who died in combat would be taken there by the valkyries – these were women who selected from the dead and brought the chosen ones into Valhalla."

"So far so good," Hawke said, with another glance at his watch. "What else?"

"One line is particularly interesting – it says that *At Midgard, the Strength of the Immortals is Inside Thor's Hammer.*"

"Odd use of the word *inside*," Lea said.

"I don't think that's a problem" Victoria asked. "They just mean that power is *within* the hammer."

"But that's just it," Lea said, frowning. "First, it's starting to look like this isn't about the hammer, and second, they don't say *within*, but *inside*."

"I don't get the distinction," Hawke said.

Victoria spoke next. "I get it – within sort of implies that the power resides in the hammer in some metaphysical way, but *inside* is saying that it is literally inside the weapon – right, Alex?"

"Right and wrong. We don't say that courage is inside you, but that you have courage within you, but Lea's right – this isn't about a simple hammer."

Hawke didn't look convinced. "If you say so, Alex."

"I think I'm right on this, Joe."

"So you're not saying that some kind of power source is literally inside the hammer?" Victoria asked.

"I'm just trying to make the point that we had this all wrong. Sala's not searching for Thor's Hammer or some bloody Tesla Coil at all."

Hawke frowned. "All right – let's say that's the case – then what is he searching for?"

Alex smiled. "Here's where it gets very interesting indeed – the poem says that after his death, Thor will travel to Mjölnir."

Scarlet sighed. "Come on, Alex, don't do a Ryan on us, please. It's bad enough I have to rescue the little toerag and use up valuable gold-finding time."

Victoria looked confused. "Mjölnir – isn't that Thor's Hammer?"

"It surely is," Alex said with a smile.

"Sorry," Lea said, "but am I missing something? We know were searching for Thor's Hammer and it's back there in the sarcophagus. What's the big deal?"

"The big deal," Alex said, her grin widening, "is that the reference specifically says that Thor will travel *to* Mjölnir."

Hawke frowned. "Travel to his hammer?"

Lea looked from Hawke to Alex. "I don't understand – the poem's saying he lost his hammer and after death he'll find it?"

Alex shook her head. "No, I don't think so – there's more. It also says his soul will break into Mjölnir."

"Is it just me?" Scarlet said. "Or is this getting less clear by the second?"

"It's not just you," Hawke said. "Alex, dumb it down please, and fast. Ryan's life is on the line."

"Sorry – it's simple. They specifically use the Old Norse verb *fala*, which means to travel, and the verb *brjóta* which means to break into something. What it's saying is that after his death Thor's soul will travel to the Mjölnir and break into it, but here's where it gets really interesting."

"It hasn't even got slightly interesting yet," Scarlet said under her breath.

"The word Mjölnir has become so famous in the Thor legend as the word which describes his hammer that people have been overlooking something so incredibly obvious."

"Make it obvious to us, will you, darling?" Scarlet said.

"Mjölnir can mean hammer in Old Norse, but it can have other meanings like cliff, or stone. I'm totally sure that Mjölnir wasn't Thor's hammer, but a reference to a cliff face on the coast that is the entrance to Valhalla itself."

Lea looked stunned. "So we're not looking for Thor's Hammer – we're looking for Valhalla after all?"

"Yes. The only reason Sala wanted Thor's tomb was because it contained the location of Valhalla. The weapons there would make a Tesla Coil look like a water pistol."

"Oh my goodness!" Victoria said.

"Are you sure?" Hawke asked.

Alex nodded. "Obviously the two things are interlinked but I would say that this poem is referring to Valhalla now, not to the hammer."

Hawke nodded in understanding. "Which makes sense because the hammer was back inside the sarcophagus and Sala couldn't have been less interested in it. Anything else?"

"One more thing – the poem talks about how Mjölnir faces Aegir."

"The God of the Sea?" Victoria asked.

"No, not in this context. Aegir in Old Norse meant not only the god of the sea, who was, of course, the Norse equivalent of Poseidon..."

Scarlet groaned and buried her face in her hands. "Please, no more of him..."

"But it also meant simply the sea. The line *Mjölnir strikes Aegir in the north* doesn't mean the hammer will hit the god, but it's a cliff face that strikes the sea, and the *norðanverðr* reference simply means northern, so that must point to the north coast, which..."

"Which must mean Norway," Lea said. "Sweden doesn't have a coast in the far north."

"Great work, Alex – but there are a lot of cliffs in Norway," Hawke said, frustration rising in his voice. "Norway has one of the longest coastlines in the world."

Alex looked down at the text and ran her finger to a particular word. "The clue is in this word *Hornungr*. I did some research on this and it looks like it's an old abandoned word for Mount Storefjell, which just means Big Mountain. This mountain is near the most northerly town in Norway, a place called Honningsvåg. If you ask me – and I guess you did – I would tell you that Valhalla was built or carved into the cliffs in the vicinity of Honningsvåg."

"Which is why we *did* ask you," Hawke said, smiling.

"But there's a problem."

She saw their faces drop.

"When isn't there?" Scarlet said.

Hawke frowned. "Let us have it."

"The cliffs in the area have suffered from a lot of erosion since the time of Valhalla, which according to most legends stands tall on the cliff tops. After significant erosion – and we're talking millions of years here – you need to start looking under the water on the coast."

"Fantastic," Scarlet said.

"But it makes perfect sense," Victoria said.

"All right," Hawke said flatly. "This means we're going to need extra gear – a submersible, plus some wetsuits and so on."

"Already organized it and it's on the way to you right now, and..." Alex stopped, her sentence cut short. She looked up from the faces of her friends on the screen to see another intruder alarm had gone off, much closer to the compound. Given the earlier intruder alert on the outer perimeter this looked like it could be trouble and she knew she had to deal with it right now.

"Guys, I think we might have a problem here, so I have to go."

"What sort of problem?" Hawke asked.

"Um... all right, I've gotta go. Talk to you later."

Alex cut the call and the screen went black. Then she turned to her other monitor and watched the flashing alert. Whoever it was must have taken Ben out and was now only minutes away from her.

*

Hawke and the others looked at each for a moment in the chilly Arctic silence and wondered what had happened back on the island.

"Well, *that* was weird."

"Maybe Maria discovered Ryan's extensive porn collection," Scarlet said.

"Not the time, Cairo," Hawke said flatly. "Ryan could be dead already."

"Or maybe," Lea said, smile fading. "Something more serious is going on?"

Hawke thought there was a good chance Lea might be right, but he knew Alex was more than capable of looking after herself – and it wasn't like she was on her own or in a dangerous location.

She was with Sir Richard Eden, a former officer in the Paras and Maria Kurikova, a Russian agent who had recently defected to the ECHO team. Not only could both of these people put up a serious defense if they were under attack, but he'd heard rumors of another Para by the name of Ridgeley who was also connected to Eden in some way and might be on Elysium right now.

Sure, he was only a Para, Hawke considered mildly, but they were still a serious élite force to be reckoned with. If this Ridgeley were there too he was sure Alex Reeve was in no danger, at least not from any external force. What worried Hawke was how the American was obviously hiding the fact something was going wrong with her legs again – something connected to the elixir he had given her in Egypt.

He knew that would need looking at, but now was hardly the time. Now, as ever, he was up to his neck in trouble and grief and he knew there was a lot more to come as well. He had to focus and look after the people in his charge who needed him right now. Then there was the fact that Ryan Bale had been snatched from right in front of his eyes. For that, Álvaro Sala would pay a heavy price.

"So where are we?" Lea asked.

"In the middle of nowhere," Scarlet said, and lit a cigarette. "As bloody usual."

Hawke looked at the sky – the sun was already climbing slowly toward its zenith. "Thanks to Alex's translation work we've got it confirmed that we're not looking for anything to do with Thor's Hammer anymore, at least not in the way we were thinking of it. The Hammer is a cliff, not a weapon, and obviously the location of Valhalla itself which Sala wants because of the weaponry that is supposed to be there."

A silence fell over the team as the implications of his words faded into the strange dawn light.

"I can't believe it – Valhalla!" Victoria said. "I know Nate must have been looking for this for a long time but I still can't get my head around it all. I'm an archaeologist, not a treasure hunter or adventurer. To me this all sounds impossible."

"We deal in the impossible every day," Lea said with a warm smile.

"Time to go," Hawke said, pointing at the horizon. "Looks like our ride's on its way." A large military helicopter was approaching them at full speed and swooping down into the valley toward them. "Let's go and get Ryan."

CHAPTER TWENTY-SIX

Nordkapp, Finnmark

The flight from Kebnekaise to Honningsvåg took them to the very edge of Europe and even deeper into Arctic territory. The transport was a long-range AugustaWestland AW101 belonging to the Royal Norwegian Air Force base at Andøya and flown by a genial young lieutenant named Trond Ljunggren who showed them aboard with a cheery wave before flying the powerful helicopter north.

Victoria looked out of the window for a few moments and then turned to the others. "Welcome to Asgard!"

They flew fast and low over some of the sparsest landscape on earth, and it wasn't long before the craziness of the last few hours conspired with the gentle roar of the chopper's engine and caught up with Victoria Hamilton-Talbot, sending her into a deep sleep.

Hawke was still fuming from his failure to protect Ryan back in Thor's tomb and stop Sala and his trained chimp Smets from taking him hostage. Not only did he fear for Ryan's life, but it also meant the enemy would be able to use him to get the location of Valhalla. Things were bad enough when they thought Sala was seeking a Tesla Coil in Thor's tomb, but now they knew he wanted the terrifying array of divine weapons in Valhalla itself things had taken a bleaker turn.

He wondered for a few seconds if Ryan was still alive, but quickly dismissed the thought for the reason he had just considered. Ryan Bale was no fool, and he would know how to use his knowledge to keep himself alive until the rest of the ECHO team could put together a rescue plan. But like everything else in life, it would all come down to a matter of timing. Hawke knew better than anyone that one screw-up could mean the difference between life and death, and having Ryan's death on his conscience was unthinkable. He had a duty to protect everyone in his team, and that included Ryan Bale.

They'd made use of the flight time by studying some classified oceanographic surveys liberated from the CIA by Alex Reeve, and after putting their heads together they'd chosen the best place for them to start their search for the missing Hall of the Slain. The maps had revealed an ancient landslide exactly where Alex had described, and closer study showed what looked like a tunnel obscured by an underwater cliff.

Whatever it was, it was large – around fifty meters wide and thirty high – and it hadn't taken the ECHO team long to decide it was what they were looking for. The only problem was that Sala was also looking for it, and he had a substantial head-start on them.

They raced ever closer to the coast, and Hawke rolled his eyes as Scarlet clambered forward to the flight deck to get more intimately acquainted with some Norwegian bedroom vocabulary.

He turned to Lea. The former Irish Ranger hadn't been herself since her last journey to Ireland and Hawke knew why, but he also knew there was little he could do to change things.

When they finally reached the coastline, they saw they weren't the first, but none of them was surprised by the revelation. Sala was not only in the lead but had Ryan's mind to exploit, and now a remarkable vessel was rising and falling in the sea's tumultuous swell. On the deck Hawke saw half a dozen men, some studying the coast with binoculars from the portside of the vessel. Written along the bow in black letters was the word "Rán".

"What the hell is that thing?" Lea asked, astonished.

"It's a Migaloo," Hawke said.

"A what?"

"A submarine-yacht. The latest must-have for the mega-rich. No international villain would be without one."

"I've never seen anything like it before," Victoria said, her eyes crawling all over the beautiful vessel in the water below.

"It's a pretty amazing piece of kit," Hawke said with appreciation. Contains a library, gym, bar, cinema – you name it. Plus it can dive to two hundred and forty meters as well."

"What does Rán mean?" Lea asked.

"Goddess of the Sea," Victoria said. "I can't believe how enormous it is!"

"So big, in fact," Hawke continued, "that it has its own mini-sub."

"Now you're just joking with us," Lea said. "A submarine with its own submarine?"

Hawke nodded. "Yeah – a Triton 1000/3. This is for the seriously discerning ego."

"I'll say," Lea said. "How much?"

"The whole package is over two billion," Hawke said flatly.

"How much?!" Lea said.

"That's absurd," Victoria said. "That's even more than Daddy has."

Scarlet emerged from the cockpit with smudged lipstick and raised an eyebrow. "And how much has Daddy got?"

"If Sala's already got two billion," Lea interrupted, "just imagine what must be in Valhalla."

"My thoughts exactly," Hawke said.

Lea looked anxious. "Anyone see Ryan down there?"

Hawke ran his eyes along the smooth, long deck. "There!" he shouted.

"Is he all right?"

"He looks fine," Scarlet said. "But I'm worried he might have bored Sala to death thereby denying me the pleasure of killing the bastard."

Lea pointed out of the chopper's open door. "Woah – looks like they're diving!"

Hawke watched anxiously as the Migaloo prepared to dive. Sala was dragging Ryan toward the aft hatch.

"Listen up," Hawke said. "I'm going down there to get Ryan before that thing goes under. After I touch down you get this chopper to shore and start to unload the sub."

"But our sub's shit compared to that!" Scarlet said.

Hawke looked at her, but before he had time to respond their chopper lurched violently to starboard as Trond increased power to the rotors and executed a sharp turn.

"What the hell's going on?!" Hawke shouted through the headset.

Trond's reply was calm but grim. "We're under attack!"

Hawke stepped into the cockpit and saw another chopper racing from left to right and turning hard to make another sweep at them. It was a Eurocopter Super Puma. Its portside plug-door was wide open and revealed a man inside who was operating a nasty-looking M60 machine gun.

"It must be Sala's transport!" Hawke shouted. "And there's a door gunner just waiting to drill us full of holes and send us into the sea!"

"What do you want me to do?" Trond asked.

Hawke put his hand on the young man's shoulder. "Keep this bird in the air, Trond – Lea and Scarlet will do the rest."

Hawke stepped into the main cabin and told the others what was happening. Lea told Victoria to strap in and stay out of the way while Scarlet loaded up a Heckler & Koch MP7 and pulled a coin out of her pocket.

"What's that for?" asked Lea, looking at the small copper coin.

"Got it in my change back in Stockholm." Scarlet nodded her head at the heavy machine gun mounted at the door of the chopper. "We're tossing for the M2."

"Tails," Lea said.

Hawke rolled his eyes as the coin flipped over in the air and landed on the back of Scarlet's wrist. She smacked it down with the palm of her other hand and grinned when she saw the sombre profile of Carl Gustav XVI looking back up at her. "Too bad – it's heads and that means I'm having the M2!"

"Great," Hawke said. "Let's get on with it then shall we?"

He opened the side door and Scarlet swung the long perforated barrel-shroud of the M2 out into the cold, rainy Norwegian air. On the other side of the chopper, Lea opened her door and cocked the MP7 while Victoria looked on in abject horror.

"I say – it's not going to be too loud is it?" she said.

Ignoring her, Hawke secured a descent-control nylon Type 4 rope inside the chopper and slipped on a pair of double-leather rappellers' gloves He checked the hookup, rappel seat and rappel ring as Trond evaded another burst from the Puma's M60 and navigated their chopper over to Sala's yacht-sub.

As they approached the Rán, Hawke checked the anchor point connection – or what rappellers liked to call the donut ring – one final time and then dropped the deployment bag out the door of the chopper into the rain, swinging his legs outside.

Trond swooped the chopper down to one hundred and fifty feet and gave the signal to go. Outside they heard the *clang clang clang* of the Puma's bullets striking the side of their chopper's steel exterior and Trond began to pull up to evade them.

Scarlet swung the M2's barrel at the Puma and returned fire. The noise of the heavy machine gun was intense but muffled by their ear defenders. The spring-activated ejector spat out the empty .50 caliber shell casings as she raked the bullets all over the side of the enemy helicopter, forcing them to break off their attack and pull away. "I could do this all day!" she shouted.

"Now!" screamed the Norwegian pilot.

Hawke looked up at Lea. "Back in a jiffy," he said, and pushed away from the chopper. He used his guide hand to control his descent and was on his way.

Buffeted wildly by the downdraft of the AW101's mighty rotors, he looked above and saw only gray skies and rain, and the muzzle-flash of the M2. Below there was only the slim outline of Sala's submarine-yacht as it sailed toward the coast and prepared to dive.

Hawke used his brake hand to slow the descent and then when he was low enough he released himself from the rope, crashing into the tumultuous ocean and disappearing into the black waves.

Times were getting interesting, he thought.

*

Lea watched Hawke disappear into the raging sea but had no time to dwell on his safety. In the cockpit, Trond was working like a devil to evade the Puma's vicious attacks, muttering Norwegian expletives every now and again when he had time to take a breath.

On the other side of the chopper, Scarlet Sloane seemed to be having a whale of time firing the M2 whenever she got a shot good enough to justify the ammo, while strapped in at the rear a terrified Victoria Hamilton-Talbot was sitting with her eyes closed and mumbling what Lea presumed were prayers.

Now, Lea stared out into the dark stormy sky. Her hair whipped around in the hail-streaked Arctic wind as she used the MP7 to pin down some goons who were standing near the Rán's forward escape hatch and taking pot-shots into the water.

They must have seen Joe! she thought to herself as she raked the sub's outer casing with bullets. In contrast to the pressure hull beneath it, the light hull was made of steel only four millimeters thick. Its only function was to provide a smooth hydrodynamic contour to the sub's design. Lea's bullets chewed into it with ease and made the men dance around like fools as they tried to evade the rounds.

She continued firing with quiet determination. Somewhere down in all that gloom was the man she loved, but her thoughts were interrupted by the chopper veering violent to the portside. She reached out to grab hold of anything that would save her, but it was too late.

She tumbled out of the helicopter into the dark, freezing night.

*

Hawke swam toward the Rán. The storm was rising and the swell was difficult work as he plowed onward with the salty spray lashing his face. On the deck, Sala looked less than impressed at the sight of Lea Donovan drilling holes all over the deck casing of his two billion dollar rubber duck. He began ranting and raving at Smets, barking orders to go below decks and get the sub underwater.

By now, the storm was raging and knocking the Migaloo all over the place. By the time Hawke had touched down beside it, the sub was already partially submerged and the sea water was beginning to slosh over the deck. At the bow, the freezing water was churned into milky bubbles by the forward hydroplanes and with every second it moved deeper into the water.

Hawke knew he had to act fast. In a few minutes there would be no submarine – just him and an awful lot of freezing, tumultuous water. He'd paddled ashore from subs enough times in the past to know how quickly they could vanish from sight, and he didn't fancy it happening in the middle of a storm.

Then he watched grimly as Sala, Smets and Ryan disappeared inside the aft hatch and went below decks.

He knew the deck would be awash in seconds now, and he swam hard for the rear of the boat. As he swam around to the hangar he heard the sub's klaxon ring out the unmistakable sound of a diving alarm. This was followed seconds later by the sound of men screaming and the other airlock hatches slamming shut, and he knew from long experience in the Royal Marines and Special Boat Service that Sala had ordered a crash dive. This was a maneuver used by sub captains to submerge beneath the surface as fast as possible to avoid being seen or even to avoid colliding with another vessel.

With the bow planes at the maximum possible downward angle, Hawke knew the crew would be flooding the forward ballast tanks as fast as they could and forcing the submarine down into the icy water at double quick speed. He only had seconds to react. Being stranded in the hangar when the sub dived was a bad idea, so he sprinted across to the hatch door and spun the wheel to open it. He swung it open just in time to see a man running toward him with his fist raised. Hawke dodged the blow, ducking to one side then he brought his fist into the man's face and knocked him out in one punch.

With seawater rushing into the hangar, Hawke slammed the door shut and secured it before moving along the corridor in search of Ryan, but he didn't have to look for long. A few moments after entering the corridor he heard the sound of Ryan shouting at some of the men, and then the sound of a heavy punch which was followed by silence. It seemed to be coming from the control room up on the right.

Hawke peered into the room and his eyes confirmed what his ears already knew – Ryan was being held captive by one of Sala's mercs and it looked like he'd been struck in the face. The young computer hacker from London could add a black eye to the wounded arm this mission had already given to him.

Sala was nowhere to be seen, and neither was Smets, but he counted only one guard in the room alongside a handful of technicians.

Hawke entered the small space and marched right up to them.

The man recognized Hawke from Thor's tomb, and reacted fast, grabbing Ryan and reaching for something to use as a weapon, but all he could find was a pen which he fumbled, sending it to the floor with a clatter.

Hawke made his move.

CHAPTER TWENTY-SEVEN

Joe Hawke pushed Ryan out of the way and lunged forward hard, punching the guard in the stomach. The man doubled over in agony but the former Commando gave no quarter, powering a devastating uppercut into his lower jaw which cracked shut hard and broke several of his teeth.

The merc staggered back with a wild look in his eyes and waved his arms frantically behind him in a bid to find something to arrest his fall. His right hand caught the edge of the forward auxiliary switchboard but slipped off, and he fell down hard, scarring his back deeply on the corner of the low pressure air manifold gauge. He screamed in agony as he tried to stagger back to his feet.

A technician stood to confront the Englishman but Hawke knocked him out cold with a single punch. "Sorry, no time for introductions..."

Another of the men looked at his unconscious colleague and ran from the control room, presumably to get back-up.

Hawke knew he had no time to waste and padded forward, snatching a wrench from the top of the diving control station. "If you want to fight someone, then have a go with me and leave the kid alone, got it?"

The guard was up now and stared at Hawke hard with a bloody smashed-tooth grin. He wiped a gnarled hand across his mouth and left a smear of engine grease and blood on his face. "You will pay for this!" he said, spitting a thick glob of blood on the mesh floor.

Hawke glanced at Ryan's black eye and then back to the man. "If you think I owe you something, then come and get it, you dick!"

The man's beady eyes swivelled around the control room in search of a weapon, but before he found one Hawke stormed forward and swung the spanner at him a second time, striking him across the nose. This produced a terrible wet crunching sound that made Ryan wince.

With more blood now pouring from his smashed nose, the man's face warped into a rictus of hatred for Hawke. His eyes wide now, and neck veins pulsing with high-pressure blood, he stormed forward, nothing on his mind but revenge.

Hawke showed no mercy, lashing out with the spanner again and hitting the technician on the right temple with a savage backhand swipe.

The man staggered backwards and crashed into the dive controls, sending the sub lurching forward to the sea floor.

"That's handy," Hawke said, pulling the unconscious man from the yoke and levelling the submarine. "Right, let's get out of here!"

Ryan looked confused. "Aren't you forgetting something?"

"Like what?"

"We're underwater!"

Hawke tapped the depth gauge. "We're only at twenty meters, mate. You've seen You Only Live Twice, right? These gauges here indicate Sala put in a nice bespoke torpedo room."

"Yes, but..." a look of horror and disbelief spread over Ryan's face. "If you mean the scene where Sean Connery is fired into the Sea of Japan as a human torpedo, forget it!"

Hawke shook his head in disappointment. "Where's your spirit of adventure?"

They ran to the torpedo room and Hawke slammed the bulkhead door shut. It was a modest affair for a private submarine, presumably built so the Andorran could take out commercial ships, but today it would serve another purpose. With Sala's goons hammering on the internal door, Hawke swung open the hatch of one of the tubes. "In you go."

Ryan peered inside. "But what about you?"

"I'll fire you out, then open the hatch and swim out the same way."

"Won't that flood the submarine?"

"Sort of what I'm aiming for, Ryan, but they could contain the flooding easily enough so let's hurry. Get in!"

"I cannot believe I'm doing this! At least Bond got to meet Blofeld at the end of it."

"Listen, hurry up or..." Hawke paused and looked at Ryan for a second, a smile growing on his face. "Wait, you don't think you're Bond in this scenario, do you?"

"Well..."

"Put this on." Hawke smiled and let it go, handing the younger man a lifejacket. "Hold your breath and the second you're outside the sub make for the surface. It's going to be choppy up there but I'll be right behind you."

Hawke slammed the hatch door and fired Ryan into the sea. It wasn't as risky as it sounded – he'd left submarines that way many times before. It was a standard manoeuvre for naval Special Forces all over the world.

With the men working hard to force open the internal hatch, and the sub still diving, Hawke spun open the hatch door and stood well back as the pressure differential forced the seawater through the tube and into the torpedo room. It quickly flooded into the small space.

The flow velocity of the water was tremendous, so he didn't have to wait long until the water was level with the top of the torpedo tube. Then he pulled himself inside and took the deepest of breaths as he went. Hauling himself through the torpedo tube took all of his strength but then he was clear and swimming to the surface.

When he left the sub they were at twenty-five meters which was nowhere near his deepest freedive without breathing apparatus. His record was eighty meters below sea level, which he'd done off the coast of Bermuda many years ago. Now recognized as a serious sport, freediving had a lengthy pedigree stretching back to ancient cultures when they used the skill to gather pearls or sponges.

For a trained Special Forces frogman like Hawke, leaving a sub at twenty-five meters and swimming to the surface was meat and potatoes, but the feigned casual manner back in the torpedo room with Ryan was to conceal his concerns about the young man's safety. This would be very deep for Ryan, plus it was freezing, dark water, he had no light and a wounded arm.

Freediving was fun, but not without its risks. At serious depths the body could suffer from a variety of problems ranging from hyperventilation to shallow-water blackout which struck without any warning signs.

There was a lot to consider, including the salinity levels of the water you were diving in. Freshwater and saltwater freediving had their own challenges. Most divers had two forces to consider – upward and downward. A diver's buoyancy was determined by the saline levels of the water, which meant that the less salt the easier it was dive, because bodies floated more easily in saltwater.

But less upward force caused by the lack of salt meant more downward force when the diver was trying to reach the surface again. In a saltwater environment it was easier for the diver to float back up, but much harder in freshwater.

Hawke knew that the Barents Sea had three distinct water masses, each with their own salinity levels. The warmer water from the Atlantic was higher, as was the colder water coming down from the Arctic, but along the coast the saline levels were lower. This made it easier to dive but harder to reach the surface, and as he and Ryan were on a strictly one-way trip from the sub to the surface this was to their disadvantage.

Now, Hawke swam to the surface, straining his eyes through the gloom to find Ryan, but all he saw was a wild, heaving ocean looming above him like a snarling beast into whose jaws he would soon swimming.

*

Lea clung to chopper's portside skid for her life as Trond turned sharply in the air to give Scarlet another opportunity to hit the Puma with the M2. The skid was wet and slippery in the freezing Arctic rain but her cries for help went unheard. Trond was in the cockpit struggling to evade the enemy's bullets while Scarlet was occupied behind the noisy machine gun. Victoria's ears were covered by a chunky pair of defenders and her eyes were clamped shut in terror. If she fell now, no one would notice for a very long time.

She made the cardinal error of looking down and saw only her Heckler & Koch MP7 as it spun down into the raging black sea hundreds of feet below her. She was dimly aware of the pale glow of the Rán's conning tower lights as it slowly sank beneath the waves and she prayed Hawke had gotten safely aboard.

She made another attempt to pull herself back inside but Trond was climbing hard into the sky and she slipped back over the skid, now hanging on at arms' length as the helicopter was shrouded in the low storm clouds. The smell of the chopper's exhaust fumes wafted over her and a wave of nausea almost made her throw up, but she focussed and kept her head together.

With the fumes past now, she blinked to get the drizzly water out of her eyes and took a deep breath. Her fingers, wrapped tightly around the icy metal skid, were tired and wanted to let go but she knew that meant falling to her death. She thought of her father. He had fallen to his death too. The only difference was someone had pushed him over those cliffs and she knew she couldn't die until she had found out who and why.

She was dragged back to life by the sound of the M2 going nuts on the far side of the helicopter and then she heard Scarlet's voice screaming with joy. Trond pulled level and then began to descend, allowing Lea to take advantage and use gravity to climb up over the skid and clamber back inside the helicopter.

Looking through Scarlet's door on the other side of the chopper she saw the Puma spinning around uncontrollably. Flames and smoke poured from its rear rotor as the pilot struggled to keep it in the air.

"You're going down like a fucking sycamore seed, baby!" Scarlet shouted, and celebrated her shot with a solid-gold air-punch.

Lea moved over to her and watched as the Puma spun closer to the ground. "Nice shooting."

"Where were you? You missed all the fun."

Lea took a deep breath and tried to slow her pounding heart rate. "Just hanging out on my own for a second."

Victoria opened her eyes and looked at them both. "Did I miss anything?"

*

When Hawke reached the surface a cold rush of air hit him in the face followed by a blast of sea spray. He was in a deep trough now, surrounded on all sides by towering walls of gray ocean. High above, he saw a crest of rising water which folded over and crashed down on top of him.

Seconds later he was atop an enormous crest of seawater, struggling with all his strength to maintain some kind of even buoyancy in the raging swell. To his left, he saw a massive, smoking fireball burning on the rear rotor of a chopper and for a heart-stopping moment he thought it was the AW101 about to crash into the sea with Lea and his friends on board.

Then he realized it was the Puma, and that Scarlet must have taken it out with the M2. He watched it drop into the ocean a few hundred yards away where it landed with a low crashing sound. A sombre column of smoke rose from the water but was quickly dissipated by the wind.

Fighting the power of the sea, he gasped another deep breath as he scanned the water for any sign of Ryan, but saw only the AW101 as Trond spun it around over the cliffs and headed back in the direction of the burning Puma wreckage. They were obviously making a fly-by to ensure it was dead.

Then Hawke saw Ryan, rising on a crest slightly further out to sea than he was – he looked disoriented and scared. The SBS man estimated the wave length at

231

about thirty meters, so he got swimming as fast as he could. He headed down the slope of the water into the trough and then powered himself up the other side until he was on the same crest as Ryan, but when he got there his friend was unconscious and bobbing helplessly up and down in the freezing water. The only reason he was still on the surface was the lifejacket Hawke had given to him as he climbed into the torpedo tube.

Hawke swam behind Ryan and hooked his arm around his chest before beginning the arduous swim back to shore. A nice little rip current had started to develop and no matter how hard the Englishman fought to reach the safety of the shore, they were pushed further out into the freezing ocean.

Hawke's mind raced with options, but then the best of all presented itself to him when the AW101 turned from the sinking Puma and flew in their direction.

"Stay with us, mate!" Hawke shouted as a line was winched down from the side of the helicopter. Still clinging to Ryan, he grabbed hold of the line and fixed himself into the harness. Moments later they were ascending toward the chopper.

"You missed all the fun!" Scarlet said as she helped Hawke get Ryan into the chopper. He clambered in after him and swept the water from his hair, rushing over to Ryan who was still unconscious.

Scarlet stretched Ryan out on the floor of the chopper and began to give him the kiss of life.

Lea ran over to Hawke and kissed him.

"What was that for?" he asked.

"I thought you were dead."

"Never! But how did you find us?" Hawke asked.

"Infrared detector on my helmet," Trond said calmly over the headset from the cockpit. "If I hadn't been wearing this you would be halfway to Russia by now."

Ryan spluttered back to life and doubled over on his side as he coughed the seawater from his lungs.

"You're going to be all right," Scarlet said, placing a hand on his shoulder.

Ryan was clearly rattled, but knew he had a reputation to maintain. Through the coughing and wheezing he looked up at Scarlet adoringly. "I can't believe…" he began.

"What?" Scarlet said.

"That I've been kissed by the woman who shot the President of the United States!"

She sighed heavily and pushed him over.

"But didn't you feel the spark?" Ryan called out.

"I've been more turned on blowing up a sex doll."

Victoria looked disgusted. "Oh, how dreadful!"

Ryan got to his knees and tried to get his breath back. "You've blown up a sex doll?"

"I see we're all up to our usual speeds and settings," Hawke said, reaching his arms around Lea's waist.

Scarlet rolled her eyes as they kissed a second time. "Is that really the best use of our time?"

"Cairo's right," Hawke said. "We need to launch the submersible right away," he said. "They've dived in the Rán and they'll be halfway there by now!"

Trond waved a one-finger salute in acknowledgement and turned the chopper back to shore. Moments later, the enormous military machine was slowly descending over the sea to the bottom of the cliffs and touching down on the freezing beach. The rain blowing in from the Barents Sea was cold and heavy, and reduced daylight visibility to the point that it almost looked like twilight, but none of that mattered to Hawke.

He had a mission to complete and nothing was going to stop him.

CHAPTER TWENTY-EIGHT

Getting inside the complex was easier than Lexi had anticipated. Her first thought was to use the door she had seen 'Ben' exit from when she set the alarm off in the yard, but when she got there it was shut again, and locked. Clearly they knew the island was now under attack and had initiated some kind of silent lockdown.

She had finally gained entry to the place via a skylight in what turned out to be the food stores. She lowered herself gently to the tiled floor and after helping herself to a sip of bottled mineral water from the shelf, she refocussed her mind and readied her weapon for the next stage of the mission.

Her attempt to obtain any kind of schematics for the complex had failed miserably – it was as if the place didn't exist. There were no authorities on the island she could ask after all, and every one of her foreign intel agency contacts had come to nothing. This meant that from this stage onwards she had to feel her way forward step by step – improvising as she moved silently along the complex's corridors in search of her final target. Anyone who got in the way between her and Eden would also have to be eliminated.

She stalked down a long utility corridor leading from the food stores to what was obviously the generator room. For a while she considered sabotaging it and plunging the place into darkness, but while that sounded like a good idea at first it would not only give away her current position inside the complex, but also give her a disadvantage. The ECHO team knew this place better than she did and they would certainly have access to better night vision tech than her handheld monocular.

In the cool, air-conditioned silence of the complex, her mind drifted back to her training back in Beijing, and the monstrous figure of Shi Keyu. Shi was her boss and chief training officer, and his fondness for ancient Chinese military strategy was well-known in the academy.

"Remember, Xiaoli," he had said. "The supreme art of war is to subdue the enemy without fighting."

If his scowling, pock-marked face hadn't been less than ten inches from hers she would have rolled her eyes. His endless quoting of Sun Tzu, the Spring and Autumn Period Chinese military strategist and commander, was also well-known in the academy.

Now, she couldn't shake him out of her mind.

The time he had caught her smoking in her room and made her do a hundred push-ups. Even now she could still see the reflection of her face in the polished toecaps of his boots. The time he had reprimanded her in front of everyone after she had failed to recite accurately Sun Tzu's five basic factors of military strategy. She could still see his bloated, sweating face even now after all these years.

She glanced at her watch – she had been on the island less than half an hour so far. She smiled and thought of Shi Keyu one last time. Shi Keyu who was dragged kicking and screaming from his Jiaozi dumplings one night to face execution by firing squad for crimes against the state. As she closed in on her objective, she heard the ancient voice of Sun Tzu as he whispered in her ear: *Quickness is the essence of the war.*

Ahead of her she heard whistling. She stopped in a heartbeat and pushed herself up against the wall, hiding in the shadows of a Chinese windmill palm. Good choice, she thought, but her appreciation of the plant-life was cut short when she saw the unmistakable figure of Maria Kurikova as she glided across the small window in the kitchen door and opened the refrigerator. It was definitely the Russian woman – blonde hair tied back, blue eyes, tall and elegant. Too elegant for an FSB goon, she thought. Perhaps she was descended from the Russian aristocracy.

But Kurikova's provenance hardly mattered now. All Lexi was thinking about was how to take her out of the equation. As far as she was concerned she wouldn't be able to have a serious shot at taking Eden out until the Russian woman was out of the way. She might look like a Tsarina, but Lexi had seen her in action and it was no joke. Her assessment of the situation was that if she tried to hit Eden while Kurikova was still standing things might get nasty.

She racked her mind thinking of possible plays, and then the ghosts returned to her once again out of the ether. *Appear at points which the enemy must hasten to defend; march swiftly to places where you are not expected...*

Not expected, indeed.

Looking above her she saw an air-conditioning duct grille. Standing on the side of the palm pot she pushed it open and climbed inside until she was concealed within the duct, and then she shuffled forward slowly and silently, dragging both Shi Keyu and Sun Tzu behind her.

Over the kitchen now, she peered down through the grille in the ceiling and watched as Maria finished making her sandwich. Lexi noted that she had left her gun on the couch in the sunken living area.

Big mistake, she thought. This is too easy.

Taking a deep breath, she coiled her legs up and then released them like a spring, powering the grille out with her boots and dropping through the hole behind it. The grille clattered to the floor with a metallic crash and Maria almost jumped out of her skin.

Lexi hit the ground and Maria reacted in half a second, just as Lexi knew she would. She spun around and reached out for the gun but it was too late. She had left the weapon too far away and made herself defenceless.

Lexi raised her gun and squeezed the trigger without a second thought, blasting Maria dead-center in the stomach.

Maria screamed in shock and agony. "What have you done?!"

"It's war, Maria, and you're dead."

Without blinking, Lexi fired a second time across the chest and Maria screamed in pain and she staggered backwards toward the fridge, staring in horror as her white shirt turned blood red. "How could you?!" she screamed, her voice trailing away.

But Lexi was already gone, running up the circular staircase on her way to the upper levels. She knew this was the location of Alex Reeve's research center, and consequently the nerve center of the ECHO team, and aside from Eden himself it was the highest value target on the island.

All warfare is based on deception, Xiaoli said the ghost of Shi Keyu. Lexi ignored it as she climbed silently up some wooden steps and moved along the mezzanine toward the research center.

"Lexi?" Alex looked startled as she turned from the computer to face her. Her face changed when she saw the gun in Lexi's hands. "Listen, just take it easy, all right? You don't have to use that..."

Lexi had heard enough. An ice-cold darkness had descended over her mind once again, just like the one she had felt when she'd called the Ministry's Internal Affairs Department about Shi Keyu's extra-curricular activities with a woman from the Japanese Public Security Intelligence Agency. He was arrested a day later.

Without a moment of hesitation she fired the gun at Alex, striking her across the chest and upper arms and sending her flying around in the swivel chair. Alex screamed in shock, but it was over faster than she knew.

It wasn't something Lexi wanted to linger over, so without glancing back, she moved stealthily along the corridor on her way to Eden. She'd already calculated that at this time of night he would either be in his bed or in his study, and the bedroom was her first port of call. She silently opened the door and switched on the lights, but the bed was made and empty, which meant only one thing – Sir Richard Eden had run out of hiding places.

Lexi Zhang raised her gun and stalked silently along the corridor to the final objective. Her mission's end was behind one more oak-panelled door, and she intended to see it through to its logical conclusion.

She saw there was a low light on inside the study. Was he still awake – reading perhaps? Not a crazy idea, she thought. Maria and Alex had still been awake after all. But then again Eden was older than they were – perhaps he'd simply fallen asleep with the lamp on. For a long time she simply listened at the door but after a few minutes she decided he must be asleep.

She pushed the door open slowly and saw she was right. There, stretched out on his long leather couch beneath the Louvre windows at the side of his desk, was the mission objective: Sir Richard Eden MP.

CHAPTER TWENTY-NINE

Hawke was first to emerge from the AW101 and was immediately whipped in the face by the driving, icy wind. "Still summer, I see," he said as he helped the others from the sliding door on the side and walked around to the back of the chopper.

Trond opened the rear cargo ramp from inside the cockpit and the hydraulic motors slowly lowered it to the wet, gravelly sand on the beach. When it was fully extended Hawke climbed up into the back of the chopper again and began the process of unstrapping the mini submersible from the helicopter.

"We don't have much time," he said, casting a suspicious eye out into the ocean. "Going by the surveys we studied, Sala should be able to get the Migaloo all the way through into Valhalla, but if not he's always got the Triton. Either way he's well ahead of us."

When it was free, they all worked together to roll the mini sub out the back of the helicopter and push it down to the sea on its trailer. The wind was rising again, and as a consequence the sea was getting rougher by the minute. The Barents Sea was what was known as a *marginal sea* – a body of water bordered by various peninsulas or islands and attached to a larger ocean, in this case the Arctic Ocean. Rich in hydrocarbons, today it was filled with rigs plundering its many oil and gas fields but Hawke and the others now knew it was also home to a much richer treasure – the Hall of the Slain, Valhalla itself.

When the sub was in place, Hawke gave Trond the signal and the mighty helicopter powered up. It buffeted them all in its downdraft as it lumbered up into the leaden Norwegian Arctic sky and disappeared from view into the low storm clouds above them.

Alone now, they hurried to move the sub to the correct depth and released it from the trailer. Hawke climbed inside first and began the process of firing up the engine and instrument panel as the storm grew in power all around them. Even this far in the bay, he felt the sub being knocked about by the swell of the sea and knew it was time to dive. Calling the others on board they closed the hatch and he piloted the submersible out to sea.

Scarlet stared at the poky interior of the mini-sub with anxious eyes. "This thing is safe, right?"

"Of course it is," Hawke said, tapping the yoke with pride.

"But it really doesn't look very safe," Victoria said.

"Trust me," Hawke said with a grin. "If it suddenly implodes at crush depth you won't even know what's happened."

Ryan laughed, then winced in pain and gripped his arm.

"That's just Joe's way of dealing with stressful situations," Lea said.

"This is why I joined the SAS and not the bloody frogmen," said Scarlet, looking once again around the creaking interior of the sub as it continued to dive into the black ocean.

"Well unfortunately, Cairo," Hawke said without taking his eyes off the controls, "Valhalla is underwater, so today we'll just have to do it my way."

"That's what worries me," she said, and then jumped. "What the hell was that?!"

"It's just the hull compressing, Cairo. Like when you crush someone's skull between your thighs."

"But that kills them."

"But unlike you, I'm in control of the situation, and the sub is designed for much greater depths than this, so why not relax and enjoy? This is probably the only time in your life you will be sailing in a mini-sub to Valhalla."

"If you say so," Scarlet said, unconvinced. "I suppose a cigarette…"

"No, you cannot smoke in here," Hawke said flatly.

"I was *joking*, frogman."

Knowing how much Cairo Sloane liked to smoke to calm her nerves, Hawke had his doubts, but made no comment as he navigated them deeper and turned into the mouth of the tunnel. The submarine started to jolt and bang around.

Scarlet reached out for something to hang onto. "What the hell's going on now?"

"We're sailing into the wake vortex of the Migaloo – no need to panic."

"Wake vortex?" Victoria said.

"A submarine moving through water is a lot like an aircraft moving through the air, so it creates a wake vortex behind in the same way a plane does."

"So this is just turbulence?" Ryan said.

"Got it in one, mate."

Lea gazed through the tiny window, amazed. "I wonder how far ahead Sala is?"

"We'll find out soon enough," Hawke said. "I can see a change in the light up ahead. They must have surfaced in an underground lake and fired up some glow sticks. No way is that natural light at this depth."

Moments later Lea was the first to see it – the hull of the Migaloo was fifty meters ahead and perfectly still in the water like a dead whale-shark. "There they are!"

Hawke nodded and his response was immediate, shutting down the engines and filling the ballast tanks with compressed air. Slowly and silently the mini sub made its way to the surface, and when they breached it they saw they had been right – they were in a cavernous underwater lake.

"I can't see Sala," Lea said.

Hawke peered through the porthole. "No, but judging by the green glow coming from that tunnel over there it's pretty obvious where he's gone. Let's get moving."

Hawke unscrewed the hatch and they clambered out of the mini sub and dropped down onto the shore of the underwater lake. They were at least a hundred yards from the Migaloo and hidden behind a stalagmite-covered ledge protruding from the cave wall, so Hawke considered it safe to fire up a glow stick.

They stuck together as they moved deeper into the complex, and if this place really was Valhalla, the Hall of the Slain, then it was greater than any of them could ever have imagined in their wildest dreams. Despite it having slid beneath the ocean floor, its construction from the interior of the cliff cave was still obvious, and most of the impressive structure had maintained its integrity.

They made their way along the tunnel in which they had seen the glow of Sala's glow sticks. At the end of it there was still so sign of the Andorran, or Smets, but they were now face to face with the deepest cave hole Hawke had ever seen.

He was staring at an enormous gorge complete with not one but two powerful underground waterfalls. Towering above them was a cave hall hundreds of feet high, its ceiling adorned with monstrous stalactites which twisted and pointed to the ground like melted fingers.

Lea was amazed. "This is more than a cave system, Joe – this is a bloody underground canyon!"

"Look!" Ryan cried. "A bridge!"

They made their way across the bridge – a rickety affair which was strung across the gorge hundreds of feet high between two ledges carved into the side of the towering cave hall.

From here they moved through a short second tunnel at the end of which their short journey came to an end.

They had reached Valhalla.

From their elevated position at the tunnel mouth, they were able to look down at the legendary location from on-high, and what they saw stunned each of them into silence.

They were looking at what had once been an opulent hall, with ornate architecture stretching from a marble floor all the way to a vaulted ceiling covered in intricate frescos portraying gods and goddesses. All around the room were doors and archways leading to separate tunnels, and with no sign of the enemy, they presumed Sala must have disappeared into one of them.

It was more beautiful than any of them had imagined but the entire place was disjointed, broken into two by the force of the landslide which had sent it tumbling into the freezing embrace of the Arctic Ocean. It was as if an enormous step had been designed into the middle of the main hall, or it had suffered a massive earthquake. Now, what had once been the most sacred place of the Norse gods resembled the wreck of the Titanic and a sense of broken, sad decay settled over everything like a dust.

Despite that feeling, Hawke knew they had finally hit the jackpot.

ROB JONES

Everywhere they looked they saw treasure far beyond anything they had ever seen before, up to and including the vault of Poseidon and the tomb of the Thunder God. Towering golden idols of gods and goddesses none of them recognized, piles of silver and gold jewellery – goblets, plates, knives, and countless weapons – shields, swords and axes.

"A veritable shimmering golden hoard!" Victoria said, her eyes sparkling like twin diamonds.

"This place is something else," Lea said, her voice trailing into the distant darkness. Crowning it all were the very walls themselves which sparkled and shone golden in their flashlights. "Are those walls made of gold?"

"They're made of golden shields," Ryan said, shining his torch on them and then up to the ceiling. "The Skáldskaparmál, the ancient dialogue between the Norse god of the sea Aegir and Bragi, the poetry god, said that when the gods gathered here the light from their swords would illuminate the feast, reflecting off the golden walls."

Hawke swept his flashlight over the vast hall as the others began to explore among the piles of treasure. He could hardly believe what she was seeing – what had started off as an investigation into a murder had turned into the discovery of the millennium. Everywhere he looked was a cornucopia of priceless ancient relics and treasure, but more than that, this was Valhalla, the legendary Hall of the Slain. He still had trouble believing any of this could be real.

This was yet more solid evidence that the history they thought they knew was wrong. The gold, swords and axes all around them told another story altogether, a story where myth was reality and reality was myth, a story that others had known all along, and worked

244

ceaselessly to suppress from the common knowledge of mankind.

"All I wanted was enough loot to buy a little island of my own," Scarlet said in amazement. "But there's enough filthy lucre here to buy a much bigger island – like Hawaii maybe."

"If anyone else said that," Hawke said from deeper in the cave, "I'd presume it was a joke, but with you I just can't be sure."

"I'm going to get my island, Joe, and when I do it's going to be paradise. You'd love it, I know you would."

"I'm not sure Hawke would love an island with a ratio of five hundred men to one woman," Ryan said.

Scarlet shone her flashlight right into Ryan's face. "If you're that worried about it you can always come and make that ratio five hundred to two."

"Yes, very drole, and get that bloody thing out of my face."

"Give it a rest, you two!" Lea said.

They made their way down a series of cracked stone steps toward the hall. Hawke tried to imagine what it would have been like when it was still in the cliff looking out to see. After a few stumbles on the crumbly steps, they finally reached the main hall, and Hawke thought he heard a noise emanating from one of the tunnels branching off from the main area. He spun around and shone his torch down it.

They were looking along a passageway which stretched away into gloom. A statue loomed at the end of it.

"Ryan?"

Ryan shone his torch down into the darkness. "Thor. That part of Valhalla must be Bilskirnir – Thor's Hall. According to the legends, each of the gods and goddesses had their own part of Valhalla reserved for them after they fell in battle. That's what all these arches are about."

"This is unbelievable!" Lea said.

"And what's that down there?" Victoria said in awe.

"What is it?" Ryan said.

Victoria was mesmerized. "Oh my goodness – it's the Warrior's Field – the Folkvang..."

"The what?" Ryan asked.

"I read about it in my research – it's where the Norse goddess of love and prophecies resides – the ninth hall of Valhalla. It's called the Sessrumnir or the Room of Seats." She began to wander toward the glow of the tunnel. "If I'm remembering right, it's where... it's where Freyja would decide who among the slain would belong to her and who would go to Odin... I *must* see it!"

"Stay where you are!" Hawke said. "No one wanders off while Sala's on the loose."

Hawke meandered further into the darkness and moments later he called out to them. "Look here!" He shone his flashlight up on the far wall and illuminated a massive statue which towered at least fifty feet above the ground.

"What is it?" Scarlet asked.

"*Who* is it, you mean," Lea said.

"It's Odin, the highest god in Norse mythology," Ryan said. "He has many names – Havi, Grim, Vak – you name it, but it call comes back to the same thing, and the same god."

Their flashlight beams danced over the statue's ancient, carved face, up his long beard and over the solid, square bridge of his powerful nose. Two blank stone eyes stared out across the vast hall.

"Definitely in the right place then," Scarlet said with a low whistle.

"You could say that!" Lea said.

"Rich's going to wet his pants when he hears about this," Scarlet said. "And this time, can we *please* get some of this stuff back to Elysium before that little shit Kosinski turns up and takes it back to DC?"

Hawke turned and swept his torch over the group. "Where the hell has Vikki gone?"

She was nowhere to be seen. "She must have gone to see the Folkvang," Ryan said.

"Damn it!" said Hawke. "I'll have to go and get her."

"Wait – check this out!" Lea said, shining her torch across another statue. This one was a woman, standing nobly in the dark silence. On the pedestal at the base of the statue was a large wooden box, untouched by decay.

"I wonder what's inside it?" Scarlet said, leaning forward.

"Drop your weapons and stay where you are!" a voice said from behind them.

Hawke spun around to see Francisco Sala standing in the archway to Thor's Hall.

"Sala!"

The Andorran stared at them coldly. "Welcome to Ragnarök – the Doom of the Gods."

CHAPTER THIRTY

Lexi Zhang moved with no sound at all across the plush rug of Eden's study. Very nicely appointed, she thought. The walls were smooth white plaster in keeping with the tropical feel of the place, but they were decorated with the trappings of various ECHO missions – a beautiful Mayan tapestry, an antique Indian sculpture of Shiva, and above the desk what looked suspiciously like Raphael's missing *Portrait of a Young Man*, but she couldn't be sure.

But either way, the treasures in this one room were all the evidence she needed to confirm that the ECHO team seemed to know their way around the world and got results. It also explained their long-running feud with Eddie Kosinski at the CIA. His little collection was well-known to the Chinese intelligence agency, who also, of course, had their own to keep them busy.

She drew closer. This was the moment that would change everything, but then as Lao Tzu once said, if you do not change direction, you may end up where you're heading. Very gently, she placed the barrel of the gun on the sleeping man's right temple.

"*Bang...*" she said quietly with a voice as soft as silk.

Eden opened his right eye and smiled warmly at her. Then he opened his other eye and gave his wristwatch a quick glance. "Faster than Maria, but slower than Hawke."

"Damn it!" she said, lowering the paintball gun to her side. "I really wanted to beat Joe!"

Eden got to his feet and shook her enthusiastically by the hand. "Congratulations, Lexi. You've passed the final selection test. You're now formally in the ECHO team!"

She was pleased, but still reluctant to show it. Tonight she had joined a new family, but she had also left an old one – a powerful one, and that meant she would have made powerful enemies in the process.

"So how do you feel?" he asked, clapping a congratulatory hand on her shoulder.

"I'm happy, I think."

Eden laughed. "I'd never expect a straight answer from you, Lexi. Shall we go and join the others? I'm sure they'll want to congratulate you."

"Why not?" she said with a smile.

They gathered in the main living area and Ben brought everyone a cold beer. He was still covered in red paint from the attack on the roof. "Those damned paintballs hurt more than you think!"

"So how did you do it?" Maria asked. She too still had the remnants of the paint on her top, as did Alex, but both women were overjoyed at the new addition to the team.

"Simple." Lexi tapped her temple. "I simply set up a scenario in my mind in which Beijing had ordered me to kill all of you. We are trained never to fail a mission and always to see it through to its end. I told myself my mission was your assassinations and planned it exactly as I would if it were any other professional hit. This way, I took no risks and gave it my all." She lowered her voice and sipped some of the lager. "And this is why you are all covered in red paint tonight."

"I'm glad you're on our side!" Alex said.

After a pause, Lexi replied. "So am I."

"And by the way," Maria said, feigning a frown, "that second shot really hurt. I thought we agreed no hitting above the waist?"

"We did," Lexi said coolly. "But where's the fun in that?"

*

Eden yawned and sipped his beer. It had been a long day, but now at least one of his objectives had been achieved – Lexi Zhang had turned her backs on the Chinese Ministry of State Security and formally joined ECHO. He knew she would have made serious enemies in doing so, but they were a family and he took nothing more seriously than the responsibility of protecting that family. She would make a quality asset – of that he was sure – and he knew everyone in the existing team had voted unanimously for her inclusion into the covert organization. Her flawless attack of the island tonight would only compound the respect they all felt for her.

Now his mind drifted to Lea and the others. They had flown to Florida to help Victoria Hamilton-Talbot, but for some reason they were now somewhere in the Arctic Circle – at least that is where he had to presume they were because that was their location when they had last contacted Elysium. He knew they were more than capable of looking after themselves, and he tried to relax, but the burdens of his work weighed heavily on his mind.

In particular, he never stopped worrying about Lea. To him, she was almost like a daughter, and to make matters worse, he had recently received a call from the rest of the ECHO team who were currently in Mexico. Alfie had called to say they were still in Acapulco but their target Morton Wade had started for the jungle ahead of the anticipated schedule.

Wade was as depraved as they came, and Eden knew he couldn't let him out of his sight. That meant sending someone in after him, but most of the team were in the Arctic and neither Alfie nor Sasha were trained for the work. To say they each had a valuable skillset was the understatement of the century, but neither was ex-military and sending them into the jungle after Wade would be a death sentence. The nearest man capable of doing the job was Ben Ridgeley and he knew he'd have to send him into the jungle soon, but now the young former Para was enjoying a cold beer with Alex, Maria and their newest member Lexi.

Let him have his beer, Eden considered. He can fly into the jungle tomorrow.

CHAPTER THIRTY-ONE

Lea watched Sala creep slowly toward them in the same way she might keep an eye on a lizard as it crawled across her patio. There was something about this man that set off all her alarm bells – something about him that was different to any of the others. As he drew closer, Smets and a handful of other men joined him from the shadows.

Instinctively she drew closer to Hawke, who stood up to his full height and squared up to the Andorran. "So pleased you could join us, Sala."

"Ah, Mr Hawke and the rest of the A-Team – you're here at last."

"Yes, we got delayed because someone tried to blow up our helicopter," Scarlet said, arching an eyebrow. "Fortunately, I'm a better shot than they were so now they're all flakes of fish food."

Sala gave no reaction other than to move over to the statue of the woman and run his hands over its smooth, cold thigh. "This is Iðunn," he said, glancing at the statue of the goddess with appreciation, almost as if it had once been alive. "She was the Norse goddess of youth and apples and in both the Poetic Edda and Prose Edda she was described as the keeper of apples. You may know that these apples conferred eternal youthfulness on those who ate of their flesh."

"Now I can see why they're part of our Five a Day," Scarlet said.

Sala ignored her. "The box you see at the base of her statue is called an *eski* – an ancient container carved of ash wood in which she kept her apples. These apples were consumed by the gods when infirmity crept over them like a shadow in their old age. After eating the apples, their power and youth were restored." Sala turned to face them. "Do you know what the oldest question in the world is?"

Scarlet glanced at his long, black hair. "Are you wearing a rug?"

Sala looked at her, his eyes narrowing in confusion. "The oldest question is simple – what good is immortality without power?"

"Like you Cairo, I'm starting to wonder if megalomania is infectious," Hawke said.

Sala dismissed the Englishman with a casual wave of his hand and glanced with unadulterated avarice over the hoard of treasure, swords and other magical weapons stretching over the vast space. "The answer is that it is no good at all. Can you imagine a life of eternal poverty, or eternal impotence?"

"No, but I bet you can," Scarlet said, glancing at his groin.

"Silence! I will not be mocked! You think this is just some kind of joke, but this only tells me you know nothing about what you're tangling with. You're like stupid little children who have discovered a loaded gun in the forest and are playing with the safety catch. Eternity is a serious business, and immortality without power is worse than death."

"So that's what you're here for?" Hawke asked, his voice echoing in the hall. "You killed all those people to get to a source of the elixir here in Valhalla?"

Sala laughed. "Hardly. There is no elixir here in Valhalla – at least not the sort you found in the Ethiopian mountains."

The ECHO team shared a worried glance. "You know about that?"

Another cackle. "Of course," he said, his face turning sour. "When you broke into the tomb you cost me more than you could ever imagine."

"Imagine my sorrow," Hawke said.

As he spoke, Smets and a team of men were moving the gods' weapons from the Hall to his submarine. They seemed to be concentrating on the impressive collection of swords which had been thrust into the ground in a large circle around the Odin statue.

"I always loved the swords..." Sala said, his eyes following their progress to the sub. "And now they are all mine."

He watched with glee as the men moved on to another part of the hall.

"You're amassing quite the collection of doomsday weapons, Sala," Hawke said. "Planning something we can all enjoy?"

Sala looked at Hawke with dead eyes. "That one is Ichaival, Odin's bow, this here is the sword of Freyr... all of them mine now – all of them my weapons, with which I will defeat the real enemy of this world."

Lea nudged Hawke in the ribs.

"What is it?" he asked.

"Look – the Tarnkappe."

"Eh?"

"It's the rest of Sigurd's magical cloak," Ryan said from his other side.

They watched the surreal sight of Leon Smets carrying the rest of the cloak of invisibility from the hall and handing it to a sailor.

"Tell me," Hawke said, "Are all you megalomaniac nutcases part of some kind of club? Do you have a union or something?"

Sala ignored him. "Now, sadly it is time for you all to have an unfortunate accident." He turned to Smets. "Are the charges set?"

Smets nodded confirmation.

"Charges?" Ryan said.

"Yes, when we arrived my men planted several kilos of plastic explosives in the most vulnerable areas of this hall. When they explode the ceiling will collapse and the whole cursed place will be crushed under thousands of tons of sea water."

"What are you talking about? You can't blow this place up!"

"Why not?" Sala asked with a scowl. "It's been done before."

"What do you mean?"

"You couldn't possibly understand. You didn't honestly think this place got here because of natural coastal erosion?"

"But it's Valhalla!" Ryan said.

"And?"

"Shouldn't it be National Trust or something?" Scarlet said.

Ryan rolled his eyes. "Come on – you can't destroy the greatest archaeological find in history."

"The greatest archaeological find in history to *you* maybe," Sala said sourly. "To me this place means nothing, and today I shall do what the others failed to do all those millions of years ago and erase it from the face of the earth."

"Others?" Lea asked. "What others?"

Sala looked at her, the grin on his face turning bitter. "You have so much to learn about this world, Lea Donovan… it's a shame you have only minutes to live."

"All of this for these weapons?" Hawke said. "What next – you want to destroy the armies of the world?"

Sala laughed. "Destroying the armies of the world is easy, Englishman. Making war with a mortal is like wrestling with a puppy. No… these weapons are for a much more ancient and bloody conflict. Smets! Don't forget those axes!"

"When you're dead, Sala," Hawke said with calm determination, "I'm going to file you under Just Another Nutcase."

Sala gave a cold laugh and nodded his head. "More humor – I respect that so let me give you a little of what you seek."

Scarlet lit a cigarette and blew the smoke into the cold air. "That's very magnanimous of you, Álvaro."

Sala cut her a cold glance. "You will be dead soon enough so I see no harm in putting you out of your misery. Yes, my name is Álvaro Sala, but during the Spanish Civil War I was Francisco Rivera." He grinned as he watched their faces in reaction to his words. "When I lived in Ancient Rome they called me Atilius. Now, you get closer to the truth after so many struggles."

He leaned closer to the statue of Iðunn and caressed her smooth stone shoulder. He pulled an apple from the eski and Lea was shocked to see it glowing bright gold as if it were electric. He bit into it and chewed slowly, a warped grin spreading on his gaunt face. Seconds later his pallid complexion began to take on a rosy glow. "How would you find the taste of the truth if you really knew it – sordid horror or fantastic beauty?"

"You're crazy, Sala!" Lea yelled.

"So you have said, but I think not. Now I will bring the Doom of the Gods to this place as it should have been done so long ago."

"You mean Ragnarök?" Hawke asked.

Sala smiled with condescension. "That is a term whose meaning you could never hope to understand."

The silence following his words was met by the sounds of Victoria returning from the Folkvang. "It's amazing down there! I found the Brisingamen – the necklace jewellery of fire that Loki stole... Loki! And it's right here in my..."

Her words startled Sala, who spun around to see the English archaeologist standing right behind him with the strange, shimmering necklace in her hands.

"Ah – Dr Hamilton-Talbot, the erstwhile archaeological academic turned grubby treasure hunter. I see you got here in the end." As he spoke, one of his men collected the eski and marched away to the Migaloo with it.

"Oh *my*..." she said in her sparkling crystal Oxford accent.

Sala smirked and waved the barrel of the gun casually toward the others. "Get over there, and give me that necklace on the way."

Victoria moved slowly toward Sala. She gently extended her hand and held out the glistening jewellery.

He bit into the apple, keeping it in clenched in his mouth as he brought his hand up to take it from her. He studied it for a moment and then turned to Lea. "You never found the gods, Lea Donovan... but you will surely die among them."

"Go to hell!"

He turned to Smets. "Kill them all now, starting with Hawke."

Smets raised his gun and aimed it at Hawke's head. He pulled back the hammer and slowed his breathing.

Time seemed to stand still.

Then he swivelled and aimed the gun at Sala, firing several shots into the Andorran recluse's heart.

Sala's eyes widened in terror as he registered the betrayal and everyone jumped with shock as the shot echoed loudly in the cavernous space. Sala gasped and doubled over, clutching at his chest where the bullets had torn inside him.

Lea screamed and took a step back as Sala fell to his knees, blood bubbling up his digestive tract and pouring from his mouth. She thought he had a vaguely vampiric quality as the bloody trickled over his teeth and ran down his chin, but then he fell forward and landed with a dry thud in the dust.

"That's you over and done with, old man," Smets said.

"I wouldn't be so sure about that," Hawke said, staring at Sala's dying body with widening eyes.

Just as they had seen in the Ethiopian Highlands when Maxim Vetrov had met his maker, something very unnatural was now happening to Álvaro Sala. His corpse began to jolt as if being flooded with electricity, and his skin was turning the color of putty and beginning to fall off in strange, dry peels. He strained his head upward in search of the apple, and spying it on the floor ahead of him started to crawl toward it, but as he moved, parts of his skin began to peel away and fall off onto the floor.

Smets took a step forward and kicked the apple out of his reach.

Victoria Hamilton-Talbot staggered back in disgust, yet unable to take her eyes away from the terrible scene unfolding before her. "What the hell is this?" she asked her voice barely more than a whisper. "What the hell is going on?"

"We don't know," Hawke said, still eyeing the gun in Smets's hand. "We saw something similar in Ethiopia. It's got something to do with their lifespan."

"Their lifespan?" she asked. "What do you mean?"

Then, with what little he had of his strength, Sala pulled a black box from his pocket. It was a small remote control device with an inch-long aerial on the top and one modest silver button.

"Bloody hell!" Hawke shouted. "He's going to blow the place up!"

"I think not," Smets said calmly. "At least not yet."

The Andorran tried to take his revenge and used what was left of his exposed thumb bone to push down the small button but the Belgian hit man darted forward and kicked the device from his rapidly decomposing hand. A terrifying, hollow howl croaked from his deteriorating body as he watched Smets pick up the device, but then he died, and what was left of his face collapsed in the dirt.

CHAPTER THIRTY-TWO

"He's dead!" Ryan said.

"Yes," Scarlet said coolly. "How very inconsiderate of the old bastard."

"Did he activate it?" Lea asked.

Hawke shook his head. "No – it didn't send a signal and it would be on a timer anyway. There's no other way for them to clear the place out and then blow it without getting to safety first – am I right, Leon?"

"Shut it, Anglais."

Ryan sighed. "I'll take that as a yes – that was a close one then!"

Hawke gave him a condescending glance. "Yes, except for the simple fact that... "

Scarlet finished his sentence. "That now we know the place is rigged with explosives and we don't know how many there are, or where they are, or when Monsieur Smets here intends on detonating them."

"Exactly," Hawke said.

The veins in Sala's neck were now tearing out through his rotting skin, but there was no more blood. Now, nothing but a strange black dust poured from them as the deterioration of his dead body accelerated. Even Smets was now stunned into silence by the spectacle.

"It's like some kind of macabre time-lapse," Ryan said in amazement.

"He's right," Hawke said. "We're seeing death, but speeded up."

Now, Sala's intestines were spilling out from his skeleton and tumbling onto the floor, all dry and turning to a kind of powder.

"Whatever the hell it is," Scarlet said, "it should have a bloody 18 Certificate on it. I'll never be able to eat Pad Thai again."

Ryan pushed his glasses up on the bridge of his nose and moved cautiously forward. "We're watching some kind of organic decomposition, but on super fast-forward."

Lea raised her hand to her mouth. "Oh *God*, is that his heart?"

A desiccated heart dropped from the safety of Sala's ribcage and hit the dust with a little thump, and seconds later the remains of his skeleton crumbled to powder and began to blow away in a breeze blowing from the depths of the cavern.

"It's like what we saw with Vetrov but with one critical difference," Ryan muttered. "Vetrov died when he took the elixir, but when Sala got shot he tried to reach the apple – to take more elixir to *stop* himself from dying. What's the difference?"

"Search me," Hawke said flatly. "But we've got to find out."

"What the hell did I just see?" Victoria asked.

"You saw what happens to an immortal when he dies," Hawke said flatly.

"He needed the apples," Smets said. "Without them he couldn't have lived to wage his war." He turned to Victoria and threw her one of his pistols. "Here, ma chérie... take this."

Victoria deftly caught the gun in one hand and pointed it at Hawke, aiming the muzzle squarely at his chest.

"Bloody hell, I didn't see that one coming!" Hawke said.

Smets walked slowly toward Victoria, a malevolent smirk on his face. They held each other and kissed much to the disgust of the ECHO team.

Then Victoria Hamilton-Talbot spoke. "All of you – stay where you are and raise your hands!"

"Victoria?" Lea asked.

"Drop your weapons – now!"

Lea took her Glock from the holster and lowered it gently to the floor. Across the hall she watched Hawke and Scarlet follow suit. Ryan, who was unarmed, simply raised his arms into the air.

"Fuck me!" Ryan said. "So all that stuff back in Florida about searching for a Tesla Coil was all just blarney?"

Victoria winked at him. "Got it in one, *babe*." She waved the gun menacingly at them. "The prize was always Valhalla and its gold and weapons. Nothing less."

"What about Nate?" he asked.

"Nate and I had been searching for Valhalla together for years but I needed more than knowledge than he could give me. I knew the only way Dickie would ever send the famous ECHO team to assist me was if something terribly serious had befallen me, so Leon and I cooked up the plan to shoot him in Canada. It worked a dream."

"But you had the flash drive!" Lea said.

"Yes but we knew we would need an insurance policy if we were unable to decode it – and what better insurance policy than having the ECHO team do our work for us."

"But what about the answer-phone message – the death threat?"

"Leon, of course…"

Leon Smets gave a proud nod of his head and a theatrical bow full of mockery. "All theater, mes amis."

Lea stared with anxious uncertainty as the Englishwoman covered everyone with her gun in a slow, casual sweep before training it once again on Hawke. For the first time, Lea saw the truth in Victoria's eyes and that truth looked like hate and avarice.

"I'm sure," Victoria said quietly, "that you know what's coming next."

"You're going to perform a Vaudeville rendition of My Fair Lady?" Scarlet said.

"Shut up, and step away from your weapons – all of you!"

Scarlet turned to Hawke. "Never trust a woman with diamond ear-rings worth more than your house, that's what I always say."

"Enough! Get over there!"

Victoria waved the gun menacingly in their direction and then pointed its muzzle toward the treasure.

"So what happens now?" Hawke asked.

"I want you to start filling Sala's Triton up with some of this gold, starting right now. He wanted the weapons but all we're interested in is money."

Scarlet gave a nod of agreement. "Understandable."

"What then?" asked Hawke.

"Then, Leon and I are going back to the surface and you're going to live out the remainder of your short and pointless lives in here, with your beloved gods. When I return to the world I'll be sure to tell Dickie how brave you all were."

"And how are you getting back to the surface?" Hawke's voice was heavy with scepticism.

"I'm not a complete fool, Mr Hawke. I've trained on Tritons in the Keys, so I know what to do, and there's always Leon."

"We'll just follow in our mini-sub."

"I don't think so, because I'm going to destroy it before I leave, and I know the Migaloo is useless to you because it requires a full crew to pilot it. Now, get going!"

Hawke picked up a large golden plate studded with emeralds and handed it to Lea who in turn handed it to Scarlet. Slowly they started their march back to the subs.

Lea looked over her shoulder at the archaeologist. "Who are you Victoria? Is that even your real name?"

"Of course it is, I'm not bloody Poison Ivy, you know. Just get on with it – I don't want to spend all day here. Leon and I have an early retirement to fly to."

*

Hawke heaved a trunk of gold over to the Migaloo and began to load the precious cargo inside the Triton mini submersible in the back of it. They had been slaving away for an hour now, hauling various pieces of treasure and other significant artefacts from the Hall to the lake where the subs were moored up. If Victoria's plan was executed how she wanted and she forced him to destroy their mini-sub, that would cut off their only other escape route.

He looked up as he worked and watched the traitor as she surveyed their labor. She was now standing beside Leon Smets on a ledge at the side of the cavern running parallel to the water and keeping them under strict surveillance. He wasn't exactly sure how Sir Richard Eden knew this woman but he thought maybe it was time for the old man to review his list of friends.

While the former SBS man's mind raced with potential tactics – and none of them seemed particularly conducive to a successful escape – he saw not everyone shared his concerns. Even under threat of immediate execution, Ryan couldn't contain his excitement as they uncovered one amazing ancient relic after another.

"Check out this incredible spear," he said, peering inside one of the chests. "How did they make such a thing?"

Scarlet sighed "As pressing as that question is Ryan – and believe me it will certainly keep me up many a night – I think we have other concerns at the moment."

"Hurry up, you idiots!" Victoria shouted.

After filling the Triton until it was almost dangerously overloaded, Victoria had Hawke pilot it out of the Migaloo and position it near the underwater exit where they had arrived. He sailed it past their mini-sub and returned to shore.

"Right," Victoria said, turning to Hawke. "Get the C4 out of your bag in the mini-sub and set them to explode in thirty seconds or I shoot Lea." She turned the gun on Lea and cocked the hammer.

Hawke clenched his jaw but knew he had no alternative. Following Victoria's orders to the letter, he climbed inside their mini-sub and pulled some explosives from his C4 supply. Then he placed them on the most vulnerable points in the sub and inserted blasting caps.

As he clambered out of the sub, Victoria flicked her hand at him. "Give me the detonator, now."

He walked toward her, ready to take her down if he had half a chance, but she wasn't taking any chances. "Not so fast, Superman," she said, taking a step back. "Put it on the floor and kick it over to me."

He did as he was told and a moment later she held the detonator in her hand. She turned to face them and raised the detonator. "Any funny business and I'll blow up your little sub right now! Now get back in the Hall!"

Lea was closest to Victoria as they turned to leave, and without any warning she lunged at her, but missed the gun and fell forward onto her knees.

Victoria turned the gun on Lea and squeezed the trigger. Ryan leaped in front of her and tried to grab the weapon but the archaeologist fired three more times. The sound of the gunpowder exploding so close to them in the enclosed space was deafening.

Ryan fell to the floor in a heap, and in the chaos Hawke punched Smets hard. In one move he smashed his jaw and disarmed him but the Belgian darted into a tunnel.

Victoria fired blindly at the others but quickly ran out of bullets. With no time to reload so close to the enemy, she turned on her heel and sprinted into the darkness of one of the tunnels behind her. In her panic she had dropped the detonation device for the C4 Hawke had put in the mini-sub.

"I'll have that," Scarlet said, snatching it from the ground.

"She's getting away!" screamed Lea.

Hawke watched as Victoria receded into the darkness while Scarlet ran to Ryan. She pulled up his Batman t-shirt and after studying the wound she looked up at Hawke with a rare expression of anxious doubt on her face. "This is bad, Joe."

Hawke's mind filled with a desperate déjà vu as he recalled the terrible day Lea had gotten shot in the Tomb of Eternity. He couldn't believe it was all happening again, but now to Ryan instead.

"Lea – get into your Dad's research, fast. We know he was a student of Norse healing and we're in the heart of Valhalla. Scarlet – look after Ryan while Lea's looking for something to help him – and don't forget that Smets could be anywhere."

"Sure, but what about you?"

"I'm going give Lady Victoria Hamilton-Talbot a course in SBS etiquette."

CHAPTER THIRTY-THREE

Hawke crossed the bridge by the waterfalls and sprinted for the tunnel leading to the subs. Smets could wait, because right now the priority was stopping the treacherous Victoria. He knew she was planning on taking the Triton back to the shore where presumably the plan was to catch up with Trond and tell him the rest of them had been killed. That didn't leave him much time to stop her.

If she got away in the Triton and somehow destroyed their mini-sub on the way out, it could block the exit tunnel and they would be trapped. Underwater cave systems like these had viciously strong currents and there was a reason why cave diving was considered a potentially deadly sport. He knew even he would have a seriously hard job getting out of this one, never mind Lea and Scarlet. A badly wounded Ryan Bale stood no chance at all.

He reached the other end of the tunnel a few moments later, and was just in time to see Victoria Hamilton-Talbot sprinting across the cave toward the subs. The Triton packed with gold was at the far end, but the mini-sub packed with C4 was closer and when he opened fire on her she had no choice. Desperate for cover and with the Triton another thirty seconds' sprint away she clambered inside the explosive-laden mini-sub. She had obviously decided to cut her losses and try to escape with her life, leaving both the gold and her lover behind to face oblivion.

Charming, he thought.

He drew his gun and fired single-burst shots at the woman as she retreated inside the vessel, carefully avoiding striking the sub. She saw him and didn't hesitate to return fire, blasting her gun in his direction.

Bullets whistled past his head and smashed into the cave wall behind him. He dived to the gritty floor, softening his landing with a classic parkour break-fall roll. Using his shoulder to redirect his forward momentum he pivoted over and came to a stop on the other side of the tunnel behind the cover of an enormous boulder.

He rubbed the dirt from his eyes and ducked as she fired another burst of bullets at him. He didn't know how he was going to do it, but he had to take her out of the game.

*

Lea frantically ran toward Eir's Hall. She had seen enough bullet wounds in her time to know Ryan's were fatal, at least from any conventional medical point of view. His only chance was if she could find something from this weird world of the gods like the elixir that had saved her life in Ethiopia. She knew Sala had sent the apples back to the Migaloo but with no idea what they would do to Ryan's mortal physiology she decided to trust her father instead.

Hurriedly, she burst into the small chamber and started searching for anything she could think of that might be able to help Ryan. Her father was a good man – she knew it in her heart – and if he had researched Eir in her capacity as the goddess of medicine and healing she knew there must be something in here that could help Ryan.

She flicked her phone and desperately scanned through the uploaded copies of her father's research files. Somewhere in here she knew she would find the answer. Scrolling past the unsettling reference by her dad to the Athanatoi, she navigated to the section on Eir. Her eyes crawled over the words as she wildly sought a way to save her former husband's life.

*

Scarlet held Ryan's head in her lap as he continued to bleed out over the dusty, ancient flagstones of Valhalla. His face was ashen now, and covered in a thin veil of sweat.

He struggled to speak through the rapid, shallow breaths caused by his failing heart. "I knew I'd get you one day, Cairo."

For once, Scarlet Sloane couldn't think of anything to say. She was watching a valued member of the team die in her arms, but it was more than that. Ryan was young – he had his whole life ahead of him.

"Stay with me, Ryan."

"Why, are you going somewhere?"

She laughed, and hoped its fraudulence wasn't obvious to Ryan. "Not me, you tit. I'm talking to you so you don't go and do something stupid like croak in my arms."

"Hey Scarlet," Ryan said, his voice weak now. "What did Arnold Schwarzenegger say when a man made from spaghetti served him coffee?"

"Stop talking Ryan – for once in your life."

"Pasta barista, baby!"

Scarlet looked at him stony-faced. "You don't say things like that in public, do you?"

Ryan coughed some blood and gripped her hand. "I'm scared, Cairo."

"No need, Ryan. We're going to get you through this. Lea's on the case and you trust her, right?"

"As long as there's no cooking involved, then yes."

"That's the spirit."

She noticed he was starting to pass out and she gently tapped the side of his face. "Stay with me, Ryan. Lea's almost here."

She looked over her shoulder but saw Lea was nowhere in sight. She had no idea where she was or what she was doing – she could have been shot and killed by Smets or Victoria for all she knew – but she had to keep Ryan alive as long as possible. "Did I ever tell you about the time I went to Rich's place in the country?"

"He has a place in the country?"

"Sure – just outside Oxford."

"A little two-up, two-down affair, no doubt?"

"A little more than that. It's got fifteen bedrooms and it's set on ninety acres."

Ryan began wheezing. "He's not one to do things by half, is he?"

"I only ever went there once. It was when he was thinking about recruiting me to ECHO."

"So just after the last Ice Age?"

"Do you want to hear this story or not?"

"Sorry…" more coughing.

"He'd just had a terrific row with the Prime Minister because they'd decided to cut his department over in MI5. His valet accidentally backed my Jag over his topiary peacock – you wouldn't think a box hedge could make such a mess of a color-coded bumper."

"Was he angry?"

"Not nearly enough – he said it was barely a scratch."

"I meant about the cuts to his department, Scarlet."

Scarlet knew what he meant, and smiled. Making jokes in tough times was what she did best, but this was testing her to the limits. She looked at her watch and then back up to Ryan's cold, clammy face. He was running out of time fast.

*

Hawke kept up the assault, his bullets ricocheting off the sub's hatch and flying into the roof of the cave with a gentle thud. In response, Victoria emptied her magazine at him, firing wildly until the bullets were gone, and then she slammed shut the hatch and began to turn the wheel to secure the airlock.

With no longer any danger of getting shot, Hawke sprinted for the sub which had now begun to move slowly away from the lake's shore and out into the middle of the water.

He launched himself from the shore's edge and leaped with all his might at the mini-sub, slamming into its smooth exterior and sliding down the hull casing toward the icy water. He reached out with his arms for anything that would arrest his fall but the hull was perfectly hydrodynamic so he continued his slide.

He scrambled diagonally across the casing with a view to using the bow planes as a foot rest, and it worked. He came to a stop on the large, metal plane and caught his breath. Inside the mini-sub he saw Victoria's face lit low in the orange glow of the internal lights. A fiendish smile crossed her lips when she saw how he had saved himself and she instantly moved to the controls.

Seconds later the bow planes tipped forward, presenting the former Commando with two problems. The first being his footrest was now at a sharp angle and much harder to cling to, and the second being that the sub was diving under the water.

He knew he had only seconds left before she took the mini-sub beneath the waves and then she would be gone forever. At the front of the sub now, he was able to walk up the shallower degree of the bow casing and run up to the safety of the deck. Inside, Victoria looked panicked and speeded up the dive, but it was too late.

Hawke was now on the central portion of the sub's deck and climbing up what passed for a conning tower on the mini-sub. He began to unwind the airlock wheel and then he opened the hatch. With the freezing water now up to his knees, he dropped down inside the sub to find Victoria waiting for him.

She was turning in her chair at the controls and pointing a gun at him in the cramped space. All around he could see the C4 he had positioned but without the detonation device it was of no more use than modelling clay – and the device was in Scarlet's hands.

The sub continued to dive but Hawke realized with some degree of relief that the gun in her hand was the same SIG Sauer P226 she had used to keep him pinned down on the shore. He decided to gamble that she couldn't possibly have reloaded it while she was diving the sub, and lunged forward.

She squeezed the SIG's trigger, but nothing more happened than classic dry firing as the hammer struck the empty chamber.

"Allow me," he said, knocking the gun from her hand. He bent over and picked it up.

She frowned. "I always thought you had a disarming personality. Listen – there's no need for us fight each other. What do you say to us getting out of here together? I can be very *accommodating*."

She leaned forward and ran her hands up his arms. Moving closer now, she parted her lips and tried to kiss him.

Hawke pushed her away with the tip of his forefinger and scowled.

"Sorry, but I have a long-standing policy never to date shits who shoot my friends."

Crestfallen, she flounced back to her chair, but then snatched up a spanner and took a chunky swipe at Hawke. He ducked and the heavy tool struck the air-conditioning controls with a loud clang.

Hawke reacted in a heartbeat and rammed the butt of the pistol into her face, knocking her back into her chair. She righted her balance and wiped the blood from her mouth.

"You should never hit a lady!"

"Thanks. When I see a lady I'll be sure not to hit her."

Before she could reply, he turned the pressurization system on and smashed the controls to pieces with his butt of the SIG. With the C4 option unavailable, and no rounds left in the gun he had only one choice. "You shot a very good friend of mine. I don't let things like that pass."

"What are you doing?" she asked, her eyes wide with fear as the realization of her fate stretched over her like a dusk shadow.

Hawke picked up the spanner she had tried to kill him with and tested its weight and length in his hand. "At least we get to find out how you react under some real pressure. Goodbye, Victoria."

He swung the hatch down and jammed it shut with the spanner. Then he jumped into the water and swam back to the shore. Behind him, just as the mini-sub sank beneath the waves he heard an enormously deep explosion as the pressure inside it reached its maximum level and detonated the vessel.

Without looking back, he sprinted back along the tunnel toward Ryan and Scarlet.

*

Lea ran her eyes over the tiny iPhone screen and muttered a thank you to her father. She was looking at a scanned and uploaded image of a pencil sketch her dad had made decades earlier. It was a flower, with delicate apple-white petals and a thin fern-green stem. Beneath the drawing were the words: *Eirflower & the healing ritual*.

She had no clue what an Eirflower was, but she knew Eir was the goddess of medicine and she liked the sound of a healing ritual. By the time she got to the small chamber she knew what she was looking for.

Eir's Hall turned out to be a modest affair but no different from the other chambers and halls they had seen since their arrival in Valhalla. There was a statue of the goddess at the far end, looming peacefully above a generous hoard of belongings and tributes. It was surrounded at its base by a ring of green and white candles, unlit and standing silent sentry in the ecclesiastical reverence of the icy chamber.

Acutely aware that Ryan's time was rapidly running out, Lea began her search for the magical Eirflower. She had only her father's rough sketch to go on, and fighting back the urge to ask how he knew of its existence, she moved with speed and diligence through the articles strewn around the chamber.

She lifted a bag of silver coins from its place on the floor beside the statue, sure that she had uncovered the resting place of the ancient flower. She found nothing but dust and continued her search.

Lea grew more anxious with each passing second as she rummaged around the chamber in the gloom. Everything in here was lit a ghostly green color by the glow stick she had placed at the pedestal of Eir's statue. There was no danger of it burning out – it was brand new and would last for hours – but the idea of Leon Smets creeping up behind her in the dark was a persistent fear she couldn't shake off.

She checked her watch and knew that time was running out fast. She too had seen the gunshot wounds when Scarlet had lifted Ryan's t-shirt, torn into his stomach in three savage punch-holes. She had watched men bleed to death in the desert in her time in the army and had a pretty good idea that Ryan was on borrowed time.

Then, in the green luminescent glow of the stick, she lifted an enormous golden feast plate to find a low, wooden chest tucked out of sight around the rear of the statue. She lifted the lid and the chest creaked open like an old Brigantine weathering a vicious squall, but inside she found what she was looking for.

CHAPTER THIRTY-FOUR

"You get anything?"

Scarlet was staring up at Lea with a look of grave concern on her face. She was still holding Ryan's head in her lap but now he was unconscious and as pale as a ghost.

"I think so, yes."

Lea dropped to her knees and showed Scarlet the Eirflower. It shimmered in the darkness of the hall.

"What the hell is that?" Scarlet said eyeing the strange flower with contempt.

"The Eirflower. According to Dad's research, the goddess of healing used it in some kind of ritual to cure the gods when they fell ill."

"But Ryan isn't a god."

Lea looked at her. "It's all we have, Scarlet."

Scarlet nodded in response. "And how does it work?"

"According to Dad's notes, the eirflower ritual involved making it into some kind of wine or tea."

"Excellent," Scarlet said with a palpable absence of enthusiasm. "I'll just put the kettle on while you open the Hobnobs. I thought I saw a packet behind that boulder."

"No time for your attitude right now, Scarlet. *Obviously* we can't make a sodding tea out of it, but the point is it was *imbibed* by the person requiring the ritual. Dad also says the consumption of the eirflower was accompanied by a sacred promise to take better care of your health and live a healthier life."

"Seriously?"

"That's the way Eir did business, apparently."

"I can accept that. My life moved into the Twilight Zone a long time ago."

Lea plucked a petal from the glistening flower and swallowed with anticipation as she pushed the flower inside Ryan's lips. "We promise Ryan will live a healthier life."

"And stop wanking," Scarlet said.

Lea shot a sharp glance at her. "Oh for *fuck's* sake, Scarlet! Can't you see he's dying?"

"You don't have to tell me, darling. I've been the one sitting with him while you were digging the garden for this petunia. It's just my way of dealing with shitty situations."

"I'm sorry."

"How's he doing?"

They both turned to see Hawke. He was jogging to a stop a few yards behind them and now crouching down beside Ryan.

"We don't know," Lea said. "I've given him a sacred healing flower. It used to keep the gods alive when they were injured so we're keeping our fingers crossed."

"And we had to pray that he would live a healthier life," Scarlet said sarcastically. "Apparently it helps."

"What about Her Nibs?" Lea asked.

"She was squeezed for time," Hawke said. "So she won't be bothering us again."

Then they heard the sound of Ryan coughing – gently at first and then more loudly. Some color had begun to bring his face back to life, and his eyes began to blink open.

"Ryan?"

"I... where...?"

"Don't talk," Lea said, pushing his hair away from his face. "We gave you a magical healing flower and it looks like it's working.

Scarlet leaned forward, her voice suddenly serious. "But only on the condition that you stop wan…"

Suddenly a savage explosion ripped through the other end of the cave system, nearly knocking them over. Chunks of rock crumbled away from the roof of the Hall and fell to the floor with a mighty smack.

"Sala's revenge," Hawke said. "That little bastard Smets must have hit the timer."

"We have to get out of here!" Scarlet said. "If that thing blows the rocks down between us and the sub we're all dead."

Another explosion tore through the cavern, this time bringing down tons of rocks and blocking the tunnel between the fleeing ECHO team and the subs in the first cave.

Hawke raised an eyebrow. "You were saying?"

While aware of the explosions and the conversation between Hawke and Scarlet, Lea's mind was still focussed on Ryan. She watched in awe as the bullet holes in his stomach began to fade and heal over, almost like watching a wound heal on fast-forward.

"That's what it looked like when we gave you the elixir back in the Tomb of Eternity," Hawke said, placing his hand on her shoulder. "But not as fast."

Lea stared at the process in amazement. "So whatever's in this flower must have similar qualities to the elixir."

"Which is why we'll be taking the flower back to Elysium for analysis," Scarlet said, turning to Ryan. "How's the patient?"

"I'm feeling much better," he said, while still obvious weak. "Another kiss from you should see me right." He pouted at her and his closed his eyes.

"In your dreams, boy."

"Ah – but what dreams…"

"Urghh!"

"Okay," Hawke said firmly. "Time for us to get out of here. Ryan – can you walk?"

Ryan nodded. "I think so, but I'll need help."

"Good job you've got your mates here then," Hawke said, helping the younger man to his feet. "Let's get back to the lake."

"Great plan," Lea said. "The only problem being the hundreds of tons of rock that are now in our way."

"Not a problem," Ryan said quietly. "But we're going to need the Tyrfing."

"The *what?*" Scarlet said.

"The Tyrfing," Ryan repeated. "It's a magical sword…" he stopped and opened his eyes wide. "I don't know what's going on inside me right now but it feels…*weird.*"

"The sword, Ryan," Lea said. "Focus on the sword."

"Ah yes – the Tyrfing. It's a magical sword mentioned in what's called the Tyrfing Cycle. Svafrlami was none other than Odin's grandson, and after trapping Dvalinn and Durin, the two dwarves, inside their cave…"

"Are you going to recite the whole of Lord of the Rings?" Scarlet asked impatiently. "Because if you are we really don't have time and I don't see the relevance."

"It's not the Lord of the Rings, it's Norse mythology, which means it's real, and the *relevance* is that Odin's grandson ordered the dwarves to forge him a sword that could cut through iron and *stone* – capiche?"

Scarlet gave him a look. "I think I preferred it when you were unconscious."

"And how do we recognize this sword?" Hawke asked.

"Luckily, neither Sala nor Victoria got around to swiping it – it's over there!"

Ryan pointed a trembling finger to a heavy sword leaning against a pile of gold coins.

Hawke snatched it up and weighed it in his hands. "Pretty solid piece of kit."

He stepped over to the fallen rocks and swung the sword above his head, preparing to strike the rock. It made a whistling sound as it cut through the air.

"By the Power of Grayskull!" Scarlet shouted.

Hawke lowered the sword and gave her a look. "Really? Now?"

"Sorry. It's a problem I'm working on. Ask Lea."

Hawke shook his head and swung the sword again, this time bringing it crashing into the newly fallen rocks. They burst apart as if he had shelled them with a heavy-duty mortar cannon. He swung again and a third time, each time smashing his way deeper into the rock, then with the final swing the rock-face burst open and water rushed through the crack into the cave.

"Ah…"

Rapidly the tunnel flooded with water.

"What is it with you and water, Joe?" Scarlet asked as she desperately clung on to a rock.

"What do you mean?"

"Wherever you go there always seems to be an increased risk of getting caught in a flooded cave."

"Rubbish!"

"It is not rubbish. If Sammy Cahn were writing lyrics for you instead of Sinatra we'd all be walking around singing Come Drown with Me."

"You know what, Cairo?" Hawke said, pushing water out of his eyes, "If you were twice as funny as you think you are, you'd still be absolutely and totally not funny."

"Hey!" Lea snapped. "Maybe a little more looking for an escape route and a little less hilarious banter?"

"Hilarious?" Ryan said. "I've seen more hilarious documentaries on the bubonic plague." He tried to laugh at his own joke but the pains in his arm and stomach brought him up hard with a wheezing cry.

"Don't you start, you pathetic little ferret!" Scarlet said.

"Hey! I am not pathetic!"

"Everyone, can it!" Hawke said. "Lea's right – we need to focus on getting out of here... I think I see a way!"

With the torrent of spray in his face, Hawke strained to climb through the waterfall and clamber up inside the narrow fissure at the top of the cave. Looking into the rushing water he could just make out the vague but indisputable pattern of very dim lights up ahead. "Must be the glow sticks in the cavern with the subs," he said.

Hawke pulled himself up and through the narrow crack, straining his eyes to find an exit from the chamber. Forcing himself through the water he pushed his head out the other side and saw the Triton sitting innocuously in the water.

"All right!" he called back. "Follow me – we're back in the first cave with the subs. This water is draining out of the lake."

They followed behind him and found themselves in the large cave at the start of the complex. Sure enough – there was the Triton.

They moved over to it as fast as they could go while carrying Ryan.

"We have a problem," Scarlet said, looking above her head. As she spoke an enormous crack appeared in the roof and a massive jet of water rushed down into the cavern. "Just like Sala threatened – the place is flooding with sea water!"

The crack grew wider and the water increased in velocity. Now it was up to their knees and rising fast.

Hawke looked at the water rapidly approaching his waist. "We have lots of problems Cairo. Tell me yours."

"The Triton's full of Victoria's loot. It's gold, Joe. It weighs a ton and we haven't got time to unload it. There's only room for two people in here."

Hawke thought fast. "Not a problem – you and Ryan take it and Lea and I will take the Migaloo."

"I thought Victoria said that needed a crew?" Ryan said.

"Nah, she was talking out of her arse."

"Great plan," Scarlet said. "Except I don't know how to drive the Triton."

Hawke shook his head. "SAS…" He climbed inside and activated the Triton, quickly explaining how to control it. "It's simple, and we don't have time to piss about so hurry up!"

"I saw a TV show on this," Ryan said. "I know what to do."

"God help us," Scarlet muttered.

They climbed inside and Scarlet gripped the controls as Ryan closed the hatch and sealed it. Hawke and Lea watched it slip beneath the surface of the underground lake and then they swam toward the Migaloo.

*

Scarlet followed Hawke's instructions to the letter. She had never piloted a Triton or any other kind of mini-sub

283

before and knew this wasn't the time to screw things up. It was, he had explained, only a case of steering the thing through the tunnel with the diving planes and horizontal rudders and then blowing the seawater out of the ballast tanks with compressed air when you wanted to surface. He had shown her how to do that and it seemed simple enough, she hoped. That plus Ryan's helpful Discovery Channel contributions meant they were able to make their way to safety.

She steered the small sub through the tunnel and finally she saw what passed for daylight in this part of the world. In her excitement, she over-steered a shallow bend in the tunnel and grated the side of the sub along the rock. A terrible, ear-piercing screeching sound filled the tiny cabin.

"Women drivers..."

Scarlet looked at Ryan. "What did you just say?"

Ryan swallowed. "Um, that you're a first-rate submariner and thanks for saving my life."

Scarlet's scowl turned to a smirk. "That's what I thought."

On the surface now, she brought the machine to a stop and called into Elysium to report. Eden was briefing Ben and Lexi on Mexico, but Alex was there to take the call.

The line was crackly but the message easily understood. Vincent Reno was out of his operation and he'd regained consciousness.

"I knew the old bastard would pull through," Scarlet said, relieved.

Alex smiled and continued. "You might also like to tell Hawke that I have it on very good authority that the British Foreign Secretary will be publicly announcing his retirement in a few days' time."

Scarlet took a moment to digest the news. She knew what this would mean for Hawke. "Matheson's bailing out, eh?"

"Yes, and I know Joe has some unfinished business with him."

You can say that again, she thought. "I'll pass it on when they catch up with us, Alex."

Scarlet ended the call and sighed.

"All good?" Ryan asked.

"That depends on who you are," Scarlet said.

Ryan looked confused. "What do you mean?"

"Matheson's retiring."

"Ah."

"Exactly."

Scarlet put a call through to Trond and arranged for him to fly out and pick them up, then she opened the hatch and stood with her upper body out in the fresh air.

"So what now?" Ryan asked.

"I'm going to smoke a cigarette," she said. "And then count my gold."

"You mean *our* gold."

She smiled and dragged on the cigarette. "Yes, of course I do."

CHAPTER THIRTY-FIVE

Barents Sea

A few minutes later Hawke was taking Sala's luxury submarine-yacht to the surface when an idea crossed his mind. He stopped at periscope depth and swivelled the lens towards the west. According to the GPS they were now sailing north from Finnmark.

"What is it?" Lea asked, concerned. "Not more trouble?"

"Not at all," he said. "Just checking up on the Triton. I spy a rigid inflatable making its way over to them. Looks like it's full of Norwegian sailors – hope they survive Cairo."

Lea rolled her eyes. "Give a man a fish and he'll eat for a day, give him a submarine and he's got to play U-Boat captain for a week."

Hawke swung the periscope up and turned to Lea. "Talking of a week, at this rate we're only seven days' sailing from the North Pole."

"You can't be serious!"

"Sure, why not?"

"Because Ryan says there's a massive hole there leading to the center of the earth."

"You're kidding?"

Lea shrugged her shoulders. "If not that, think of the others – they'll be worried sick! They'll think we got caught in the cave system and risk their bloody lives trying to get us out."

Hawke thought this was a pretty solid point, so he asked Lea to radio the Norwegians and let Scarlet know they were both fine and had decided to take a few days out. Scarlet, Hawke suggested with a grin, could pass the time counting the gold coins with Ryan and if that failed to amuse her there were always the Norwegian sailors.

As Lea made the call, Hawke set the autopilot and dried his hair with one of Sala's monogrammed towels. Then he turned the radio on and the plush cabin was filled with the sound of 1970s easy listening. "I see they're bang up to date in this part of the world." He started to go through the galley in search of something that seemed to elude him.

Lea switched off the radio and joined him. "What are you looking for?"

"Just a little something to set the mood." He smiled broadly and nodded his head in appreciation. "Ah – I knew old Sala was a man of discerning taste."

"What is it?"

Hawke turned around with a bottle of champagne. "A 1998 Clos d'Ambonnay, chilled to perfection. He must have been saving it in anticipation of discovering the golden apples and all those divine weapons."

"And instead he got turned into fertilizer. Go figure."

"Shame to let it go to waste though."

They moved to the VIP bedroom and Hawke turned the bottle to pop the cork out. "Nothing wrong with a few bubbles from time to time."

Lea smiled and slid up on the bed, but then her face changed. Hawke watched her smile change to a terrible rictus of fear.

"What is it?"

"I thought I saw…"

"What?"

"A ghost…"

"Eh?"

Then she screamed and Hawke turned to see the looming figure of Leon Smets moving toward him. He was carrying a roller speargun, and moved menacingly toward the Englishman. Hawke spun the champagne bottle around and turned it into a weapon.

"So you're back from the dead again then, eh?"

Smets said nothing, but grinned malevolently as he fired the roller gun.

Hawke jumped aside and the spear flew past him, slamming into the walnut veneer door of the drinks cabinet. A thick vertical split formed in the door. "Bloody hell, man!" Hawke shouted. "You could kill someone with that!"

"I think that's the idea, ya eejit!" Lea called out.

Smets ran forward, now wielding the speargun like a club. He took a heavy swipe at Hawke and the gun whistled past his head before smashing into the top of the cabinet and obliterating a sherry decanter and a good portion of Sala's finest quality stemware.

Hawke regarded the damage with disappointment. "Now, that's just irresponsible."

"You killed Victoria, *putain!*" Smets hissed. "I will gut you like a mackerel."

"Not sure mackerels can gut things to be honest, Leon," Hawke said. "They haven't got any thumbs."

Smets screamed and lunged at the Englishman once again, almost frothing at the mouth with rage, but Hawke easily sidestepped the attack and brought a fist up into his stomach as he ran past him.

The Belgian doubled over but took the punch as he had taken a thousand others in his life before snatching a botte of wine off the carpet and staggering back to regain his balance.

"How the hell did he get on the ship?" Lea cried out.

"How the hell should I know?" Hawke called back. "And it's not a bloody ship it's a boat. How many more times?"

Smets swung at him wildly with the wine bottle.

"No one outside the navy cares, Joe."

Hawke dodged the bottle. "You could give me a hand, you know!"

Smets smashed the bottle on the end of the bed and waved the broken end in Hawke's face before charging at him again. The bottle flew toward his head but the SBS man was too fast, ducking to one side and bringing his forearm up to block the assault.

Hawke brought his other hand around and smacked Smets's wrist hard with a karate chop. The Belgian cried out in response and released the champagne bottle. It hit the carpet and rolled under the bed, but before Hawke knew it Smets lunged at him again.

The Belgian's heavy, calloused hands were wrapped into two solid fists now, and smacking into Hawke's head and chest. Knocking the Englishman back several feet, Leon Smets kept up a furious barrage of punches and kicks.

Hawke regained his balance and began the fight back, landing a chunky overhand punch on Smets's jaw, sending the Belgian flying off his feet, but he put out his hand behind him and stopped himself from hitting the floor. Then he crouched down and compressed his body before swivelling his hips and propelling his right foot toward Hawke.

Hawke recognized Smets was using Capoeira, the deadly Brazilian martial art which specialized in disguising lethal kicks inside other less dangerous moves. Now he was drawing on his entire body's mass to fire his boot into Hawke's flank like a lead weight on the end of a coiled spring.

Lea screamed out, and Hawke knew a successful strike would have powered a ton of force into his chest and smashed his ribcage, but he was trained in identifying moves like this. He evaded the flying kick with half a second to spare, tottering backwards and crashing into the wall-mounted plasma TV at the foot of the bed.

Smets was fully charged now and back on his feet, swiping uppercuts and shovel hooks at Hawke and anything else he could think of as he stormed forward to finish the Englishman off, but Hawke wasn't going out that easy. He moved forward with his fists raised to meet the Belgian.

Smets pulled a second bottle from the cabinet and smashed the neck off, leaving another lethal razor-sharp weapon in his hands. He moved forward, a devilish grin on his sweaty face, but then things took a different turn.

Hawke heard it first – the smacking sound as the bands on the speargun struck the tip of the muzzle and fired the lethal barbed spear forward at a ferocious velocity.

The next thing he saw was the tip of the spear protruding through Smets's abdominal muscles. The weapon had entered through his back and ripped through his entire torso.

Hawke knew it took a long time to reload a roller gun, but it was unnecessary, because now blood was bubbling out of the Belgian's mouth as he looked down at the wound with a look of frightened confusion on his face.

Before Hawke could make another move, Lea brought the speargun crashing down on Smets's head, striking the top of his skull with the stainless steel trigger guard. Smets went down like a sack of potatoes.

"Glad you could join the party," Hawke said. "At last."

"I was waiting for you to finish him off. What took you so long?"

Hawke gave her a look as he grabbed the Belgian by his ankles and dragged him toward the stairs to the lower deck.

"What are you going to do?" Lea asked.

"Show him how the SBS like to have fun."

Hawke dragged him down the stairs and into Sala's torpedo room.

The evidence of where he'd flooded it earlier was still obvious, but the clean-up had been good and it was all good to go.

He opened the hatch of one of the torpedo tubes and began to heave the heavy Belgian inside, literally loading him into the tube like a torpedo. As he went inside, Smets began to come to, and started moaning and then lashing out.

But Hawke moved fast. He forced the struggling man inside the torpedo tube and after taking a few kicks to the face finally wedged him in far enough to slam the door shut. The tube was basically part of the boat's pressure hull, a little like an airlock, and as Hawke secured the internal watertight door and flooded the tube with seawater he heard the sound of Smets's boots as the fatally wounded Belgian ferociously pounded against the door in a bid to escape.

With the pressure in the tube equalized to that of the sea outside the hull, Hawke activated the expulsion system as he had done with Ryan, forcing high-pressure seawater into the rear of the tube and blasting Leon Smets at great velocity into the icy water. That plus the speargun wound ought to be enough to take him out of the game, he thought.

Hawke ran up the metal steps from the torpedo room and returned to the opulent luxury of the main deck. He was met by the sound of yet more easy listening and Lea had lowered the lights.

"Honey, I'm home."

Lea peered over his shoulder. "Is he gone?"

"Sadly, yes. A shame because it turns out he was a real blast."

She looked at him confused. "Sorry?"

"Never mind. Now, where were we?"

She untied her hair and shook it free. It tumbled down over her shoulders and shone in the warm, low light of the cabin. "You were about to pop your cork."

"Oh, *really*, Donovan. I hope the quality of conversation's going to be better than that because it's several days until we get to the North Pole."

She frowned. "You're not serious about that?"

"Sure, why not – where's your spirit of adventure?"

"Won't we get trapped under the ice or something?"

Hawke shrugged his shoulders and peeled off his wetsuit. "I don't see the problem. That's the one place on earth you can't hear Ryan Bale."

"I heard that too," she said. "But I'm still not sold on the idea – can't we go to Tahiti or somewhere instead?"

Hawke reached the bed and passed his hand over the stubble on his chin as he pretended to contemplate her suggestion. "No – the North Pole it is – I'm sure you'll feel on top of the world before you know it."

She rolled her eyes. "And you haven't even fired your torpedoes yet."

Hawke moved beside her in the bed. "You really are incorrigible."

He slowly unzipped Lea's wetsuit and moved his hands up her body as he started to kiss her. They rolled over in the bed and the Rán's autopilot submerged the luxury vessel beneath the icy waves, pushing her toward the Arctic north.

THE END

AUTHOR'S NOTE

With Joe Hawke and his friends safely out of trouble (for now, at least...), this seems around the right time to talk about where I'm trying to direct the series. I have plans (and plots...) to varying degrees of detail for many more Hawke novels, and very specific detail for the next two. I can reveal the first of these will be called The Aztec Prophecy (Joe Hawke 6) and deals with a very grisly theme indeed.

My rough idea is to bring together the various baddies who seem to have slipped the net through the series so far and re-unite them into some sort of dream-team (or should that be nightmare-team?) in Hawke 7. Here, the ECHO team will face their toughest challenge yet as they try to stop their greatest enemies from discovering the dark truth about the world in one of its most mysterious locations – a truth that has been lurking there for a very long time indeed... Or something like that, because it's not written yet... although I will drop a hint now that a major character or two might get brutally killed in Hawke 7 (at least according to my plot outline ;)...)

In other news, I'm also planning a separate international mystery thriller totally outside the Hawke universe, and with luck I hope to release that later in 2016 if I can, but it's all very tentative at the moment.

Anyway, please let me thank you for coming so far with me on Hawke's journey, and I hope you're enjoying it as much as I am. As ever, look out for updates on my website, Facebook page or Twitter account, and also as ever, I reply to all emails even if it takes me a few days to respond. I always appreciate constructive messages from readers and enjoy interacting.

My thanks to you, Dear Mystery Reader,

Rob.

JOE HAWKE WILL RETURN IN
THE AZTEC PROPHECY

Printed in Great Britain
by Amazon